Penny's Loft

Jennifer M. Lane

Cover design by Leigh M. Morrow – plotbunnies.net

Copyright © 2019

Published by Pen and Key Publishing

jennifermlanewrites.com

ISBN: 978-1-7334068-4-0

ACKNOWLEDGEMENTS

Thank you to Sunyi Dean, Shelly Campbell, Essa Hansen, Alia Hess, Leigh M. Morrow, and Cheryl Murphy.

CHAPTER ONE

"How many LEGOs did you eat?" Penny put her pen light back in the pocket of her lab coat and nudged the boy's chin, closing his mouth. She held up a hand to count backward from five and tucked in her thumb. "Was it this many?"

The three-year-old boy shook his head and blond curls bounced. "Free," he said.

"Three. That's not many. Were they the big green sheets or the little tiny onesies?" Penny pinched her fingers together and wrinkled her nose. The boy giggled. Kids who weren't really injured were the second-best part of being in medical school, right after the ones who were that she could mend with a lollipop.

"Little blocks. Like blueberries."

The boy's mother clutched her purse in both hands and perched on the edge of the padded chair. "His sister was building food out of them. That must have been where he got the idea. I turned my back for one minute to take a call. Another one of those telemarketers. My parents are older, and I have to answer the phone, you know?"

Penny had seen it before, the guilt of a parent and leaving a child unattended and returning to find the unimaginable. She'd bandage the wound, and they'd show signs of relief, yet the fear of things far worse would stick with them for days.

She removed her gloves and dropped them into the trashcan by the sink. "Kids are sneaky. It's not your fault. It should pass through him in three or four days, and he'll be fine."

The woman didn't look relieved, though. Her knuckles were white, her fingers digging into the tan leather of her purse. "Larry's going to kill me."

"Is Larry his father?" The woman wore no rings.

Her nod was small. Almost imperceptible. "He's on his way." It sounded like a threat.

Penny had been trained to see the signs. A woman whose fear was disproportionate to the situation. Certain scrapes and bruises on a child. Little Bobby seemed unharmed, except for the assault on his esophagus from a LEGO or two. But something about the woman's demeanor said she wanted to be gone when Larry arrived.

"I had to call him. Last time…" she trailed off, white lines appearing on her leather bag as her nails went against the grain.

The hospital had an officer trained to deal with abuse, and Penny was obligated to report it, but she needed a little more confirmation of her suspicion before she called in the big guns. Starting a spiral of paperwork could throw a child into a system that he didn't belong in, and it could damage a woman's reputation if all she had was a nervous tic.

Sometimes it was better to be upfront about things. "I'm not a full-fledged surgeon yet, but I do have a duty to report if I think there might be something going on. Is there anything you want to say?"

The woman was still looking at her bag when the curtain yanked to the side, and a man Penny assumed was Larry stormed into the room, nearly tripped over the trash can, and hovered over Miss Hopkins. She looked like a puppy who peed on the floor, assuming a stance of ridicule and shame.

He spit his words loud and fast. Accusations about terrible parenting and neglect.

Penny clapped her hands to get his attention. She knew better than touch him or raise her voice and make things worse, but at the clap of her hands, Bobby began to cry. Miss Hopkins raised her hands to cover her ears, which seemed to cause a demon to rise within Larry. He swung into the stainless-steel tray that sat atop a cart. Metal forceps and scissors hurled into the air and Penny lunged, covering the boy with her body.

The boy's primal fear unleashed and he screamed into her chest. She held him close.

"Shh. It's okay. People are coming. It's okay."

They had to be. There was no way all that racket went ignored by the nurse's station. It was only twenty feet away.

Her back was to the curtain. The sound of it ripping from the rail and falling to the floor was a welcome one. Peeking at the floor, she saw the shoes of a police officer. One was always stationed at the hospital. Orderlies in their white slacks rushed in behind him. As they wrestled with Larry and calmed Miss Hopkins, Penny lifted Bobby and carried him to the nurse's desk. His little form trembled, and he settled on her lap as she fell into an old office chair that had lost its seat padding years before.

"Do you like lollipops? I always keep a magic stash back here. They're really good for soaking up the tears."

She tugged open a drawer, and candy slid against the front. She plucked a green one with a looped paper handle and ripped off the wrapper. "Here you go. Can you tell me a story? Do you have a kitty at home? Or a doggie?"

Bobby clutched the popsicle in his little fist. Between gulps of air that wretched his body, he said, "I had a kitty, but Larry took it."

That man really is a monster. She wanted to curse but knew better than to say it out loud.

Penny never had a pet as a kid. The security deposit cost too much, and her mother couldn't afford it on a single mother's income. But she'd always wanted something to cuddle that relied on her. And this man was destroying everything in this boy's life.

"Penny? Is this Bobby Hopkins?"

She straightened her back and lifted her chin to see over the high counter. In the background, the emergency suite was empty. Instruments strewn across the floor, the cart on its side. Blood splattered on the torn curtain where Larry must have put up a fight on his escort to a police car. Someone ran a piece of yellow tape across the entrance. It would be photographed before it was cleaned. And before her was Rebecca from child services, her arms out ready to take the boy.

Penny cleared her throat. "This is Bobby. He was just about to tell me if green was his favorite flavor or not. Bobby, this is Rebecca."

In a sea of doctors and nurses in pastel scrubs, Rebecca wore yellow scrubs covered in puppies. Her hair was pulled back in a curly ribbon barrette, and she wore a wide expression like a Broadway musical cast member. She held out her arms.

"I know where your mom is. Do you want to go see her?"

Bobby nodded and slipped off Penny's lap to the floor. He walked around the counter to the bubbly child protective services work.

"Someone will be by for your statement, Penny. Hang tight."

"Will do. Carry him, if you can. He wants to be close, and he's really scared."

And just like that, the little boy was gone.

"You did good in there." Cassie wheeled next to her. "Nice instinct, protecting the kid."

"Thanks. What else was I supposed to do?" Knock Larry upside the head with the tray, for starters?

"More paperwork. Aren't you overjoyed?"

"Poor little boy is full of LEGOs and tears, and all this place is worried about is paperwork." Penny pulled her ink pen from her lab coat pocket and stuck the cap in her mouth.

Cassie scowled and turned back to her computer. "That's a disgusting habit. Really."

"As if you don't look at a thousand bowel movements a day."

"Lee says he thinks you have one of those stress-related oral fixation things."

"Yeah, well if Lee saved his diagnosis for his patients, I wouldn't have a Lee problem on top of my stress problem."

"You know he has a crush on you, right?" The corner of Cassie's mouth curled into a smile.

"Ever the matchmaker. Thanks, but no thanks. I have one goal. Surgeon. Anything else is a distraction." Anything else would break the promise she made to her mother in her dying days, that she would get a good education and become a surgeon, to keep more kids from losing their parents. Many years had gone by since then, but she'd never lost sight of that goal.

"You look exhausted." Cassie nudged a drawer with her knee.

"We've got energy drinks stashed in there."

She stifled a yawn. "I hate those things. It's gonna take a lot more than an energy drink anyway."

"Maybe you need a vacation. Some place warm. A little long-weekend fling? Or a long little-weekend fling?"

"Funny. But no." Penny shook her head, and red curls came loose from her hair tie.

"You have been doing a lot of doubles lately."

"I wouldn't have to if Lunsford had put me on rotation at the start of the semester instead of giving me a week off for no reason. Then my grandmother died, and I had to make that up. I didn't even know her. I said I only wanted one day off, but they gave me the week anyway for bereavement. Now here I am. Doubles forever."

"Sorry, Penn. It's been a rough semester for you. It'll all work out. Maybe you can find a way to sneak in a little calm. Some aromatherapy. Tracey swears by a hot bath at the end of the day with lavender in it."

Penny rolled her eyes. "Hard to find peace in an apartment with neighbors like mine. I just have to get through school, be a surgeon, save my pennies. Someday I'll be able to afford a penthouse condo. I've never lived in one, but I hear it's the American dream."

"Well, I'm gonna have to leave you to your dream. This ER is full of patients, I'm down a room, short two nurses, and all this paperwork doesn't file itself." Cassie spun in her wheelie chair and scooted across the tile. If it weren't for Cassie keeping an eye on the residents, helping them avoid mistakes and route paperwork in the right direction and for stepping in to defend them and take the blame when they made simple mistakes, Penny would have found herself on Lunsford's bad side twice as often. And if not for Cassie's banter, Penny would probably lose her sanity.

Her phone buzzed in her pocket. "Shit." She dug for it past the pens and her stethoscope. It was forbidden on the floor, but she'd forgotten to leave it in her locker.

New email. Fifteen new notifications on top of the sixty-three she hadn't read yet. She scrolled through them, deleting the spam. It was a gratifying purge, watching spam from shoe retailers and life insurance scammers fly out of her inbox. The only things left were from school, a few memos from the hospital about medical errors and needlestick procedures. And the email that had been sitting in her inbox for ten days now from some guy she didn't know with the subject line "Eliza's Will—Info about Ramsbolt Antique Shop."

The subject line glared up at her like the kind of unfinished business that gets worse the longer it's ignored. The kind that would take forever to unravel and stress her out for days. It was her favorite kind to ignore, in fact. But now that she'd opened it, there was no going back. At least she could get a sense of what she was up against while she waited to give her statement about the psychotic dad who'd scared that little boy, abused her instrument tray, and caused her a ream of paperwork.

A few files were attached to the email. A scanned letter from her grandmother. A copy of the will.

What was I just saying about distractions?

Her face grew hot with anger. Her mom had always kept her from Ramsbolt. Said the town was small and junky, and her grandmother's antique shop was nothing but a hoarding store, that the woman never sold anything. If her mom was right, it was probably packed to the gills with crap.

I'm so sorry for your loss, the email said. *Everyone here loved her, and she's been missed the last two months.*

Months. Had it been that long since her grandmother died? Since she drove to Ramsbolt in the rain just in time for the burial, hid beneath an umbrella while people she never met put the grandmother she never knew to rest? She'd been ashamed of running off so soon, rushing back to the city and back to work. Like she turned her back on some ancient mourning ritual that was supposed to make her feel something about the loss. But the truth was, she only saw the woman once, and she had no interest in Ramsbolt.

She opened the second attachment first, the letter from her grandmother. A black and white scan of a missive in ink, in the shaky scrawl of an aging hand. Still more legible than half of what she saw from fellow doctors. The edges were blotchy, and the thin lines of her writing were broken up by the scanner, but her name was clear at the top of the page.

Dearest Penny,

It shall probably come as a surprise to find yourself in the possession of a cluttered antique store. But with your aunt and mother both gone, you—as Arvil tells me—are the rightful heir. I'm ashamed to have left you with so much jumble and debt to dispose of.

Who was Arvil? How much debt? A wave of heat washed over her, and anger rose with it. She had enough debt of her own between school and that stupid credit card she almost maxed out when she was young and hungry. As if she wasn't still young and hungry.

My hope is that you'll be able to sell the stuff, sell the store, and make a tiny profit to put toward school. Wherever you are, whatever you're doing with your life, may it be some small help to you.

Some small help? Penny swiped the apps closed and turned off the screen. Who did this woman think she was, throwing herself into Penny's life after not being a part of it? This was more than a distraction. It was a disaster. She stuck the cap of the pen in her mouth and squeezed it tight between her molars.

"That can't taste better than tater tots. Wanna go get lunch with me?" Lee leaned across the counter and peered down at her. "Whoa, you look like someone just handed you an accreditation visit and a massive pile of complicated medical histories to read."

"Yes, and worse." She nodded toward the cordoned-off room. "A guy flipped out on his ex in front of his kid."

"That's not so bad. Happens all the time. Come eat with me. I hate eating alone. You can tell me about the worst part." His puppy dog eyes would have given him away if she wasn't already aware of his sentiments. He didn't care one bit about eating alone. "Besides, you look like you could use a break."

"Can't. I have to stick around until the cops take my statement. The worst part is this email I just opened that I got two weeks ago. My grandmother left me some store full of junk and a lot of debt, and now I have to figure out what to do about it. I've been pulling a string of doubles. I'm tired. I just need more than a break. I need like a month off."

"You got an email from a lawyer two weeks ago and didn't open it until now? Christ. I know you've been exhausted and working a lot, but you've gotta read your email more often."

"I still haven't read the will. Just the email. And it wasn't from a lawyer. Some guy who lives in town. Anyway, how's the world of addiction counseling?"

Lee shrugged. "Fixating. Pun intended. But don't deflect. You do that. You like to avoid things. You really should read that will and take care of that."

She feigned a dramatic collapse on the desk. "It can wait. I'm really ticked off though. Who the hell just gives somebody a store without asking? Like I don't have enough on my plate to be dealing with the end of her life. It's like some kind of revenge for my mother not wanting to be a part of hers, and now I have to go up there to that god-awful town and dig through all her trash."

"Where is it, the store?" Lee's beeper went off, and he dug it from his pocket.

"North. Much north. Little town called Ramsbolt."

"Never heard of it. Guess you'll be up to your elbows in a rural vacation, then."

"Lord, no." Penny waved at Officer Wilson as he approached the desk to take her statement. "Hell will freeze over before I step foot in Ramsbolt, Maine."

CHAPTER TWO

Penny knew the walk to The East End by heart. It usually brought her relief, pounding down the sidewalk on the west side of the hospital. Leaving behind the wounds she couldn't heal and the scars that sometimes felt like they were too big to live with. The beeping of machines over the screaming of a patient, a wailing loved one, and a frantic doctor whose demands weren't met soon enough by someone who couldn't read his mind. Stacks and stacks of forms to fill out that fed the lawyers and accreditation agencies and registered patient satisfaction but had nothing to do with patient care.

Right at the light. Two blocks down. The nightclub was tucked between a marketing place that did its own graphic design and one of those urban churches that fills in old retail space. Redeemer of something or other. Music blasted through the door when a group of guys pushed their way onto the sidewalk, laughing. Penny held the door for them and slid in against their wake.

Working third and first shifts meant arriving at the bar for drinks before rush hour. It was too early for a cover charge, so Bradley, the usual bouncer, wasn't in his chair by the door. She went straight to the bar, where Dave guarded a row of bar stools and drinks belonging to the regular crowd, ready to order liquid relief. The room was dark enough to separate the patrons from the reality outside but light enough to show its own scabs. It looked sleek and modern at night, people dancing in clusters, resting drinks on polished tables. But the harsh light of early evening showed all the flaws. The scuffed floor and scratched bar top. It was honest, and Penny liked it that way.

"You're late tonight." Dave was an EMT whose shift let out at the same time as hers most days. He cradled two thirds of a beer in his hand, his papery skin peppered with spots, belying his age by at least a decade. He removed his hat, and wisps of white hair swirled beneath the ceiling fan.

Penny chose the empty stool next to him and let her tote bag fall to the floor, but only because the floor wasn't sticky yet. She hoped he didn't ask her how it was going, because that stupid antique store wouldn't leave her alone, and the last thing she wanted was to talk about it. "Got a lot going on. Still."

"Not missing anything. Band canceled, so they called in the karaoke guy. He'll be late."

"Good. More time to enjoy the radio hits." Penny stole a napkin from the tray and nodded to the bartender, who was busy pouring beers for three women at the other end of the bar. Black jackets and heels, hair perfectly arranged. Lawyers, probably. "You gonna sing for once?"

Beside her, Dave shifted his weight to the beat of a Top 40 song by a high-pitched woman. "Not unless you're buying me supper." He nudged her with his shoulder. "But it might look like a date, and I don't want to make Lee jealous."

"Funny. Anybody else here yet?"

He gestured toward the back. Sunlight streamed through a door at the top of four stairs. "Yup. Out back, smoking. Scott and Lee. Jenna. Marnie's in the bathroom, I guess. Might be out there with 'em."

"How can people who work in hospitals smoke? I don't get that." Penny kicked her bag under her chair. "Especially Lee. He treats addictions. You'd think he'd know better."

"Usual?" The bartender twisted a towel and threw it over his shoulder.

Penny nodded. "Thanks."

"I got a theory it's an affirmation of life thing." The bartender tilted an empty glass under a tap and filled it with golden IPA. "You guys are all stressed out, dealing with death and illness. It's like grabbing the reins of your own mortality." He placed the glass on Penny's napkin. "Tab?"

"Please." Penny sipped. Crisp and hoppy, she had to admit that a cold beer made a nice transition from blood loss and near misses with death to turning off her brain at the end of the day. At least it was some liquid wishful thinking. "We all have our vices, I guess."

"Yeah, so what's up with you?" Dave picked at the corner of his eye.

Don't mention that stupid store. "Losing my mind lately. Bunch of double shifts. Just trying to hold it all together until this residency is over."

"Is it three years you got left?" Dave moved his coat and made room for the returning smokers. They brought with them the acrid whiff of affirmations of life.

"Two and a half." Penny buried her nose in her beer. "For this round, anyway. Then I get to the good part and dig into my surgical specialty." Some days, it felt like it would take forever to reach the end. She tried not to think about it. She'd get there by taking it one day at a time, whether she counted them or not. She'd wanted to be a doctor since she was a kid, since George Clooney made hospital scenery look good, and she stitched up every wounded doll in her toy box. Since her mom got sick, and she learned she had a natural bedside manner. It sparked a fire in her to heal the wounded, so no kid would ever lose a loved one too soon again.

Marnie clicked her way across the empty dance floor on towering heels, back to her seat. Scott, Lee, and Jenna followed in her perfume haze. Marnie slid onto the barstool next to her and crossed her legs, the dainty toe of one shoe perched on the chair rung, the other flicking the air.

"I heard they came down on you last week about forgetting paperwork." Marnie had been a coiffed administrator since Penny met her, though some people said she was frumpy before she got addicted to reality makeover shows.

"Can you help me understand something?" Penny rubbed at one eyebrow. "What is it with you office people and your paperwork?"

"We love to make your life difficult." Marnie gave Penny's elbow a playful nudge.

Lee pulled a stool from the end of the bar and wedged it between her and Marnie. Another gesture in the battle for her affection. The less attention she gave him, the more he sought it. If only she could settle on whether she enjoyed it or not.

He leaned toward her. "It's the hospital, the lawyers, and the federal guidelines. There are a million people we have to keep happy. If you follow the rules, they'll leave you alone. It's not that hard, once you get the hang of it."

"Yeah, well. I don't wanna get used to it. I wanna finish school and get on with the fulfilling part of healing my patients. Paperwork just doesn't do it for me, ya know?"

Lee wasn't doing it for her today, either. He was nice enough. Attractive. But they had nothing in common. He had his life together, and she was doing a mediocre job of faking it. His attention was flattering, but she couldn't afford to take any focus away from her goals. At least that's what she told herself. Plus, she had this whole antique store mess on her mind.

"Where have you been, anyway?" Scott reached across Jenna for the carafe of bar mix.

Penny swallowed a bitter sip of IPA and wiped her upper lip. "Ramsbolt and work."

Scott raised an eyebrow. "Rams-what?"

"Ramsbolt? It's where my grandmom lived."

Lee tossed a balled-up napkin down the bar. It bounced off Dave's beer. "Don't be rude, asshole. Her grandmother died. She went to a funeral."

"I didn't know that." Scott waved a hair-thin bar napkin in surrender. "Sorry, Penn."

"No big deal." Penny took off her glasses and settled them on the bar. "It was a bit ago."

"How did it go, anyway? Was it as bad as you thought it would be?" Jenna gave her sad eyes. The kind that said she didn't really care how the funeral went, she just wanted to express the right amount of social sympathy.

"Nah, but I got out of there fast. It's a small town, and everybody knew her. It would have been awkward, talking to all those people who knew her." Penny centered her drink on her napkin. She came for the escape, not the recap. It felt good to get some of the weight off her chest, though. It had been a while since she complained about work, life, patients, and hospital drama with her after-work drinking buddies. It felt good to know other people walked the same planks and tried to mingle reality with the surreal truths of the mortal coil.

"Tell them the good news." Lee bumped his knee against hers.

She tried not to recoil, though she wanted to smack him. Nothing about the news was good, and she didn't want to talk about it.

Dave winked at her. He must have spotted Lee's nudge. "What good news?"

But Lee filled them in. "Penny got the golden ticket. Did you read the will yet?"

She slouched and let the air deflate her with a deep sigh. "It's not a golden ticket. It's a horrendous tumor of debt and disaster, and I really don't want to talk about it."

"You didn't read the will, did you?"

Marnie was all ears. She leaned down to peer past Lee. "You inherited something, and you haven't read the will? You could have a million shares of stock or the world's biggest shoe collection."

"Something like the former. But none of it is in my size. Look, my mom and grandmother didn't get along. I never met my gran, and Mom died when I was in high school. I lived with my godmother until I graduated. I don't know anything about Ramsbolt or that store or her debt, and I don't want to. I just want it to go away."

Marnie's eyes sparkled. "But it could be Eden! It could be your ticket out of this rat race."

"I like this rat race. This race is just one hurdle on my way to the thing I've wanted my whole life. Inheriting that woman's hoarding store and all her debt is like stepping out of the race and walking into a cupcake store. On top of rent I can't pay, school that costs a fortune, work that makes me crazy—for now—and all the paperwork, I have this giant wave looming over me. It's not Eden, Marnie."

Penny bowed her head and let it hit the bar. Her beer sloshed in its glass.

"Oh, Penn." Lee patted her back with one hand and sipped his beer with the other.

"Hoarding store was kinda funny though." Marnie stifled a laugh and poked at a chunk of ice with her lipstick-stained straw.

Penny raised her head and shook her hair out of her eyes. "When my mom was a kid, it was packed with stuff. Floor to rafters. Used junk she couldn't sell 'cause nobody wanted it the first time around."

"Can't you just call a lawyer or something?" Marnie arched one eyebrow.

"In Ramsbolt?" Penny leaned back in her chair, studied the exposed vent work along the ceiling through her blurry vision. "Maybe. I dunno. I don't think there *are* lawyers in that town. I'll have to go up there again at some point. Not sure when I'll find time for it. It's already tight, fitting in all my hours for this semester."

"Maybe it'll fit into your family leave stuff. Come by my desk." Marnie examined her nail polish. "I can help you with the schedule and get you the time off."

"I might take you up on that."

Lee wagged a finger at her, his eyes wrinkled with a smile. "It might not seem like it right now, but you're one of the lucky ones."

"Lucky? I don't feel so lucky."

Marnie sipped something peach, leaving more lipstick prints on the straw. "I think you *are* lucky. At least you know what you want to do with your life. Most people never find out. Think I'm passionate about making sure there are enough nurses scheduled for Saturday? And the amount of shit I get from people?" Blond curls swished when she shook her head.

Marnie had a point.

"I'd say you're lucky." Dave turned on his barstool and faced her, one eyebrow furrowed. "I wanted to be a podiatrist but got bored with all the books. Now it's drug overdoses and heart attacks, cutting people out of cars. People bleeding all over their bathrooms. Misery. All the time. There's no joy in it. Most people just keep going in the wrong direction until they're totally broken, like me. That's what I'm sitting here for. Because after all I saw today, all I see every day, the last thing I want to do is go home and face the television by myself." Dave gripped his beer so tight his knuckles turned white. "Don't compromise. Promise me that won't be you. Me? I'm too old for a life change, but if someone gave me a hoarding store, I might have moved in."

Penny offered him a sad smile. She often considered the things he saw in the course of a day and how he dealt with the impact. In the emergency room, she had the benefit of being busy, surrounded by others who saw the same things. The trauma came to her. But Dave rushed to meet it head on each time, and when it was done, he climbed back into his ambulance with his partner and waited for another call. Another victim.

She patted his arm. "Sometimes we end up where we're needed the most, and that isn't always where we planned to be. But I promise, Dave. I won't compromise. Now save my seat. I gotta pee."

She slipped from her barstool and walked to the back, toward the neon signs for the restrooms. It was nice to vent, but she came to get away from all that. She didn't hear Lee skipping to catch up until she stepped into the hallway.

"Penn, I wanted to ask you…"

He leaned, his shoulder against the wall, head tilted. Just enough shaggy brown hair falling into his eyes to give him an air of mystique. Backlit by the pink neon light, he looked like the suave worst-choice in an '80s teen movie. But that look. His clients must get sober just to please him.

"Don't, Lee. Not this again. You've been chasing me for half a year, and I'm not in any position to—"

"It's never going to be the right time. Give me a chance. Three dinners."

"I don't have room in my life for chances."

"Okay, one dinner."

"It's not a negotiation."

"Did I piss you off by letting your secret out?"

Truth was, he hadn't. She even felt a little better for having talked about it. She wouldn't let him know that, though.

"It's no big deal. Don't worry about it. But dinner is a no. I need to focus on my education. I can't afford distractions. It's nothing personal."

"Rejection is always personal to the one being rejected." The curl of his lip and the fine lines at the corners of his eyes said he wasn't too hurt, but Penny could tell she'd struck a nerve.

She gave the bathroom door a push, and yellow light flooded into the dark. "I'm nothing more than an addiction. First you can kick me, then you can kick those cigarettes."

CHAPTER THREE

A kitchen table was no place for a thirteen-year-old girl to start her high school education, not by her mother's estimation. But the master bedroom of their tiny apartment wasn't any place for Penny's mom to recover from chemotherapy, either. Visiting nurses weren't covered by the world's worst insurance, and Penny had no intention of leaving her mom home alone, sick in bed. After that first bad day when her mother couldn't keep anything down and couldn't walk to the bathroom alone, Penny got special permission to learn from home.

The kitchen table was a whirlpool of textbooks and notebooks, homework and healthy foods, cancer research, pamphlets on chemo recovery, and bottles of pills. For Penny, the apartment became a churning pit of trying to make her mother feel better and feeling guilty when she couldn't. A silence had fallen over them. Sometimes ominous, thick with Penny's fear of losing her mom, and her mother's fear of leaving her daughter alone in the world. Sometimes it was a healing silence, smoothing over a violent bout of pain. It was broken by sickness, by tears, and by visitors.

Brenda, Penny's godmother, lived down the hall. She stopped by every night after work, before she ran home to make dinner and live her life. Sometimes she brought presents. Word find books and trashy novels, snacks, and casseroles. She made sure they ate and popped dishes the neighbors brought into the oven. She drove Penny's mom to appointments. Some nights she was a welcome break from the gruesome hold that cancer held on their lives, and sometimes she was a reminder that life went on, and Penny's mom would probably be denied the rest of hers because she'd waited too long, the doctors missed the signs, and though her breasts were gone, the cancer wasn't. And it was going to win. Then Penny would be expected to drag her possessions down the hall, into Brenda's apartment, and continue on, day to day, as if this had been the plan all along.

Fourteen years hadn't been long enough for Penny to learn how to handle it all, but sitting at the kitchen table in the stillness, while her mother slept, and the neighbors crept down the hall and laughed through the walls, she could immerse herself in a biology textbook and settle her mind with learning.

While her mother slept, Penny lost herself in a chapter about cell structure and function. At the knock on the door, she spun her head. Dirty casserole dishes lined the counters. No use trying to hide them now.

"Penny? Are you two home?" Kim. The woman from upstairs who wore the world's worst perfume and lived with all the cats. She always brought food, though. More dishes to wash.

Penny opened the door wide and motioned for quiet. "Mom's sleeping."

"I'm not sleeping." Her mother's voice wasn't strong, but it didn't have to make it far. "Is that you, Brenda?"

"It's Kim from upstairs. I brought some lasagna." She held out a white dish with blue flowers, covered in aluminum foil. Penny bit back a cringe. There was no way of knowing what her mom could eat or when she'd eat it.

She reached out to accept it. "Thank you. Mom really liked the tuna casserole you brought."

Kim patted her on the arm. "I'll bring you another later this week."

"I'll wash your dishes real quick. I'm sorry I didn't get to it. I—"

"Think nothing of it. You have so much on your plate. Pun intended." Kim wore the same sad smile everyone gave her. The one that said they accepted the excuse, and they wouldn't want to trade places. Penny's face grew warm, and she turned away. She didn't want to be forgiven or overlooked or pitied. She wanted to be accountable for her mother's well-being.

"Kim? I'm glad it's you. Can you come back here? I want to ask you…"

Kim moved on to the bedroom, toward the favor she was eager to perform. It was always the same. People eager to please, to take on a minor inconvenience when what they really wanted was to know that if their turn ever came along, they'd get the same kind of support. They wanted reassurance that in a world that shunned the sick and dying, they wouldn't be left alone, clinging to their humanity as it slipped away.

Penny closed the refrigerator door, sealing the lasagna away with the mac and cheese and some kind of kugel made with potatoes. She found Kim's dirty dish among the rest and ran water in the sink to wash it. Not so much that she couldn't hear her mother and Kim, though.

"I couldn't possibly accept it." Kim turned down another of her mom's gifts. From her bed facing the window, she'd been giving away everything not bolted to the floor, promising the furniture to anyone who would accept it.

"It really doesn't mean anything to either of us. Everything will have to go. Brenda's taking care of Penny when I'm gone, and she doesn't have room to store all these things. Penny won't want this old stuff, anyway. She'll want nice new things someday. Just the dresser? Are you sure?"

Penny had heard it before. The pleading to take away their things. Begging them to take it now or put their name on it and come back for it later. After. When it was all done. Her mother would beg them to take their meaningless junk, and shell-shocked neighbors who hadn't come for a shopping trip would offer awkward denials. Penny didn't argue.

She'd visited Brenda's half a dozen times. Counted the steps from one apartment door to the other. Forty-eight from her bedroom to the one she'd move into once her mother was gone. She knew that the books and the relentless studying were how she would get through the grief. That she'd pour all her anguish into something productive and live the life her mother wanted for her. She hoped when the time came, she'd be studying books for another semester and not the ones piled on the table. Just one more semester. At least.

"Poppy. Please. I couldn't." Penny cringed again. Her mother hated her name. Poppy. A flower known for memorializing the dead. She'd hated it even before she was dying. "Are you sure you want to give so much away? Maybe Penny will want these things."

The contents of her mother's stomach hurled into a bucket she kept by the bed. It came without nausea. Without warning.

"Sorry, Kim." Penny set the dried dish on the table next to her biology book and stepped into the room. "Mom doesn't get much warning sometimes."

Kim stepped back, inching to the door. The usual change was in the air, a visitor's shift from her mom's awkward questioning to their polite repulsion. It would be easy to let her off the hook: she'd had enough practice, but Penny's focus was entirely on her mother.

"It's almost time for your medicine, Mom. Hold on, and I'll get it together for you." She set the box of tissues on the bed and left for a damp washcloth, Kim on her heels.

"Before I forget." Penny put the yellow dish in Kim's hands. "It was delicious. Mom really loved it."

Kim didn't meet her eyes. "I can bring another next week."

"She would like that. We both would." Penny turned away and dampened a washcloth. "Thank you for the lasagna. It will be great this week once her stomach settles, and we—"

Penny turned from the sink, but Kim was gone, replaced by her biology teacher.

"By the look of the woman running from the apartment, I'd say you have two patients on your hands."

Penny wound the washcloth in her fists. Mrs. Poulson was not a welcome sight. She could send Penny away. Say she was too young to do this alone. Send her to live with Brenda and force her mom into a hospital. Mom didn't want to be in a hospital. Maybe it was hard caring for her, trying to figure out the right thing to do to ease her pain, and maybe it did make her sad sometimes, but it was the right thing to do, to care for her mother at home. Almost like it was her destiny.

Penny twisted the washcloth into a tightrope. "That's just Kim. She's a neighbor. Mom isn't feeling well." She stepped past the teacher and into the bedroom. "Here you go, Mom. Do you want anything else?"

Her mom had pushed herself up in bed, her skin pale and speckled with sweat. "No, thank you. Is that your teacher?"

The bed was only a few steps from the front door. There was no way to conceal a visitor from her mother. "It is. Mrs. Poulson. I should go talk to her."

"Send her in to see me when you're done? I want to ask questions."

"Ask her what? Please don't try to give her things. No one wants our stuff, Mom. They have their own stuff."

"I want to ask about your schoolwork."

Her schoolwork was perfect, but Penny didn't want her to worry. Keeping the teacher away would only give her something to agonize over. "I will. I'll send her in."

Penny tucked her shaking hands into her back pockets and stepped into the kitchen, into Mrs. Poulson's scrutiny. The woman hovered over her open textbook, her tight gray curls barely moving as she turned the pages.

"Cells. You're ahead of the class already." The teacher pulled two books from her tote bag and laid them on the table. "I brought you these. I didn't want to overburden you, but I also know that when things get tough, I like to read. Maybe I'm silly like that. Learning new things is a great distraction for me."

At least she wasn't there to criticize. Unless it was a ploy, to distract her and strike. "Learning is a great distraction for me, too. I have plenty of time to learn, so it's not hard. What books are these?"

"One is from Ms. Bailey. Something about Shakespeare for your honors English class. The other is from me. I had a feeling you'd be ahead. It's all in the syllabus. Ms. Bailey says she hopes you're doing well. Sends her best to your mom."

"Thank you. Tell Ms. Bailey I'll get this back to her in a week or so?" Penny pulled a blue folder from beneath her notes. "These are the homework assignments and tests. They're all scanned and emailed, but I thought you might want the hard copies?"

Mrs. Poulson waved a hand. "It's okay. You can keep them for your records, if you want. Do you still have a visiting nurse?"

The place didn't look like it. Dirty dishes, food containers, and an overflowing trash can. It looked like a teenager was in control. "We do. She comes two days a week. That's what Medicaid pays for. We'd have to pay for more than that, and we don't need it anyway."

"I get it. She wants to be home. Not in a hospital. I would, too."

"And I don't want to leave her. Not yet. I won't."

"It's hard work, caring for someone who's terminally ill. And you're so young." Mrs. Poulson's eyes were narrowed. Penny straightened her back against the inspection.

The words bit into her. Terminally ill. They didn't use those words in their tiny apartment. The knowledge of it hung in the air, but it wasn't discussed. Not yet. "Being here with her keeps me focused. I don't worry that she's alone. We take it as it comes. There are a lot of good days. And I'm not caring for her by myself. There's Kim and the neighbors and my godmother, Brenda." Penny kept her voice low, though she knew her mom was close enough to hear. "Are you here to send me away?"

"Send you away? Why would I send you away?"

"I thought." Penny lifted her chin and shoved her hands back into her pockets, her palms hot and sweaty. "I don't know what I thought. Forget I said anything."

"I came to bring you the classwork. And to see how you're doing. All of us, all your teachers think highly of you. We want you to succeed, but not at the mercy of your own well-being."

"It's fine. I promise."

"Can I see your mom? Does she like visitors?"

Penny stepped back and nodded toward the door. Mrs. Poulson approached her mother with more confidence than the neighbors. She moved like a nurse or a doctor. Maybe there was something about studying all that science that took the fear out of being around illness.

"Knock, knock."

Penny watched from the table as her teacher took a seat in the plastic lawn chair they kept by the bed.

"I thought I'd peek in and say hi. We met once a few months ago. I'm Penny's AP Biology teacher. Tanya."

The bed creaked, her mom adjusting. "I remember. It's nice to see you. Is she doing well? She studies a lot. I hear her out there clicking away on the laptop all day."

"She is doing well. She's ahead of the class—"

"She wants to be a doctor." The bed creaked again. Penny could see Mrs. Poulson accept her mother's hand. "She's so smart. Her teachers have always said so, and her grades have been perfect. A natural healer. She could cure cancer one day. It's so important to me that there are people in her life who make sure she's invested in her education. People who keep on her and don't let her slip. Know what I mean?"

"I do. I—"

"She could change people's lives. The world, if she sticks with it. I need to know that people will make sure she goes to college and picks the right one."

"I promise. Your daughter has a gift, and I promise you, her teachers will not let you down."

CHAPTER FOUR

Penny hung the clipboard at the foot of her patient's bed and put a cup of ice chips into the woman's hands.

I hate these conversations, she thought. *How can you tell someone not to be afraid when there's every reason to be?*

"I didn't want you to wait too long, so I got you some ice myself. Mrs. Accardo, we have your EKG results, and we'd like a little more information." She was careful not to say *but. But* was nothing but a verbal house fire. Everything after might look like soot and ashes, but it would be full of fear, the past, and a future she'd miss out on. Penny hated *but.* "We're going to send you up for a blood test and an X-ray. Were they able to get your daughter on the phone?"

"I don't know. I haven't talked to anybody."

The furrowed brow. The hands twisting the blanket. The eyes darting for the door. Mom would do that when she got bad news. When they told her the tumor was only getting bigger, and cancer had spread to the lymph nodes. Mom had clutched at the hem of her shirt like she was trying to loosen the chains, and when her eyes went for the door, Penny'd been sure she was about to bolt.

She placed a hand on the woman's arm. "Everything will be okay. Rest easy. I'll go find out for you and order the test."

"Do I have to go for the test before she gets here? I want to see her before the test. I don't want to be alone. What if..."

Penny gave her a gentle squeeze. What if she died before her daughter showed up? What if the test results were bad, and her daughter wasn't there to hear it? Even worse, what if she was?

"Even if you do have to go for the X-ray before she gets here, it only takes a moment. We'll make sure the two of you are connected. We're good at keeping track of patients."

"What if I die before she gets here?" The woman's eyes filled with tears, and her lip quivered. She turned her face away. "I have so much to say."

Penny gave her the same reassuring smile she'd given to her mom a thousand times or more. "Listen. You are not going to die today. Not on our watch. I'll be right back with some news about your daughter. I know it's hard to do right now, but try not to think too much. In ten years, this will be just another memory."

Penny closed the curtain when she left the room and stepped up to the nurse's desk with a stack of forms. Her phone buzzed in her pocket.

She checked the screen, but her attention was still on her patient. "Hey, Cass. I'm ordering tests for the woman in seven. Do we know if anyone reached her daughter?"

Cass handed the form to another nurse who leapt for the computer. The wheelie chair spun from beneath her when she stood. "She's about ten minutes away. I'll let her know, since I was the one who spoke to her daughter. Aren't you pushing the envelope with your cell phone in your pocket? You're supposed to leave that in your locker."

"I usually do. I drank too much wine watching Netflix last night and was running behind this morning. I forgot to leave it with my purse. It's been buzzing all day. Oh, and she's really upset. She's having a hard time putting thoughts into words, so you might need to spend an extra second with her." Her phone buzzed again in her hand. "Oh my God. Why are they still calling me? This same number has called me six times today." She accepted the call. "I don't need a car warranty or health insurance. Take me off your list, please."

"Wait! I'm not selling anything. Please." An unfamiliar male voice on the other end begged, edging on panic. "I'm Nate."

"Nate who?" Penny sank behind the nurse's desk, disgusted at the interruption and afraid she'd be caught with her phone and reprimanded. *No personal phones on the floor*, they always said. She'd already been chewed out once this month for not following policy. Was this some guy she met at the bar? Couldn't be. She never met people at the bar, and she never gave her number to strangers.

"I got your number from Morgan. He's the town manager. He got it off your grandmom's will, which she brought down to the office a few months before she passed away, and I was—"

"How did she have my number? I'm really sorry to cut you off. Nate, was it?" Penny's patience was fading. She had a sick patient who deserved her attention.

"Nate. Yup. I just need to know—"

"I'm at work, and I don't have a lot of time to talk—"

"When are you coming for the cat?"

Christ. Did her grandmother have a cat? "Please tell me there's not a starving cat somewhere nobody told me about."

"He's in the will."

31

"He? It's a he? I didn't see that in the will." There was no cat in the will. Was there? She hadn't read the will, so she wouldn't know. She grabbed a pen from the desk and left a furious, therapeutic scribble on a scrap of paper. If someone had told her there was a life at stake, she would have read it days ago. How was she supposed to know there was a cat?

"Well, it was a lot to read."

Penny's voice went up an octave. "There was no cat. I don't know what to do with a cat."

"Morgan hates to read small font, so documents here are really long. Who doesn't, really?"

"What am I supposed to do about a cat? Is there a shelter down there? Like, a place that finds homes for cats?" She rubbed her eye with the heel of her hand, and her sight went out of focus.

"No rescue. Not in Ramsbolt. There's the pet store that finds homes for stray cats sometimes, but Shauna, she runs the place, she's wicked full of cats. I've been feeding him, and it's getting expensive. All this caring for a cat I don't have. I don't mean to be—"

"No one mentioned a cat. Can I just pay you to take care of the cat? Like, a stipend or something?" She couldn't afford to pay him to take care of the cat, but if it was her responsibility, she had no choice.

"Now you listen here. You can't just throw away your cat."

Who did this guy think he was, burdening her with a cat? Unless she'd grown out of the allergy, cats gave her sneezing fits and made her nose feel itchy. And she worked too many hours to take on a cat. Penny stood, and the chair slid away from her. "It's not my cat! I don't have a cat!"

"You inherited this cat. Jake is a living thing, and he's legally yours,

32

and I don't know what to do with him."

She performed one of those in-through-the-nose-out-through-the-mouth breaths her yoga teacher said was calming. It didn't work. "I am at work right now. In a hospital where people are dying. I will have to call you back about the cat."

"What was that about?" Cassie returned from a paperwork mission and pushed the chair into the backs of Penny's legs. Penny ended the call and let herself fall into it.

"He was rude. This guy just calls and starts screaming at me because I haven't done anything about my grandmother's cat. I didn't even know about a cat."

"So. Why the exasperated face? Just send it to a shelter if you don't want a cat." Cassie punched at the keyboard, entering patient information into some online database that remained a mystery to Penny. "I did that when my mom died. Took her old poodle to the shelter. They were happy to rehome him. Angry little dog, too."

"Have you ever been to Ramsbolt? There are two hundred people there. There's no cat shelter. What am I going to do with a cat? I can't have a cat! I guess I'll have to go get it and make a poster or something. Maybe a shelter around here would have room for it." She didn't even know if she was still allergic to cats or if she'd outgrown it. Clearly that Nate guy didn't want it. If she went down there to get it, she'd have to face her grandmother's things. The place her mom called a hoarding store. And all that debt.

She unlocked her phone and opened her email, deleted a few pieces of spam that had rolled in. She found the email from Morgan with the will attached. The file couldn't be very big. Her grandmother had no children left. Penny was fourteen when her mom lost a fight with cancer and could barely walk when her aunt lost a fight with an RV and died of carbon monoxide poisoning in the desert somewhere. There were no cousins or spouses to leave everything to. Like she expected, her grandmother kept it simple. *With only one heir, it seems wise to leave my estate to the one person who could benefit from it the most.*

Little did her grandmother know what a burden it all was. The debt and the junk her mother had always complained about and the hassle of dealing with it at all. And now this cat. Penny chewed on the cap of her pen and slid her glasses down her nose. The bulk of the will, at a skim, read more like a treasure hunt than any set of last wishes. How to find paperwork she'd tucked in her office under the stairs. Where she kept the bills. The name of a guy who did her taxes until a decade ago when he retired. None of it useful in any tangible way. And nothing about a cat.

"You and that phone again." Lee dropped a clipboard on the counter and leaned across.

She took the pen cap from her mouth and stuck it in her lab coat pocket. "You and showing up every time the shit hits the fan. How do you do that?"

"I have good timing. Lunch?" His eyes lifted at the corners in a look that was hard to say no to.

Cass fell back into her chair, out of breath with a stack of forms to add to the pile next to her printer. "The woman in room seven? Her daughter's here. They're going up for the X-ray."

Penny smiled. "That takes some weight off. I'm gonna take my lunch, then. I'll be back in a bit." She slid around the counter and fell into step next to Lee. They steered down a tiled hall, following the blue line that led to cafeterias and cafes. "I have to do some research. Turns out I inherited a cat. His name is Jake. And I can't just leave him out there."

"What about the store? Did you read the will yet?"

"Of course not. Who do you think I am? I've read six textbooks, but not the will. I did look up cleaning crews, salvage companies, junk dealers. They're all too expensive and too far away. There aren't any thrift stores, charity shops, or antique shops to donate it to, either."

"Sounds like her antique store didn't have much competition."

"And somehow she still managed to create enough debt to pass it on to me."

"Maybe you can just give it all away. Cut and run, you know?" Lee waved at a man in a polo shirt and loafers without socks when they passed.

"Maybe. The people of the bustling metropolis of Ramsbolt gave it all away once before. Maybe they don't want it back again later."

And if they had it once and threw it away, what made her grandmother think she would want it? Penny had no connection to those things. She didn't even have a connection to her grandmother, who turned out to be everything her mother said she was. A disorganized woman who only cared about herself. If she wasn't, she would have taken better care of her cat.

"Nothing about this situation was going to fix itself. The bills will continue to mount and eventually, the creditors will come for you. If you don't tackle this, you can be fined for abandoning property. I know I've been teasing you, but you really have to do something about it."

"Jesus. I know. There are too many problems and not enough solutions right now, and I…" Penny's temper almost grew too big to handle, but was squashed flat by the window of the gift shop. It had closed weeks before when the church that ran it couldn't afford to keep up with the place. Since they'd been moving out fixtures and furniture. A pile of boxes and chairs, trinkets and odds and ends once sold by nuns sat surrounded by ripped up carpeting. On the ledge of the window, next to an old lamp painted with flowers, rested a figurine of a sailor statue.

She stopped dead in the hallway. She'd seen him somewhere before. Recently. The sailor with a brimmed hat, gripping a ship's wheel, his eyes fixed on some distant horizon. Where had she seen this?

"Does this look familiar to you?"

Lee hiked his messenger bag higher on his shoulder. He looked at her as if she had three heads.

"It reminds me of something. Can't remember where I saw it, though." What was the deal with the little statue? She shrugged and turned the corner, Lee on her heels. And then it hit her. "I know where I saw it. There's a statue in the middle of a turning circle in Ramsbolt. It's similar."

"Where the antique store is, right?"

"Yeah. There's just this giant statue in the middle of this roundabout and it reminded me of it, that's all."

"Do you believe in signs?"

"Not unless they're for food. Or those overhead highway signs. They're helpful." She didn't want to sit through a lunch-and-learn with Lee so he could lecture her about facing her problems head on. Her temper had already flared at him once.

"You know what I mean, Penn. A sign the universe is trying to tell you something."

"Is it trying to tell me that I'm so addicted to bagels that I'd have lunch with you?" She stuck out her tongue at him and stepped up to the end of a line of people waiting at the deli counter. It was short, but still long enough to trap her in one of Lee's psychology interventions.

"Very professional." He cocked his head to the side, his green eyes sparkling. "You're stressed out and overworked, and you're avoiding one of the major things that's making you feel overwhelmed. Maybe you're supposed to go to Ramsboro, or whatever that town is, to sort out that store so you can relax a bit and focus. Your oral fixation is getting worse, and you're probably not sleeping well either."

"What oral fixation?" Penny leaned back, away from the accusation.

"You chew on pen caps all the time. It probably relieves stress. It focuses your anxiety. If you dealt with this head on—"

"Oh, Lord. It's just a bad habit, the pen cap. I'll try to quit if it'll make you happy." She spun on her heel and faced the deli display case.

"If you want to quit, telling yourself you'll try to quit is a bad way to start. Just quit instead."

"Nice advice. I'll take it when I need it." She'd been addicted to avoiding pain for most of her life, since her mom died, and she got sucked into unavoidable loss that never ended in relief. Avoiding things never made it any better, though. He was right; she needed to sort it out before it swallowed her whole. But she didn't need Lee's opinion about it. Or his psychoanalysis. "Maybe bacon, egg, and cheese would be more filling than plain? I do have a twelve-hour shift ahead."

"You really need to let off some steam." Lee grabbed a red plastic tray off the stack and hugged it. "Wanna go to the bar after work again today?"

"If I'm avoiding my challenges, how will going to the bar help? Nah, I should go home, sit down and sort this all out. I'll feel better when I can make some sense of it all." Penny yawned and covered her mouth.

"Atta girl. Jump in there and tackle that mess. Plus, maybe some time away will help you figure out what you really want."

The woman in front of her ordered a fancy latte and dumped change on the counter. Penny turned her back to the scene and faced Lee. "And you think when I know what I want, you'll be on the list, right?"

"A guy can hope."

"I know what I want. What I want hasn't changed. I want to see patients through their challenges. Improve people's lives. I want to know that I made a positive impact on someone. I don't want distractions."

The woman stepped away with her latte, and Penny slammed her tray down on the rail harder than she meant to. It felt good, though, to make a little noise. "I'll have two everything bagels, please. One with bacon, egg, and cheese for here. A toasted one with cream cheese to go. And a cup of coffee. Please."

The man behind the counter nodded and turned away.

"Lee, I'm sorry. I don't mean to be rude. I just can't stand unsolicited advice, that's all. I gotta figure this out for myself." If he really wanted her to like him, he'd accept her as she was and not try to criticize her every move. But she stopped short of saying it.

He put his hands up in surrender. "Hey, it's not rude. I have a bad habit of intersecting work with life. Sorry."

"It's cool. I'm sorry I got snippy. I'm under a lot of pressure."

Penny paid the man for her bagels and coffee and waited for Lee to do the same. She picked a clean table with a seat by the window while Lee ordered his lunch. She would never be one of those doctors who ran around giving unsolicited advice because they always know better. And she wouldn't ever date one, either.

She pulled her phone from her pocket, pulled up her contacts, and called Marnie.

"Why are you calling me from your cell phone? Aren't you at work?"

Marnie typed in the background, her long nails clicking on the keys.

"I am. I'm on lunch. Anyway, remember how you said I should call you if I need to take time off? I'm gonna need two or three days. Can you help?"

CHAPTER FIVE

Penny left her sneakers by the apartment door, mud clinging to the soles from her shortcut in the rain and through the mulch. Her tote bag landed on the sofa with a satisfying thud, and she spun out of her jacket, shaking rain from her hair onto her T-shirt. Her drive home felt like it was as long as the day had been. Gunshot wounds and car crashes. Picking glass from a little girl's arms. Telling the mother it would be okay; they'd take good care of her daughter until the mother's surgery was over. And everyone would do their best to put the bones back in, to sew her up so she could walk again.

"You'll be dancing at that little girl's wedding," she'd said. But she'd never know for sure. Just another patient she'd wonder about on sleepless nights.

She grabbed the remote off the sofa but dropped it before she hit the power button.

She took a deep breath and a good look at her apartment. All of it, the coats and sweaters, shoes, and take-out containers were like a jumbotron, screaming out about her neglect. Living with blinders on had cost her a tidy apartment. At least the piles of clothes and containers were an easy mess to fix. What else was she too blind to see?

No television, she told herself. *No radio. No background noise. Just a few minutes of uninterrupted cleaning. Empty space, empty mind.*

With her apartment clean, she'd be able to concentrate on her mounting problems and break them down into pieces she could tackle. She was way too smart to let her grandmother's store and the mounting bills take her down.

"Okay, room. Get ready. We're gonna burn down all this mess and start with a clean slate."

She gathered an arm full of clothes and carried them down the hall, the sleeve of a sweater unfurling to her knees and into her bedroom, where she dropped them on the floor. T-shirts and jackets she forgot she owned. Pairs of shoes she wore home from the club. Bras she discarded when she walked in the door. Each pile and armful of clothes she confronted told a piece of the truth. Deep down, she was still just a scared college kid, alone in the world.

With clothes out of the way, she pulled the trash bag from the kitchen can, threw away all the take-out containers, chopsticks, and wrappers. She tied the bag closed and left it on the kitchen floor where it could stay until the rain came to an end.

Her eye fell on the calendar thumbtacked to the wall below the phone. A phone that never rang because she couldn't afford and didn't need a landline. It was a relic that came with the place. November stared back at her, as if autumn and winter hadn't come and gone. The entire year had changed, and the calendar went unnoticed. She'd bought it to help keep track of bills. Written them in the little squares on their due dates and for three weeks in April, she managed to sit down and pay them on time. But that was April. Of the year before.

She tore it from the wall and tossed it in the trash with the rest of the garbage. Who keeps an old calendar up for that long?

But her apartment was clean, for the most part. She could see the living room floor. There was dust on the end table and a fine film covered the television. She'd brushed into it at some point and rubbed a spot clean. A black streak against the gray. The beige carpet hadn't been changed in a decade. Definitely not before she'd moved in, because a stain from someone she never met peeked out from beneath her sofa. A ding in the drywall from when she brought the sofa in the first time. It wasn't like she'd moved in with much. Her television rested on the same old end table she bought her freshman year in college. Her coffee table was the old trunk her mom once kept records in. Maybe she'd be more inclined to keep the place tidy if she liked it more.

With the exception of the burgundy sofa, there was no color, no charm. Charm cost money. All she had to do was hold on through medical school, and she'd be able to buy new furniture and put it in a place that was comfortable enough to make the cost worth it. God knows all her childhood friends had figured it out. Her social media feed was a parade of perfect lives. The ones who hadn't left the city for cute little houses with cute little yards had bought condos and started families. They had gym memberships and ate at nice places, and she ate old salads from the hospital cafeteria and drank at odd-hours with lonely coworkers at a gloomy nightclub.

Like there's any comparison. You're chasing your fate. Everybody chases it at different speeds. You just chose a fate that's really far away.

She went to the kitchen, ripped a paper towel from the roll, but she had no surface cleaner to dust with, so she dug a pencil from the junk drawer and jotted a note on it instead. Cleaning supplies. She pushed it aside, next to a bottle of wine.

Wine. Why should she face all her debts, her missed school deadlines, her bills, and her insurmountable inherited predicament empty handed?

She found the bottle opener in the junk drawer and poured herself a glass. The mouthful of dry red took the edge off the long, rainy day. She left the opener on the counter and took her drink to the dining room table, where her laptop should be. Where it always was. But her laptop was gone.

It always sat there, on the table. It wasn't in her car. It couldn't be; she never took it out of the apartment. It wasn't in the living room. She'd just cleaned there. She tore the pillows off the sofa as the heat of panic started to rise. No sign of it. It wasn't in the bathroom. Not that she expected it to be. She hadn't left it on a shelf in the narrow hall closet, either. That would be the kind of absent-minded thing she'd do. In a dizzying haze, she flew into the little den. Nothing was in the little den. It was far too small for anything, even if she owned something worth putting there.

How was she supposed to work all this out with just her phone? Without her laptop, she couldn't sort the bills, set up a calendar for school deadlines. She couldn't go through the will and finish her list of things to do. She couldn't look for someone to help with this monumental disaster. It would take forever without her laptop.

The bedroom. She probably scooped it up with the sweaters and T-shirts. She must have. "Maybe I carried it in here to do schoolwork?" She pressed a hand to her stomach, relieved to have narrowed it down, wiping the sweat from her palms onto her shirt. The long, slow breath she let out was supposed to be calming, but it was shaky in her dry throat.

Too many layers of glossy paint made the bedroom door stick to the jamb. It opened with a crack, and she stepped into the mess. Piles of clothes she'd not washed since winter were scattered on the floor. At least her lab coats were on hangers, and her scrubs were in their drawers. She went to the small desk she hadn't used in months and pushed aside unopened mail, most of it junk. No laptop.

It had all her schoolwork on it. All the papers she was working on that were due at the end of the semester.

It wasn't on her bed, among the pillows and comforters. Maybe it was in her closet?

All that research. Without the laptop, she was set back so far she'd never finish school.

She flung open the bifold doors and stepped inside. Too small for a light, the tiny room was all shadows, but she found no laptop on the shelves or the floor. It wasn't in her laundry or clean clothes or on top of her dresser. It was gone. She wiped sweat from her forehead with her forearm. Could a plumber have come in to fix a leak and walked off with her laptop? She hated to think that way, but it was a possibility.

"Everything will fall apart if I don't find it."

She raised her arms and let them fall. It didn't make her feel any better.

She made fists, dug her nails into her palms to feel the sweet release of a stinging pain against her frustration. Then closed her bedroom door on the disarray.

She made a beeline for her glass, lifted it with a shaking hand, and took a sip. It sloshed in the glass when she set it down. Anxiety buzzed through her like an electric current. All the things she'd planned to do scattered in her mind, fragmented, smashed to bits. All the fears and hassles and tangles pushed aside by the horror of having lost the expensive lifeline to her education. She turned, and there, in the kitchen, sat her computer, charging cable snaking across the counter. It had been there all along, right next to her, and she couldn't see it for all the clutter.

How could I be so stupid? She grabbed the laptop and dropped it on the table next to her wine. "You could cure cancer if you got your shit together."

That was the goal, wasn't it? To pour her grief into graduating from high school at the top of her class. To getting a scholarship and grants for college and loans to pay for the rest. But most of all, to ignore anything that would delay her even for one second from the promises she made to her mother. And herself. The first, granting her mother's dying wish to get a good education so she could be a doctor. The second, the promise she made after her mother passed, before she even called the hospice nurse and piled her things into trash bags for her trip down the hall to live with her godmother. She would do everything in her power to prevent a kid ever again from losing their mother to cancer.

Penny fell into the chair at the table, and her wine rippled in the glass. She jammed the charging cable in the outlet behind her chair, plugged in the laptop, and opened it.

"You *think* you'd like to cure cancer," she said to her glass of wine, "but there's probably too much paperwork."

The more she tried to cram into her muddled brain, the more it fell apart. She'd already burst at the seams and nothing would stay until she stitched it back together.

How did it get this way? The startup screen flashed, and her desktop began to load. How had she unraveled this far. She used to be so tidy about everything.

Maybe everyone was right. Maybe she did need a break. She couldn't keep headed in the direction she was going, that was for sure.

Her laptop came to life, and her desktop appeared with all the familiar icons. She grasped at the fragments of her plan, but all of it swam, just out of focus, like fish and seaweed in muddy water. She couldn't make out the form of any of it, but she knew it was out there. Possibly dangerous, and she probably didn't want to find any of it. She ran her finger across the trackpad and opened Netflix.

CHAPTER SIX

Penny hadn't stepped foot in the university admission office since she was eighteen years old. The corridor was the same; it just felt smaller. Blue carpet, tan walls, lined with framed pictures of campus landmarks. They were supposed to evoke some sense of pride that the school was an academic powerhouse, but she'd been shaky on her feet then. Dwarfed by the academic grandeur and intimidated by the world around her. Like her guidance counselor had said, an acceptance letter meant nothing unless you could foot the bill, and there wasn't anyone to split it with. Everything had hinged on meeting with an admissions counselor, and her hopes had been higher than her expectations. She'd sat in an uncomfortable chair and explained how her mom was gone, her godmother's job as a guardian was done, and she was on her own. Then she'd walked out the door with a folder full of financial papers and a student loan she wouldn't have to repay for many years to come.

She was no less nervous this time than she'd been a decade before. Five minutes early for her appointment, she waited in a blue wingback chair and read a two-year-old alumni magazine with an article about rocks written by someone from the geology department. Something electric hummed, and if it weren't for the discomfort of being in an academic office, she could let her eyes close and drift off into a peaceful nap.

"Penny?" A door opened, and a woman pinching her glasses between two fingers motioned her in. "You need a leave of absence?"

"Not quite. I don't need to be gone that long." To sit there and ask for a leave of absence from the only goal she'd ever cared about would be a self-imposed flagellation. She sat across the desk from a woman who clearly didn't care, her eyes already locked on her monitor. To her, this was all in a day's work.

"My grandmother passed away, and I inherited a bunch of stuff. I just need two or three days off to handle it. I know I'm supposed to notify you if I need to take more than one shift away from the hospital, so here I am. Notifying you."

The woman punched at a keyboard, her eyes fixed on the monitor. "When do you need these days off?"

"Next week."

The woman scowled at her across the desk, her eyebrows pinched together in silent judgment.

"It's okay. I already worked it out with the hospital to cover my shifts. My grandmother has bills, and I don't know where anything is. She lived in Ramsbolt, which is four hours from here, so I can't just hop over there. She had a store and a cat, too. It's a mess."

The woman turned to her monitor and removed her glasses; the stern expression seemed permanently etched into her forehead. "There's family leave for close relatives. Shorter-term family leave for more distant relatives. And for anything else, you need to take a one-year leave of absence. Period. That's how it works. It's a really big task, closing an estate. Especially if she ran a business and has a lot of inventory. My grandmother's estate was a mess, and she owned a hot plate and a curling iron."

"I don't need a big block of time off or anything. I didn't even know her. It's not a grief thing. I just have to figure out what to do with this cat and all her stuff."

The woman turned from her monitor and dropped her glasses on the desk. "You just said you're the executor of her will."

"Yeah, but that doesn't mean I need a bunch of time off."

"Is there any way you can put this off until after the semester has ended?"

Penny laid her hands on the desk, at the end of her rope. Why was it so hard for her to understand? "No. There's a cat, and I—"

"A few days in a case like this usually turns into more. We've seen students be named executors of wills before, and it's harder than people think."

Penny shook her head, and her eyes fought against the fatigue to stay focused. "I am fully capable of doing my rotations, I'll just have to do some doubles to catch up when I get back."

"Have you looked at the calendar lately?"

She was twenty-five hours behind. What was looking at a calendar going to do for her? "I have a little bit to make up, but I can do it."

"I can't stress how important it is that you return before Thursday so you can declare your specialty for next year. All the hours you put in this semester will be void if you don't. The state has strict licensure requirements, and there are no exceptions to their rules. You'll be placed on academic hold. You won't have the credits to graduate. You won't be qualified to work as a physician, you'll have to repay your loans anyway, and you'll be forced to sit out two semesters. Two. If you want to come back after that, you'll have to petition your advisors to reapply. This is a very big deal."

Running her fingers across her forehead required more effort than it should. Her whole body was tired. "I will. I promise. It'll suck, and I'll be even more exhausted than I am already, but I'll double up shifts again when I get back. I'll have plenty of hours to qualify for the test."

"If you don't pass the state test, you can't proceed. You know that, right?"

Of course she knew that. It was another major hurdle in the only race she'd ever run. The only one worth running. She lifted her own glasses and rested them on her head.

The woman raised an eyebrow in a mock sense of gravity that was offensive enough to make Penny's nostrils flare. She wasn't stupid. She just needed to fix her problems.

"If you need more than three days, you absolutely have to contact us. You will miss declaring your specialty for your fourth year. It's next week—"

"I know."

The woman punched keys. Pages spit out of a printer behind her, and she grabbed them without looking.

"Sign these." She laid them on the table in front of Penny. "Maybe you can use this as a nice vacation."

Was it that obvious that even a total stranger could see the exhaustion? Penny signed the forms and slid them across the desk. "I wish I didn't have to take this break at all. I swore I wouldn't stop until I reached the end of this. Taking three days off feels like a failure, even though it's really not my fault. I'm not a slacker."

"I can tell that from your records. And your grades are at the top of your class."

"So if I miss declaring my specialty, and don't finish my hours, I'll be kicked out of school?"

"Not in so many words, but yes. You have to keep up." The woman fed the signed papers into a scanner. "Okay, you're all set." The woman's hand shot across the desk, and she shook it.

"Thank you for your help."

"You're welcome. With any luck, there'll be a Goodwill down the street, and you'll be able to do everything else from here."

Penny nodded. She'd already looked online, and there were no thrift shops, but there was no use in arguing. She needed the money anyway. Real luck would be selling it all so quickly she'd have one day to herself to sleep before she went back to work.

She wasted no time in the university's blue-and-tan hallway. Debt and the threat of student loan repayment was one thing, but the fear of academic hold, being kicked out of school, and not meeting state requirements for licensure gave her an extra push. She rushed down the hall, through the marble lobby, past its giant stone columns, onto the portico, and across the lawn, with a list of obligations running through her mind like a yoga mantra. She needed to get back to her car, to make notes on her phone. There were too many rules and dates to remember, and she'd come too far to lose it all now. She rushed through to the parking garage, hopped into the driver's seat of her Jeep, and texted Marnie.

I took care of the school part. Thanks for your help w/ the hospital.

Three ellipses flashed on her screen. *No problem. When are you heading out?*

First thing tomorrow. Will be in Ramsbolt before lunch. Back before Wed!

Bar tonite? Lee will be there...

As if Lee had anything to do with it. *Nah. I have to pack.*

Enjoy the trip! Have fun while you're there!

Ramsbolt was no vacation spot. It was the source of most of her problems. Hopefully the woman was right, and it would only take a day or two. If she didn't fix this mess, things would only get worse. And she couldn't wear scrubs and lab coats the whole time she was there, either. She turned the key, and her Jeep came to life. It was time to do some laundry.

CHAPTER SEVEN

Penny took the top off the Jeep, rolled the windows like sushi, shoved them in the back with her old banged-up suitcase, and pulled out of Otley. The traffic and red lights of the city faded behind the thick forests of Maine. From time to time, the trees would grow smaller and houses would scatter along the roadside. Another town would toss another diner on the rural road.

She didn't need a GPS to find Ramsbolt. It was a straight shot toward the Canadian border. Even if she hadn't been there for her grandmother's funeral, she couldn't have missed it when she arrived. One red light in the middle of nowhere. A cheap motel on one side of the road with a gravel lot and plastic Adirondack chairs pushed up against the faded blue siding. Next to it a crumbling gas station with a rusted awning. Across the street, a brick bar with no windows and a sign almost unreadable for all the peeling paint. She sat at the red light, the lone car on the pot-holed road, then turned left toward town.

The road to Ramsbolt was lined with houses cut from the same brick cloth. Steep roofs and bay windows, cratered driveways and broken sidewalks. The road opened to a roundabout and there stood the sailor statue again, just as she left him, profiled against Main Street. She entered the roundabout, pulled the Jeep to the shoulder, and looked him in the eye. He didn't return the courtesy.

Ramsbolt wasn't a coastal town. There were streams and lakes, but nothing to warrant an homage to a sailor. Maybe that's why she was so drawn to guy. He didn't belong there any more than she did. But it was definitely the same statue as the figurine in the hospital gift shop. If it was some kind of omen, like Lee said, she couldn't see it.

She pulled away from the curb and into the circle. "Hello again, Raaams-bolt."

When her mom had said it, she'd put a nasally emphasis on the letter *A*, mocking the little village. Penny had never pronounced it any other way. Her mother hated the town for being so isolated, and Penny saw no value in it as a place of substance or for leisure. Last time she was, she was an outsider, here for the funeral of someone she'd never met. Running late and leaving early. But this time she felt more of her mother's presence as she spun around the circle. Like she was retracing the steps her mother took the last time she ran out of town.

Around the circle, three quarters of the way. She turned right onto an empty street. Storefronts closely packed, most of them empty. A bicycle repair shop with no lights on inside next to a small engine repair shop with an Out to Lunch sign in the window. A florist that looked all but abandoned, with white trim faded to gray and paint husking from the sign over the door like chaff from dried corn, as if what was underneath had been used up long ago. A cheery little toy store that looked out of place among the crumbling paint and rusting signs of the neighboring buildings. The little shop her mother hated so much would be on the left. Just after the toy store. Penny did a U-turn in the wide street, and parked her Jeep at the curb in front of her grandmother's shop.

Junk littered the sidewalk. Old suitcases with rusted hinges, metal lawn furniture with layers of peeling paint, wooden crates and bird cages, terra cotta pots, lengths of metal fences. It spilled from the sidewalk onto the street. Nothing but crap no one wanted. The place wasn't fit for an adult without a tetanus shot, let alone to serve as a suitable home for a child. No wonder her mother hated it so much that she left and never came back.

She looked over her shoulder for oncoming traffic, as if there were traffic in Ramsbolt, and stepped into the street. The slam of her Jeep door echoed off the buildings.

The three-story building looked sturdy enough. No cracks in the mortar or rotting wood. The bricks were old, pockmarked by weather. The trim around the door, the shutters, and the upstairs windows were painted a dusty teal and faded by the sun. The entry door was fairly new, glass from the threshold to the top, but wavy glass in the upper windows hinted at the building's age. Drafty? Probably. Her mother must have endured some harsh winters.

She peeked inside the darkened store. Bound by shadows, the furniture and household crap seemed to be one mass, not separate parts she could extract to sell or discard. Chairs, wooden tables, and parts of beds stacked and twisted, like a nest of rigid snakes. Old telephones and clocks and trinkets were tucked in every crevice. Shelves of dishes and pots and pans were inaccessible, surrounded by ephemera.

She could kiss her extra day of sleep goodbye. There was no way she could clear all of this out in only a few days. There had to be hundreds of things in there. All of it looked as if it sat so long it fused together, a mass of things that no one wanted welded by their disuse and neglect.

And there, among the shambles were the unmistakable droopy eyes of a Snoopy bank, cast in foot-high plastic.

* * *

Penny got a Snoopy backpack for her sixth birthday. For a month after, every day after school, she dropped it on the kitchen floor in front of the kitchen table. Her mom would pick it up, lay it on her immaculate kitchen counter, and dig through the contents, looking for homework and notes from her teachers.

"Who is Caitlyn?" Penny's mom turned a party invitation over in her hands. Garfield the cat had a dozen candles shoved in a pan of lasagna.

"Caitlyn's in my class. She's having a party at her grandmother's house because they have a pool. Can I go?" Penny bounced up and down in the kitchen. The salt shaker wobbled on the counter.

"Stop jumping, sweetie. You'll annoy the neighbors."

"I wanna go. Can I go?" Penny pleaded, her hands clasped.

"You can go. We'll have to get you a bathing suit." Her mother left the card on the counter and returned to the bag for her homework.

Penny hopped onto a chair at the table and smoothed red curls away from her face, preparing for her after-school snack. "Why don't I have a grandmother?"

"You have one. Everybody has one. Two, actually. Is this all your homework? Spelling and geography?"

Penny nodded, and her hair bounced. "If I have a grandmother, why don't I see her?"

"Because we moved here, and your father moved away. We wanted to live two different lives, and that was that. My mother... she's too far away. Even if our old car could get there, it's not a safe place for a kid." Penny's mom pulled a carrot from the fridge and put a dollop of peanut butter on a plate. Carrots and peanut butter. Mom never gave her fun snacks like cookies. "Here."

"Does my grandmother live on a construction site?"

Her mom laughed and grabbed another carrot from the fridge. "Why would you think that?"

"You said the construction by the park was dangerous." Penny dredged the narrow end of the carrot through peanut butter.

"It's a different kind of dangerous. You'd only be bored out there, anyway. There's nothing fun for kids. Just piles of trash everywhere." She returned to the backpack. "You got an A on your math test. Good for you!"

"Yeah. It was easy. Were you bored when you were little?"

Penny's mom sat in the chair across from her. She had that look she always got when she tried to explain grown up things. "Yup. Bored and very lonely."

"You didn't go to school and have parties?" Penny couldn't picture her mom without friends. Brenda was over all the time, and they watched television together and had drinks from big glass bottles and laughed a lot. Sometimes Penny would stay with Mrs. French down the hall so Mom and Brenda could go out to parties.

"I had friends at school, but I could never invite them over because our house was too cluttered to play in. I couldn't put toys on the floor like you do because there wasn't any room."

"Why was there so much on the floor?" Penny had to pick up her toys at the end of every day. And sometimes just because she stopped playing with them. "Did you get out too many things? You always tell me to put things away."

"They weren't my things, bug. They were my mother's things. She liked things more than people. Remember the fairy tale about Hansel and Gretel?"

"With the house made of candy!" Much better than a carrot and some peanut butter.

Her mom leaned across the table, her eyes sparkling, like she was telling a ghost story. The kind that would keep Penny up at night. "They were lured into a gingerbread house because it looked so inviting, but once they got inside, the woman wouldn't let them leave. My house was like that. Only you'd get stuck in there, trapped with all that stuff. Furniture and old lamps and lots and lots of useless junk."

"Grandmom sounds scary!"

"Yeah. But that's why I couldn't have friends over. I couldn't run or play because I could break something, and all those things were more important than me."

"She doesn't sound fun." Penny wrinkled her nose. "Did you get cookies as a snack?"

"Sometimes. But before dinner? Never."

* * *

Penny cupped her hands to clear the glare and peered between them through the door. Her breath fogged the glass. "Geez. Mom was right. It's just a hoarding situation with a sign out front."

"They're closed. And you can't just park here. That's a street. For cars." A man's voice behind her made her jump.

"I know they're closed. I mean, look at the place. And why can't I park here? It's a curb. The street is four cars wide. Who's gonna come barreling down this road and not see a red Jeep?"

The man was ten years her senior, at most. Mid to late thirties. Dark hair streaked with premature grays. Dark eyes flecked with hints of gold.

He wore jeans and a sweater with a hole in the sleeve and boots that had seen their fair share of mud puddles. In one arm, he carried a paper grocery bag that rattled when he shifted his weight. Dried pasta in a box. Shells, maybe. Or Penne.

He tilted his head to the side. "The street's that wide because they wanted a trolley back in the day, but they couldn't figure out where to connect it to. There's no street parking here. You can go 'round back or park on Main Street and walk down."

"I apologize." She tried to keep the sarcasm from her voice but didn't try hard enough. "There aren't any No Parking signs in this marvelous metropolis you have here, and there's no paint on the curb. Excuse me for not reading the hive mind of the smallest town on the planet. I'll only be here a few days, and I'll be out of your hair."

"Penny?" The man stepped back, his features softened.

"Are you the guy who called me about the cat?" As if her first impression of him wasn't bad enough, the second impression wasn't all that pleasant either.

He shuffled the bag to his other hip and stuck out his hand. "I'm Nate. Sorry I yelled at you. And that you lost your gran. I'm not usually this grumpy, and I'm really bad on the phone. I've got a key for you in my store here. Did Morgan send you one?"

His store? Great. The town grump and parking enforcer was right next door. "Who's Morgan?" The name rang a bell. "Oh! The town manager guy. No. I haven't met him, and he didn't give me a key or anything. But I have his address, and he said in his email I could stop by anytime to get it."

"I'll give you the one I got so you don't have to wait. God knows where he'll have run off to. He's young, that one. Hyper." Nate gave the door to the toy store a good push. The door swung open, and an electric chime rang out. She watched through the window as he dropped the bag on the counter and dug a key from the drawer of his cash register. Then he bent behind the counter and scooped up a cat. A tan cat with a pink nose and little white feet.

The door opened, and Nate stepped onto the sidewalk. He pushed the cat into her arms. "That's Jake."

"Thanks, I think." The cat squirmed in her arms. He didn't want her any more than she wanted him.

Nate fiddled the key into the lock. "Same key works from the outside or inside. And for the back door, too. It sticks in this lock here, though." The door clicked, and he shoved the key in her empty hand. The cat squirmed in the other.

"Is this an outdoor cat at all?" His claws dug into her arm.

"Never was, but I bet he'd come back. Loved your grandmother. He only tolerates me, though." Nate swung the door open and stepped into the dark cramped store. He held the door open for her. "Kinda like the woman across the street. Just tolerates the rest of us."

Penny glanced at the dilapidated flower shop. "You mean someone runs that store? I thought it was abandoned."

"It looks that way, but it's been there for three or four generations. She's about my age. But she's a tough nut to crack. Your grandmother was a great neighbor, though."

Penny stepped into the store and into a wall of warm air, thick with the musty smell of dust and wood.

"What a disaster." Penny covered her mouth with her hand. Dust floated in the rays of light that streamed in through the door and the upper windows. Furniture and parts of furniture covered the entire first floor, stuck together like abstract sculptures. Shelves of household goods tucked among them. Narrow paths were barely accessible for the clutter that tumbled from every surface.

To her right, set back from the door, was a glass display with costume jewelry and old amber rings. A vintage cash register rested at the far end of the counter. Mirrors, drawings, and framed photographs covered the walls, punctuated by the taxidermied heads of former wildlife. A rabbit. An elk whose antlers rose to the loft above.

A well-worn trail cut through the clutter, revealing the wide-plank hardwood floors. It led from the counter to a sunny room in the back. Yellow walls and a small white table, a breakfast nook perhaps, shined like a flashlight in the darkness. Her grandmother had lived in the space, after all. There must be a few creature comforts. The path forked to the right, to a set of stairs that led to a lofted living space. She could make out the foot of a bed beyond the tree branches that formed the railing.

Penny let Jake leap from her arms onto a table. He disappeared among the legs of chairs stacked halfway to the ceiling. How did he not get lost in the maze?

As if he could read her thoughts, Nate said, "He knows his way around. Thing is, your grandmother wasn't messy. This is a pretty organized collection of things, overall. It's just cramped in here. She dusted all this, believe it or not. Nobody's been here since just after she died. It's gone downhill a bit."

Penny put her hands on the glass display and peered behind it. Stacks of wooden crates and boxes of packing material leaned against the wall. As if anyone ever bought anything to have packed up and shipped out. "Why is there so much stuff? There's gotta be more crap in here than in the houses in town."

"A lot of people lost their jobs here. They moved away or downsized. They only took what they needed. Eliza, your gran, she used to go to estate sales and buy things to sell, but when all those people moved, they brought her stuff for free that she could sell. She promised to give it all good homes, but there weren't many takers, and the ones who were just passing through were never good enough for these things. This is Ramsbolt history."

Penny stared straight up, praying nothing fell in her eyes. Chairs hung from the ceiling. Chandeliers made of crystal and glass and wood and antlers. "My mom said she never sold anything."

"She sold stuff, but not enough to clear the place out. Don't know how she stayed in business. She was the only person in town people trusted with their heirlooms, though. Place is full of things people around here used to love."

"Used to." Penny examined a wood magazine rack. One leg was barely holding on. "She doesn't even have price tags on anything."

"On purpose. She paired people with stuff so she priced accordingly. If she didn't think somebody was good enough for what they wanted to buy, she'd make up a price too expensive so they'd go away."

The annoyance accumulated, building as tension in her shoulders. She rubbed at a spot near her shoulder blade. "Seems counterproductive to running a business to me. And now this is my mess to clean up. No wonder my mom called her a hoarder."

Nate shook his head and dust danced in the air around him. "It wasn't that. She wasn't collecting it. Keeping it around did nothing for her." He stepped to the door. "I'll leave you to it. Come on by or knock if you need anything. I'll bring Jake's food by. There's probably still some in the kitchen back there, too."

Nate left, and the door creaked to a close behind him. In the silence, she could hear Jake moving through the furniture, his paws padding on the wood floor. He hopped up on the glass display and rubbed his chin on the vintage brass cash register.

How was she supposed to move all this stuff? She certainly wasn't strong enough to haul it all outside. Even if she had enough money in her savings to afford a truck to get it to the dump, she still needed to sell as much as she could to pay off whatever debts her grandmother claimed she'd left behind. Her back ached from the thought of trying to lift it all, her mind reeled with the strewn scraps of an intangible to-do list, and her lungs were choked with stale air tinged with dust.

"This is impossible, Jake. Where do I start? If I pull one chair out of here the whole thing could come crashing down. How did it even get like this?" And how was she supposed to get rid of it all in three days? "I'll start with you. Let's find you a happy home. First thing in the morning."

Then she would sell as much as she could, make as much money as she could, and face what was left when her time was up.

Penny followed the narrow footpath as deep into the mayhem as her courage would allow. The pictures told a sepia-toned story that had no meaning to her. Maybe those images connected the people to their history, but they'd thrown it all away. In one photograph, a grand estate sat, surrounded by a porch and fields of potatoes. In another, a black and white street was lined with electric lights. She recognized the roundabout, empty, before the sailor statue arrived. There were paintings of ships and drawings of birds. She stepped around a school desk carved with the names of students who worked hard, dreamed big, and got out of town. At least Penny hoped they had. But each of these things once meant something to someone. And her grandmother had been the end of the line for all of it.

It definitely wasn't any place for a child, but the way Nate told it, her grandmother was liked. If she hadn't hoarded it for personal gain, the way her mother made it sound, then she must have found some fulfillment in being surrounded by this stuff. How anyone could be content and feel any gratification in all that mess was beyond her.

"Cleaning out this place is going to be harder than I thought, Jake." No junk removal companies nearby. No salvage or scrap people for hundreds of miles around.

Just because it was hard, didn't mean it couldn't be done. She would just have to work harder to sell as much of it as she could. The risk of leaving this job undone and the damage it could do to her future was greater than she cared to calculate.

"If all of this crap came from Ramsbolt, Ramsbolt is gonna have to take it back. It might take a hell of a lot more than a sidewalk sale to get rid of all this, but the sooner I start, the sooner I can finish and blow off some steam." And it would take a whole lot more than a sordid-looking bar across from a cheap motel for her to blow off the steam from this chaos. She missed the club. She even missed Lee.

"I want this over. Like, yesterday." She turned back, aiming for the sunny kitchen, and kicked at the leg of a table, stubbing her toe. "Ow. I can't believe this shit! First you robbed Mom of her childhood. Now you're robbing me of time at school. I should be healing people. Learning to be a surgeon. Nothing about this place makes anybody feel good about anything."

CHAPTER EIGHT

Penny banged her knee on the leg of the little white table when she crossed her legs. Plastic daffodils wobbled in their vase. She steadied her coffee while she rubbed at the stabbing pain. If her eyes weren't still so puffy from sleeping in the dry store, she might be able to see her own legs better.

Coffee would help. The stuff in her grandmother's cabinet wasn't the best, but it was better than anything from the hospital vending machine. One small success in an otherwise dismal start.

Jake hopped on the table from out of nowhere and sank onto his paws, resting in a spot of sunlight from the tiny window behind her.

"You hungry?"

Jake purred and lifted his face to the sun.

She scooped dry cat food from the bag Nate dropped off. It clattered into the bowl.

"Is the heat in here gas or electric?" Penny turned up the thermostat next to the fridge. Sixty-eight felt more like fifty. "What do you care? You've got fur. Heat ducts are probably covered by furniture anyway."

Jake jumped from the table to his bowl and crunched his food. He lifted his head at a sound, faint and distant.

"What is that noise?"

Jake crunched his food.

"It's like a scratching or a—" Penny craned her neck around the corner and saw a figure at the door. "Geez. Is my Jeep in the wrong place around back, too? There's no privacy here at all. How did she live like this?"

She tied her robe tight and grabbed the key from the display counter on her way to the door. As she got closer, she could make out the features of a young man, twenty perhaps, in cargo shorts and a T-shirt. He gave her a frantic wave and a broad smile, and held out a basket wrapped in cellophane.

His muffled voice came through the door. "I'm Morgan. The town manager."

It took some fiddling with the key, but the door finally unlocked. "Things get moving pretty early around here, huh?"

Not as early as a shift in the emergency room, but she didn't need to burst his bubble. Penny held the door open and let him in. A burst of cool morning air came with him.

Morgan stepped inside, and the door closed behind him. "Welcome to our little town. I was out running around this morning, and thought I'd see if you were up. I got your key here. Though I can see you met Nate and got your hands on Jake. What a sweetie. He's a treasure." Morgan dropped the basket on the display counter and dug into his pocket. He put the key in her hand.

"Thanks. I don't mean to rush you off, but—" She was standing in her housecoat in front of a kid who was barely twenty years old. How was he the town manager? None of it seemed appropriate.

PENNY'S LOFT

He waved a hand and stepped into the clutter. "Don't worry about me. You probably think I'm too young for this job. Frankly, it's not even my job."

"So Morgan is your dad?"

"No, I'm Morgan. My dad ran for the office when Faulkner retired. Faulkner did this job for decades. Turns out, Dad hated doing it, so he paid me to do it. I've been at this for about three years now. He lets me have the salary, and he pays me a little on top of it because I said there's no way I'm doing all this for so little money. He didn't want the job back. So here I am. Morgan."

Penny raised an eyebrow. What kind of town was this that the town manager got an allowance from his dad to do the job? "Isn't that, like, extortion? Over your dad?"

"No, no. The town pays, like, *no money*. So no one else would want this job. It all works out. Anyway, that over there is your welcome basket from the town. You've got breakfast in there from Marissa's that'll still be warm if you get to it fast enough, and there's a gift certificate for the tea house in there. Coupon for the hardware store. That kind of thing." Morgan tipped back on his heels. "Looks like you'll be needing that hardware store coupon."

Penny folded her arms. "I don't want it."

"The coupon? It's just part of the basket."

"The basket. All of it. I don't want it. I'm not staying."

Morgan tucked in his chin, disbelief spread across his face. "I can't take it back now. I can't return a bagel. It's not returnable."

"Fine. I'll keep it. Thank you."

"You're welcome. Enjoy your stay, as long as you're here. Oh, and if you're wondering, there are no local taxes to worry about."

Penny bit the inside of her lip. She hadn't even thought to be worried about taxes. She tagged it onto her mental list of things to figure out, alongside getting a grasp on the debt and finding a home for Jake. Taxes couldn't be any harder than hers. She'd just use that free online software. She rubbed at the corner of one eye, afraid to ask. "Is there anything else I should know?"

"Sewer and water. If you don't have recent bills, let me know."

"Are there hidden fees or anything? I don't have a grasp on what she owed yet." She glanced around for paper, somewhere to make a note, but there was nothing but furniture and clutter.

Morgan shook his head. "Ramsbolt's easy. Not much to maintain here. Just the park at the circle, and there's no budget for that. People chip in and clean it up when it gets really bad. Mostly during the tourist season when everybody feels the need to throw things out the car window. There's a fun story from a long time ago when they wanted to put electric lights on Main Street."

"I'm okay. No offense." She put up a hand to stop him. "My brain is really full, and I'm having a hard time putting all the pieces together here. So there's nothing but sewer and water, right?"

"Right. We're too small for even school taxes. The town gets a subsidy."

"Okay. That's good news." Penny tightened her robe again. The bagel did look good. "Can you recommend a real estate agent, by any chance?"

Morgan shook his head. "We don't have one of those."

How could a town not have a real estate agent? How was she supposed to sell the store if there wasn't a real estate agent? But she should have known. Her mother always said Ramsbolt was a backward little town. She just figured it would be a backward little town that had a real estate agent and a thrift store.

She rubbed her eyes with the heels of her hands and ground her teeth together, suddenly craving a pen cap to chew on.

Morgan pointed his thumb at the door. "Any more questions before I run?"

"Yes. Is there a grocery store? I'm starving."

"Only place for groceries is the market, unless you want to drive out of town. I'd stick to the market, though. They got everything you need. You just go down to the circle and go left. That's Main Street. Store's down on the left. I'd recommend the bar, too. There's no food there. Used to be, though, back before Helen got tired of running a diner. It's just beer and whiskey and wine, now. Nice place to meet folks and unwind."

"Thanks. But I'm not staying." If that little brick building was where they went to unwind, this town could do with a little tightening.

Morgan raised an eyebrow. "Okay. Have a good day, then."

He let himself out, and the door closed behind him. Penny kicked herself for not asking how people sell real estate if there's no real estate agent in town, but she wasn't about to chase a young man down the street in her bathrobe.

Something brushed against her leg, and she jumped, clutching her robe tight. Jake bonked her leg with his head and wound himself through her feet.

"This town is insane, Jake. One park. No budget. The school is barely a school."

In the fifteen years since she lost her mom, she'd wished she could call her a million times. To be able to pick up the phone and ask advice. Standing in all that clutter, she wished more than anything that she could call and thank her for leaving Ramsbolt. "I never would have been who I am if I'd been raised here. Never would have been a surgeon. Probably wouldn't have made it to college. My mother hating my grandmother turned out to be my salvation."

In the back corner of the room, tucked beneath the stairs, was her grandmother's office, its walls made of pegboard nailed to the studs. She'd wedged a little wood desk with a phone and a notepad and a plastic trash can into the tiny space, along with a small filing cabinet. A dry-erase board was fastened to the wall with twine. Penny found a dry-erase marker in the desk and wrote *Local Taxes / Fees* on the board and crossed it out. It wasn't much of an accomplishment, but it was one worth noting. On more a discouraging note, she added "Real estate," and "Bills / Debt."

On the desk, a red light blinked. Penny flipped on the desk lamp and inspected the phone. Voice mails. "There's a nice source of stress first thing in the morning. How many of these do you think are good news?"

She grabbed a pen from the desk drawer. Its cap was clean and shiny, unscuffed. Even so, she knew better than to stick it in her mouth, but stress drained from her like sand from an hourglass when she clenched it in her teeth. She pressed the speakerphone button to play the messages, holding the pen over a scrap of paper, ready to take notes. Salespeople offering web development services. Did this place even have a website? Advertising people from antiques circulars begged for return calls as soon as possible so they could make their pitch.

"Poor woman got herself on a list somewhere, huh?" Jake wound his way between her legs. Penny scribbled down names and numbers. Not that she was going to call any of these people back.

"This message is for whoever takes over Eliza's shop. This is Cheryl from Bar Harbor Vintage. I knew Eliza from the antique circuit. I'm interested in making a purchase, and I have an offer for whoever takes over now that she's no longer with us. If this message reaches anyone who wants to sell, you can reach me at…"

Penny checked the time on her cell phone. Eight fifteen. She rang the number.

"Bar Harbor Vintage, this is Cheryl."

"Oh. I expected voicemail. Good morning. I hope it's not too early. I'm calling from Eliza's shop in Ramsbolt."

"That adorable shop in that cute little town? I never expected to hear from anyone. Is anything still for sale?"

"Still? Everything's for sale. You can have all of it. The walls, the roof, all of it. You can even have the cat."

A beeping came through the line, like a forklift. Did this woman have a store so big she needed equipment? Penny peeked around the corner at the mountain of despair. What could it all be worth? Bed frames and massive tables. People paid a small fortune for matching sets of antique chairs. There was no telling what condition it was all in, but there could be thousands of dollars of furniture in there. Tens of thousands maybe. Her throat went dry. She hadn't considered that there could be anything of value in this for her at all. What if she could make enough to pay off her student loans?

The beeping on the line subsided. "Sorry about the noise. Anyway, I don't need all of it, and I already have a cat. I buy in bulk where I can. Are you the executor of her will?"

"I'm her granddaughter. Penny. I inherited it, and it's not my destiny to run the shop, so it all must go."

"Two thousand dollars. For everything. Except the building, of course. I don't do real estate."

"I'm sorry. I may have misheard. Two thousand dollars for everything? There has to be nearly fifty years of stuff in this building. And some of it is really old. I don't know how valuable it is, but it's gotta be worth more than two thousand dollars."

"This is what I do. I have a warehouse, and I buy stuff when estates close. I clean it up, and sell it online and in my store here. I have to make a profit."

Two thousand dollars wasn't two months of rent. She hadn't seen her grandmother's debt yet, but if it had been worth mentioning, it was probably more than two thousand dollars. She flung open the bottom desk drawer. Little tabs lined green hanging file folders in orderly rows, in handwritten all caps. But the contents were in disarray. A folder labeled Phone Bills contained some kind of medical receipt. Another titled Credit Cards held an instruction manual for a microwave. She thumbed through them, fast, passing recipes torn from magazines and pages from old wall calendars.

"You still there? Penny?"

"One second. Sorry, I'm just looking for something here."

In folder labeled Insurance, she found a credit card statement three months old. The balance had two digits before the comma. Penny's heart sank. She winced and threw the bill on the desk.

"Is that a negotiable two thousand?" Even if it was, there's no way she would get tens of thousands from the woman. Cheryl's profit would be Penny's killing.

"Nope. Last chance. You just caught me at the wrong time. The warehouse is filling up, and I'm placing a bid on the contents of a massive estate in Rhode Island this weekend. I'll be out of space after that. Say yes, and I can have it all gone tomorrow."

Penny couldn't say yes. All that, shipped out of town for only two thousand dollars? It wouldn't even relieve the burden of her debt. Money was worth so much more than time. "Sorry, I can't. It's just not enough. Do you know anyone else who does this kind of thing? Buys up whole stores?"

"I'm sorry. I don't. You could call around to other dealers, but most of them have small shops. There aren't many who keep warehouses for storage. Thanks for calling back, though. Have a good one. And good luck." And Cheryl hung up. All business, that one.

"She wouldn't fit in around here, that's for sure." Penny lowered herself into the leather desk chair. Her grandmother's slender frame had made a divot in the seat.

She pulled a stack of file folders about two inches thick from the drawer and tossed them on the desk. Inside the first one she found ten-year-old phone bills. The folder claimed to be tax receipts.

"No wonder you were so far behind, Eliza. All these bills are ancient. Things are in the wrong folders."

She found the prior year's tax forms inside a folder labeled Telephone. "At least you kept up with that."

"Penny? Hello!" It was Nate. She hadn't locked the door behind Morgan when he left. The chair creaked when she stood. Her robe cinched tight, she stepped out from the office cubby beneath the stairs.

"Sorry about my casual appearance here." She ran a hand through her hair. She hadn't even combed it. Not that appearance counted for much.

"No problem. I forgot to bring Jake's bowls over last night." He held them out, and she took them. Two little ceramic bowls, one white and one blue. "The blue one's for his water. He hates if you mix them up.

Won't eat."

"Sure. Cats. Picky."

"I see you got a welcome basket. Marissa's bagels are the best. She also makes really good coffee. How long are you staying?"

Until she'd gone through the files and put a price tag on the obligations. Until she'd compressed the pile of abandoned household stuff, and it turned into diamonds that made her rich enough to pay off everyone her grandmother owed. Was it the swarm of confusion and the paralyzing tasks she couldn't comprehend that were clogging her head and making her dizzy or was it all the dust?

She sneezed.

"Bless you," Nate said. "Here are those cat bowls."

"Thanks." She tucked them inside the welcome basket and hugged it to her chest. She'd almost forgotten about the bagel. "Trust me, I am *not* staying. I'm out of here the second I can sort through her bills and sell off all this stuff. And find a home for the cat."

CHAPTER NINE

Penny found stickers in her grandmother's desk. Little round stickers in red, yellow, green, and blue. She moved through the store and stuck them on anything that looked like it would move during a sale. Blue for the cheap things. Red for the most expensive. Yellow and green for everything in between. She'd only scratched the surface, labeling just what she could reach, but if she sold that stuff for what she hoped, she'd be able to pay off the electric bill, at least. And maybe make a dent in the sewer bill.

"What about this dresser, Jake? What would you sell it for?"

Jake had no opinion. He peered from a desk to the floor below, waiting for a spider or some speck of dust to make itself known.

"Is it red expensive or yellow expensive?" She held up two sheets of stickers. "Red expensive would be, like, more than three hundred dollars. Yellow expensive is maybe, one fifty? Oh, *what's the plan*, you ask? Thank you for asking. Yes, the plan is to let people name their own price. Everything blue is free with the purchase of anything not blue. How's that sound?"

Jake swished his tail. Still no opinion.

"That's okay. I didn't expect you to be very useful anyway."

Her cell phone buzzed in her pocket. She dropped the stickers on the dresser and swiped at the screen. Lee.

She held the phone to her ear. "Hello?"

"Hey, there. Feels like I haven't talked to you in a decade." Penny put the sheets of labels in her back pocket. If she left them on a piece of furniture, she'd never find them again.

"I just talked to you. It was the day before yesterday. Aren't you at work?" Lee never called her. She couldn't even remember why he had her number.

"I am at work, actually. Remember the heart attack lady? You sent her for blood work? She didn't want to go up for testing before her daughter arrived?"

Penny sat on a Windsor chair. "No. Please don't tell me she's gone. I sat with her for so long, and her daughter was so upset."

"She's fine. Did a stint. She was discharged today."

"Thank God. I was worried for her."

"They never would have known if you hadn't ordered that blood work. Pays to be cautious, I guess."

"Paid off for her. Don't know about her co-pays."

"Anyway, I was down in the ER with an overdose patient, and I heard someone at the nurse's desk say the woman wanted to thank you, then Cassie said you were on vacation, and I had no *idea* you were on vacation, so I thought I'd call and pass it on to you. I wondered when I didn't see you at the club on Friday night."

"I'm not on vacation. I'm in Raaams-bolt. Marnie didn't tell you? How do you even have my number?"

"Got it off Cassie. No, Marnie didn't say anything. I missed her at happy hour. Are you okay in the wilderness? Do we need to send supplies? When are you coming back? Do they even have coffee there? How you will survive?"

"It's not so bad." On one hand, she wanted to beg him to come, to make her laugh and keep her from losing her mind. But on the other hand, she was happy for the distance. His affection made her warm and turning him off would be a cold necessity. "It's a small town, not post-apocalyptic destitution. I'll get by."

Lee snorted. "You talked about that place like it was right out of *Deliverance*."

"It's really not that bad. I even got a welcome basket this morning from the town manager." Not that she wanted it.

"What was in it?"

"A really good bagel." She smiled at the memory of it. Much better than hospital bagels. She'd have to find that bakery.

"But aren't welcome baskets for people who are sticking around? They give those out to every visitor?"

"Hell if I know. Strange little place. Definitely not a vacation."

"At least there are bagels. You didn't say when you're coming back."

"Three days." Penny picked at the peeling varnish of a dining room table.

"Well, we miss you. Call me when you get back. We'll have breakfast or something."

We. He didn't mean everyone, he meant himself. Penny missed him, too, now that he wasn't next to her. She missed the city, and it hadn't even been a whole day.

A bell rang out behind her, and she jumped. The door swished closed behind a woman in her forties in a pair of linen pants and a blue sweater.

She held a small bunch of lupine in a simple glass vase. Penny waved.

"Lee, I gotta go. I'll talk to you later." She ended the call. She could picture him in the break room, at the counter. Piece of wheat bread in the toaster and one of those little packets of almond butter he liked so much waiting on a plate. If she were there, she'd be at the nurses' station, trying to pawn off paperwork on one of Cassie's unsuspecting nurse's assistants. Of all the people who missed her, Cassie probably wasn't one of them.

Penny stabbed a blue sticker on a box of old metal Matchbox cars and turned to the woman at the door.

"You must be Penny. I'm Adelle." She rested the vase on the counter and tucked her hands in her pockets. She slouched, as if she were uncomfortable in her own skin. "I was fairly good friends with your grandmother, I guess you could say."

Penny slinked around furniture and put out a hand. "Nice to meet you. I'm sorry for your loss. I didn't know her, so it feels a little strange being here."

Adelle nodded. She wore a sad smile. "I can imagine. Even the most distant loss comes with a side order of all kinds of guilt." She picked up the Snoopy bank and brushed dust from the top of his head. "Eliza had a way with objects. She knew how they could change people. She said everything has an aura to it, and things have to match up right. Sometimes an object doesn't belong with a person, and she wouldn't sell it to them. She was looking for a home for this bank, waiting for the right kid to come along." She placed the bank back on the window ledge. "She sacrificed money, though. That's for sure."

"I can tell. There's a lot of debt." If the woman hadn't waited so long for the right buyers to come along, Penny wouldn't be there hoping anyone would come along at all.

"Maybe you'll have an easier time with it. Some new marketing ideas could breathe fresh life into the place."

Something had to. "I'm not taking on the store. I have to get back to life as soon as possible, unfortunately."

Adelle straightened her back and raised her eyebrows. "Oh. I don't know why I thought you were staying. What do you do?"

"I'm in school to be a surgeon." Penny said it with a broad smile, but it was met with a scowl.

"We don't need a doctor here. Or a pharmacy. We have those."

Penny put her hands in her back pockets. "I'm not moving here at all, actually. I'm going back to Otley to finish school and then moving somewhere else."

Adelle nodded slowly, her lips pursed as if she'd been offended somehow. "What's so wrong with Ramsbolt?"

Penny could tell she struck a nerve. "Ramsbolt is great. It really is. I love how it's held onto its roots. It's just not my thing. I grew up in a city, and I'm at home there."

Her chin lifted, eyes ablaze, Adelle turned to leave. "I'm fourth generation Ramsbolt, and I love it here. My dad was the town manager before he died, and I can't imagine living anywhere else. There's something to be said for a small town that holds onto its identity. Your grandmother understood that. But it's not for everybody, I guess. Enjoy your stay."

"Thanks for the flowers."

The woman pushed through the door and was gone. What had Nate said about the florist? Something about her being an acquired taste? Penny couldn't argue with that. She put a blue sticker on a box of dishes

81

and nudged them under a table with her foot. The dishes rattled when the box bumped up against an old A-frame sign.

She wrestled it from behind the box and stood it on a dining room table. It would be perfect for the sidewalk. It was all wood, in pretty bad shape. Dinged and chipped with chunks missing from the frame. With a little paint, though, it would make a decent enough Going out of Business sign.

"Hey, Jake. There was paint around here, wasn't there? Where did I see that?"

No answer from the cat. Her tummy grumbled and jogged her memory. She'd seen it after she ate the bagel, when she looked under the sink for a roll of paper towels.

Penny skirted the piles and stacks, dodging protruding chair legs. She collected the small can of paint and some brushes from a mason jar, and under Jake's scrutiny, painted in all capital letters: *Estate Sale! Everything Must Go!*

She tapped the lid back on the paint with an old hammer and left the sign to dry.

"There. What do you think, Jake? We can set this out front and wait for the crowds to rush in. Then, when this place is empty, I can get the building on the market. I can sell all this crap in a few days, right?"

The cat rubbed his tan chin on the sign.

"And I'll find you a really nice home. With some kids. Toys to play with and a place to lie in the sun. A bunch of windows. Would you like that?"

Jake swatted at the can of paint and knocked it to the floor.

"Thank God the lid was on. Silly cat. What are you trying to do to me here?" Penny's tummy grumbled again. She needed something to eat, to stock the fridge, and check in on that pet store to see if they could find a home for Jake. If the town couldn't take pity on her, maybe they'd take pity on poor homeless Jake.

She picked up the can and carried it to the kitchen, Jake on her heels. "That bagel didn't last long, and you're almost out of crunchies, kitty. I'm gonna go find that market and put some food in this fridge. I'll spread the word about the sale downtown, and maybe when I get back, that sign'll be dry. We'll put it out and wait for the after-church crowd to run in. Sound good?"

Penny grabbed her keys from the counter and scratched Jake's head. "You stay outta trouble."

A narrow door led from the kitchen, down two wooden steps, to a small concrete patio and a paved back lot. Her Jeep sat nose to nose with an old Buick that must have belonged to Nate. If only she could climb into it and head straight back to the city. Back to work and school and to the only thing that mattered, the hospital.

She let the engine rumble and settle before backing down the alley. Three quarters of the way around the roundabout, she turned down Main Street. It wasn't a bustling shopping district, and she didn't expect it to be. She expected crumbling storefronts, vacant real estate, trash-strewn sidewalks, and a street littered with cans and cigarette butts. But the street was clean, the storefronts tidy. There was free parking on both sides of the road. A few stores were empty, but most were occupied with the kinds of shops she expected in any town. A laundromat, a dentist. A pharmacy. A deli across from a pet shop. A tea shop across from the bank. Only the newsstand next to the town office stood as a reminder that Ramsbolt was decades behind the rest of the world. A hardware store occupied the widest building on the right side of the street. The widest building on the left was the market. And dead ahead, at the end of the road, stood a simple but elegant Methodist church.

Penny left her Jeep at the curb across from the market and scampered across the empty street, her mind focused on her shopping list. A box of cereal, some sandwiches, a few snacks. Just enough to hold her over for a few days.

Inside, the market was quaint and cramped. Narrow aisles of metal shelves. It looked more like a convenience store than a place to get groceries. The kind of place you'd find refuge on a road trip, but hardly the source of daily sustenance. There were no prepared foods like sandwiches or salads. No fresh flowers or fresh-baked breads. She browsed the baskets of fruits and vegetables and picked through a pyramid of apples, looking for three of the best ones.

"Welcome to town." A woman at her shoulder lifted a bruised Granny Smith from a wicker basket.

"Oh, thanks. That's nice of you." Penny placed a Fuji in her basket where it rested with her sliced ham and swiss cheese. She knew what came next and decided to head it off at the pass. "But I'm not staying."

"What a shame! So you're just here to sort through Eliza's things?" Fifty years or so her senior, the woman's voice cracked with age. Her gray curls hid beneath a scarf. How did she know? Had she known Eliza? Then Penny remembered the town was so small, she probably drove over a trip wire somewhere and started a phone chain. The creepiness was slightly eclipsed by the charm.

"Afraid so. I have to get back to life as soon as everything's wrapped up. Having a huge sale, though. Lots of free things." Penny added another apple to her basket. Two should be plenty. "Everything must go. Spread the word!"

The woman nodded a soft assent. Penny accepted her smile as a gracious well-wishing, but she knew she'd never see the woman again.

On her way to the register, she found a loaf of wheat bread, a generic brand of mayonnaise in a little mason jar, and the kind of sweet cereal her mother would never have let her eat.

The store accepted cash only, no cards or checks. She dropped her basket on the counter and dug through her wallet. Two twenties. She'd have to stop at a bank. She had to go anyway, once they were open, to figure out whether Eliza had a checking account or anything in savings.

"Welcome to town, ma'am. Are you Penny?" The bag boy swatted blond bangs from his eyes. He looked so young. Too young to be bagging groceries. She worried for her apples. "My mom ran into Nate at the post office, and he said you'd come to town."

"I am Penny. It's me. But I'm not staying." The declaration rolled off her tongue like a well-worn script. She passed a twenty to the man at the register. "I'm going to sell the place when I can. Everything is on sale, though. Big discounts. Come by whenever! It's open from dawn until I turn the lights out. Bet you could use a ton of stuff for your apartment, huh?"

"I live with my mom."

The man at the register held out her change. His dark brows furrowed over ice blue eyes. "You're selling everything? All of it?"

She offered him the biggest smile she could muster, figuring the friendlier and more welcoming she looked, the more likely they'd be to come by. So far, all she'd been doing was telling the town she had no intention of living there. "What doesn't sell is going in the trash."

His eyes narrowed. She'd said the wrong thing. "You can't just throw it all away. I think half my grandmother's furniture ended up in there.

Hate to see all that end up in the landfill."

"No, I don't want to throw it away. I need to sell all of it. I just mean that I can't afford to take it home with me."

The fighting glint in his eye made her blood boil. If the town treasured that garbage so much, they shouldn't have piled it on her grandmother. On her. They should come and take it back.

"Unfortunately, half your grandmother's furniture ended up in my grandmother's store, then she died, and left it to me. I have to get rid of it all, so I can pay her debt and get back to medical school and become a surgeon and save lives, know what I mean? So if you need anything like furniture or decorations or old pictures, you're welcome to come shop." She finished with a smile instead of the string of curse words that came to mind. "Store's open late. Hope to see ya."

She snatched her paper bag from the counter and nearly tripped on her way out the door. If the town had a police officer, he could have made a fortune giving her a speeding ticket as she tore up Main Street. She whipped around the roundabout and parked behind the store. The Jeep creaked to a halt and crunched when she pulled the emergency brake.

She mumbled to herself on her way to the back door. How dare they just assume she was going to hold onto all their crap for the rest of her life. Like Raaaams-bolt was the be-all, end-all of the American Dream. She had crap to do. She couldn't sit around here forever with all this garbage.

Jake greeted her at the back door, oblivious to her troubles.

What was wrong with these people? She threw the bag of cat food and a box of cereal into the cabinet over the counter and slammed the door. They treated this store like it was some kind of dump. Just threw all the crap they didn't want anymore in here. And now they're all like *you can't get rid of anything*. She wasn't a museum! Did she look like a museum? She already looked, and this town did *not* have a museum.

Jake hopped onto the kitchen table and perched next to the vase of Adelle's flowers.

"They made me so mad I forgot to stop at the pet store to see if they can help find you a home."

Penny stormed out of the kitchen and into the store, performing her ballet of dodging protruding legs of chairs. "Like I'm some kind of damn charity. I'm not gonna go bankrupt so I can play storage facility to a bunch of people who can't throw anything away. I swear to God."

She came to stop before the sign she had painted. It was still wet, but there was no reason to wait before putting it outside so it could bring people in. Church would be ending soon. Maybe she could pick up some foot traffic.

Any sense of fondness she felt for the history within the store's walls was eclipsed by the scale of it all. It closed in on her. Pillars of chairs and dressers. Dark wood. Dark corners. How much did this stuff weigh? Her insides twisted. She wanted to push her arms out, make some breathing room. Desperate for air, she grabbed the sign and carried it outside to the sidewalk.

She propped open the door to let some fresh air in. Maybe it would lure in some people from Ramsbolt.

"Come and get your junk before I set it all on fire," she yelled into the silence.

CHAPTER TEN

Penny pulled into the parking lot of the local bar, gravel kicking up by her tires and pinging under her Jeep, grateful it was open on a Sunday. She hadn't sold a thing all day and needed to console herself. The lot was a dry and rutted welcome mat to the only watering hole in town. She parked next to a dumpster and nearly twisted her ankle when she hit the ground.

The building was windowless and inhospitable. Little more than a brick and concrete rectangle with a door, it was the kind of place her mother warned her about. "Dear Lord, when you grow up, don't step foot in bars like that," she'd say when they passed rural dives that looked not unlike Helen's Tavern.

How could anyone breathe in there? It looked like the kind of place people go when they don't want to be seen. Hardly the serene setting to find a satisfying distraction, let alone some friendly locals who might help her offload her grandmother's stuff. But Morgan had recommended it, and he seemed cheery enough, not the type of guy to steer her to a strip club, though it was hard to picture anything else by the look of it.

She skirted the building to the front door, its wood swelled in the humid New England evening. She pulled it open and panes of rippled yellow glass rattled in the frame. The vestibule smelled like old cigarettes. Broken coat hooks drooped from cheap wood paneling and the ceiling tiles were yellowed with age. A light buzzed overhead, one tube flickering every second or two. Another door stood between her and the bar. It weighed less than she expected, and it flung wide open when she pulled on it. A bar full of people who'd been hunched over their drinks spun their heads and glared. They looked as annoyed at her as she felt about being there. Her cheeks grew warm at the attention, and she slid up to an empty seat, giving the locals a wide berth. She had to start somewhere.

"Can I get you something, hun?" Behind the bar, a woman in her sixties with a wide frame and a gentle face cleaned glasses and put them in a tray. "I'm Helen, by the way. Logan's off tonight. Not that you know who Logan is. You're not from here. You must be Penny?"

"I am." Funny. It had only been a day, and she wasn't creeped out anymore by people knowing more about her than she knew about them, but she'd already grown weary of the inference on everyone's lips that she needed to stay. As if life couldn't exist anywhere else, and hers had been stagnant. She didn't want to think that about the serene woman before her, though. She gave off the air of a grandmother eager to find pleasure with her progeny and well worth pleasing. "I'm not staying. I mean here, yes. For a drink. But not in Ramsbolt. I'm just here to close out my grandmother's estate."

"No one can fault you for that. You probably have a life to get back to. We just get really excited about newcomers. Town's so small we get sick of ourselves. So what can I get you?"

Not a soda. Nothing from a gun or a length of bacteria-laden tubing.

Something with alcohol content to kill anything it touched. "A whiskey of some sort? How about that one, the bottle with the orange label?" She recognized it from the club. Lee ordered it in his old fashioneds.

"Neat or rocks?" Helen grabbed a rocks glass still wet from the dishwasher. Penny took it as a good sign.

How did Lee take his? "Rocks on the side? In a separate glass, I guess. Thanks."

The woman moved as slow as molasses in January. Penny pulled out her phone to pass the time, an instinctive move she used to insulate herself from the world. But she was supposed to be meeting people and promoting the store. She turned off her phone and tried to look approachable without looking…approachable.

"You're Penny, then." A man two seats down looked like Maine incarnate, like he stepped off a movie set dressed as a stereotype. Plaid flannel shirt and dirty denim with a beard from ear to ear that he stroked with his right hand. On the bar in front of him sat a black leather wallet with worn corners and one of those pocketknives that could cut down a tree and repair a boat engine.

"Dan."

He stuck out a hand, and she shook it. His skin was rough but clean, and his shake was dainty. Like he knew he could crush her.

"Penny."

"Welcome to town." He tipped his beer in her direction, then returned to it to its place on the thin paper napkin. Condensation had nearly eaten through it.

"Thanks for not asking if I'm staying. I'm just here to close out my grandmother's estate. She had this store downtown. Antiques."

"That's a shame. I know that place. What'll happen to it?" One eyebrow raised, he summoned her fury at the man from the market.

She folded her arms across her chest, defending against the blow. "It's for sale."

"The building or the business?" He sipped his beer straight from the bottle.

"All of it. Come by tomorrow. Tell everyone you see. Everything must go. I'm open from the second the sun comes up until I turn the lights off at night. I don't have a lot of time either. Discounts on everything."

"What about Jake?" Dan sipped his beer and set the bottle down harder, perhaps, than he intended. He licked foam from his mustache and leaned back.

"Up for adoption. You want him?"

"Can't have a cat. Allergic." He lifted his chin, and his eyes narrowed. The light picked up hints of red in his beard. "Your grandmother loved that cat. Everybody in town knows that cat."

"True. Seems she did. But there's no shelter around here, and I can't keep him. I work too much. So if you know of anybody who might want to adopt a sweet little orange cat, send them my way. I'll throw in some furniture to sweeten the deal."

A woman with long black hair leaned and peered down the bar at her, her eyes wide with curiosity. "What do you do that you can't have a cat?" Her perky voice and broad grin were a welcome departure from the criticisms.

"I'm in school to be a surgeon. I need life to be as simple as possible so I can focus. I work a lot of hours in the emergency room right now."

"It's just a cat. It don't need affection." Dan grimaced, but the woman down the bar shook her head and disagreed. Black bangs waved above her eyes.

"No. You're wrong, there. Some cats love company. They do get lonely." The woman tipped her glass of beer in Penny's direction. "Shauna. I work at the pet store. Sorry we don't have room for Jake. We're full of cats. But I can put a sign up in the window. Somebody might take him on. People who know him like him well enough."

"Thanks." Penny's throat stung at the sip of whiskey. "Is there a real estate agent around here? I need to find somebody to list the building for sale, like yesterday. Morgan said there isn't one in town, but I just can't believe that no one in Ramsbolt helps sell houses."

Dan pointed a thumb across the bar, to an older man hunched over a newspaper. "Closest thing we got to that is Arvil down there. You don't want to talk to him about it, though. He ain't the easiest to get along with."

"People reach agreements between themselves around here." Shauna shrugged. "When I bought my house, I heard about it from Rachel at the church. She mentioned it before Sunday service when they ask if anyone has any news. You might try that? Anyway, after you find someone to buy the place, you just go down to the tea shop. Diane who runs the place is a notary. Morgan can do it, too. He does all the deed stuff, but he's hard to pin down. Anyway, mostly people just stay where they are."

"You mean the church at the end of Main Street?" Penny had stepped foot inside a church twice. Once when her mom tried to make Easter a thing and later when some high school club function met in the basement of a Catholic church. Both times she thought they were too big and echoey. No one needed to hear themselves talk that badly, especially on a Sunday morning.

"Yeah. At the end of the street there."

"That's a great idea, but I missed it. And I have to be back at work this time next week."

"There's a Monday night service. Tomorrow. It's mostly a repeat, though they change the songs up sometimes. It gives the people who work in the day a chance to do their bit."

Tomorrow. She could muster up the willpower to give a public speech in twenty-four hours.

"What about a mortgage? Don't you need someone to walk you through it all?" It was almost as if the whole town operated on some set of rules established before the turn of the century. Like she stepped into an episode of *Little House on the Prairie*.

Dan swallowed a sip of beer. "The bank. They do it. It's down at the end of Main Street, next to the church. Across from the tea place, on the right."

Maybe the bank knew of someone who would buy the place. They'd probably offer to put a sign in the window. Penny stopped herself from rolling her eyes and sipped the last of her whiskey. It burned the back of her throat. It was a shame they didn't serve wine.

"You want a refill, hun?" Helen leaned on the counter behind the bar, straddling a puddle growing from under a cooler.

"Sure. I'll take another. Please."

Across the bar, Arvil shook the newspaper and turned a page. Maybe he wasn't as bad as they said. Maybe he could help her find a buyer. She couldn't afford to be afraid of the locals. Besides, talking to him couldn't be nearly as scary as walking into the bar had been. The worst he could do was say no.

Their eyes met over a flopped page, but Helen dropped a glass in front of her, tearing her attention away. "That store sure will be missed.

Your grandmother was quite the character. You look a little like her, if you don't mind my saying."

"Empty real estate is bad for the town!" Arvil yelled across the bar.

"I'm sorry, are you speaking to me?" Penny raised her eyebrows. She was familiar with rebuke. She'd endured her fair share of testy patients, but she'd never been screamed at by a stranger across a bar before. Dan did say he was a grouch.

Arvil wagged a finger at her. "If you inherited that building and that store, you own it. It's yours. And it's your responsibility to take care of it."

Penny shifted in her seat and straightened her back. At least she could cross Arvil off her list of helpful options. "It is my responsibility, and that's why it's for sale. I have to get back to my life, and I can't afford to take on that debt." She decided not to mention that the town should have taken care of all their old garbage instead of passing it on to her, even though it would have given her satisfaction. Or that they should have logical services like real estate and lawyers like any normal town.

His voice shot up an octave. "What do you do that's so important you can't care for your property?"

Shauna giggled into her drink. Dan slapped the bar and spun his seat so he faced the door, mumbling about the night going to shit.

Penny's patience wore thin. She filled her mouth with whiskey and let it wash over her teeth, numbing her gums. It kept her from saying that it was none of his business what she did with her property, and if he cared that much, he should do something about it. She swallowed hard. "Look here. I am going to be a surgeon, and Ramsbolt is not where I intend to live. I have no intention of staying here."

"And why not? What's wrong with Ramsbolt?" Even through the

shadows, she could see his face turn red with anger. Why would someone who cared so little for her want her to stay in town, anyway?

"Arvil." Helen waved a dirty pint glass in his direction. "Shut it. Don't harass my customers. I'm not here for it today."

She turned to Penny. "If you have a sale or something, you let me know. Lotta memories in that store, but you gotta do what you gotta do. Heck, half the stuff I replaced after my divorce is probably still in there. Spent a lot of hours with Eliza at that little kitchen table in those days. I'd go to drop something off for sale or buy something I needed, and she'd make coffee. We'd sit there for hours, talking about life."

Her mom never told stories of her grandmother that painted her in that light. She'd always pictured someone more like Arvil. An angry, bitter woman who barked at kids and liked things more than people. Penny folded her corner of her napkin, marking a memory with a dog-eared page.

"Thanks. I never knew that about her. I have the store open all the time. Everything has to go. I really need the money, so I'm selling everything dirt cheap. I don't want to throw it away, but I can't carry it back to my apartment, either. I know there's a lot of history there that means something to people. Maybe you all could spread the word? I'm only here for a couple of days, and then it all has to go. One way or the other."

"That is a shame." Helen gave her a sad smile and left her tab on the bar. "Your grandmother would be sad to see it all go."

"Then she shoulda thought about that before she let it all rot in there." Arvil got the last word in, and it was one Penny couldn't argue with. He shook his paper and ducked beneath it again, leaving the room in peace.

"I'll be by in the next day or two. I do miss your grandmother, and I'll miss knowing that store is there any time I want a stroll down memory lane."

Dan leaned closer. "She was a class act, Eliza. I'm not just saying that 'cause she's gone. She was old school Ramsbolt. She could connect with people. Not like people these days sucked into their phones. She was all heart."

Penny took a biting sip of her drink, and a sad memory from childhood washed over her. Chasing paper dolls in the park. They blew from her lap in a gust of wind, and her people all fluttered away. The people of Ramsbolt had been like that when she rolled into town, paper dolls she had to outfit, to bend to her will until it was time to put them away and go back to her homework. But as it all unfolded, they weren't so flat. All these people had been part of her grandmother's life. She'd seen them from a distance, huddled at her grandmother's funeral. Up close, they would hold her accountable for her grandmother's legacy with Arvil's grit or Helen's grace. And it was their memories stacked to the ceiling in the store. She had a responsibility to all that stuff, all those people. And this cute little town. For as quirky as it was, it wasn't that bad. If three days wasn't enough to salvage her sanity and future, she would have to find a way to soften the blow before she walked away. They deserved that much.

CHAPTER ELEVEN

The whiskey wasn't enough to give Penny a headache in the morning, but it slowed her down and made her regret that third glass. Steam still poured from the little shower in the upstairs loft while she wiggled into jeans she never wore. If she kept eating Marissa's bagels, she wouldn't be able to wear them for long. Scrubs were far more comfortable, anyway.

She held the railing on her way down the stairs, insurance against tripping over Jake who rushed between her legs and down the steps, his paws thumping down the stairs.

"For being so small, you make a lot of noise." Maybe she did have a bit of a headache after all.

The whiskey gave her a lot to chew on. Like whether she should go to Monday church service and why no one in Ramsbolt wanted a cat, but it did nothing to take the edge off the claustrophobia of being in the store. Maybe not having a real estate agent would be a blessing. There'd be no crazy contracts or paperwork shuffles. There was something to be said for a good old-fashioned handshake.

The towering heaps of furniture looked worse than ever, tugged and frayed by her frantic need to put prices on things and her effort to get to smaller items tucked in the seams that people would be more likely to buy. If she could get to the bottom of the pile, if she could spread it all out so people could see what was there and maybe get some of it out onto the sidewalk, it might not feel so overpowering. Too bad she didn't have a bedroom she could shove it all into, like she did at home. All the stuff was making her dizzy. Her grandmother's mistakes and her mother's anger all jammed together with her failures.

Unwilling to tread water in the sea of stuff, she dove in. Starting with the stacks closest to the door, she untangled stools and benches from bed frames and chair legs and carried them outside to clear the space and her head. She lined the sidewalk in front of two empty storefronts, uncovering decades of furniture, paintings and pictures lost in the rubble. Dropping a stack of old window boxes at the foot of a cast iron garden bench, she rubbed at her lower back and squinted in the sun.

Thank God I'm still young enough to do all this, she thought.

"You can't leave all this here!"

Penny spun to Adelle, who leaned out the door of the flower shop.

"You can't litter the sidewalk like that. It's dangerous."

Penny waved a hand down the sidewalk. "You're kidding me, right? Who walks here? No one walks here. Besides, there was already crap all over the place."

Adelle's face burned red. "You're making this place ugly. Maybe you don't give a crap about Ramsbolt, but the rest of us do, and we don't want that stuff all over the sidewalk. What was already out here was fine. Just leave it alone!"

Just leave it alone. It wasn't about her putting stuff outside; it was about change.

"If Ramsbolt had cared enough about all this stuff and this stupid store, I wouldn't be here trying to sell it all back to you." Penny yelled back across the street, hands on her hips.

This wasn't Penny's mess. It was Eliza's mess. And it was Ramsbolt's mess. Was it too much to ask for a little support from the neighbors so she could fix this before it turned into blight? She had her own life to live.

"It's not my fault you're disorganized and can't figure out how to run an antique store. I shouldn't have to look at this all day because of your chaos. You come here and act like we can't take care of our own."

"My chaos? Your own what? It's not my fault my grandmother didn't sort her shit. I didn't even know the woman because she tried to raise her own daughter in so much mess that she ran off screaming. If you all want this stuff so badly, come get it! If Ramsbolt had taken care of its own chaos, I wouldn't be here doing it. If you love the way things are so much, why don't you buy it from me so you can run it the way you want? I didn't ask for this. I'm just trying to sort it out as best I can."

And her best wasn't good enough.

Adelle gave the door a push, and it swung out over the tiled threshold. She caught it when it swung back. "This better be temporary. You've been nothing but a mess since you got here."

"Tell me about it!" Penny threw her hands in the air. "And stop saying that. I'm not a mess. I'm here to fix this shit and go home, and this whole town is a giant roadblock."

"Ramsbolt doesn't like to get involved in other people's affairs. We don't need change, and we don't need you." Adelle stormed inside, the door slamming behind her.

If Ramsbolt didn't want to get involved in other people's affairs, it shouldn't have dragged her here. How did they get anything done with an attitude like that? No wonder they were stuck in the nineteenth century. They can't even sell anything without someone having a heart attack.

She kicked at a small wooden ladder and a rung fell off and clattered to the sidewalk.

I should be mending broken bones, not screaming at some woman on a sidewalk while trying to make a few bucks at the world's largest yard sale.

She picked up the broken ladder and rung and carried them inside, leaning the pieces against the counter. Jake ran from the kitchen to inspect it.

"I'll just have to work harder to sell this crap, and she will have to sit there and stare out that window at it all day until every last thing is gone. And why am I sweating?"

Penny fluttered the hem of her T-shirt, trying to cool down. She propped the door open to get some air moving and turned her back to it to inspect the store. Moving things outside had given her access to pathways through the junk. She stepped over crates and boxes to reach an old walnut secretary, its tall shelves tucked behind wavy panes of glass. Squinting through the doors she made out the titles of books. Old romance novels.

"What do we do with these things, Jake? Five cents each? Give them away for free with the bookcase?"

"Hello? Penny?"

She jumped, startled by the unfamiliar voice. She spun on her heels, almost tripping over a crate of old records.

"Sorry. Didn't mean to startle ya. I'm Riley. Postman. You've got a lot of mail here. Where do you want it?"

She stepped over the rubble. "Can you put it on the counter there by the door?"

"There's not really a flat surface here. I can put it back in the office, if you don't mind me moving those boxes to get to it? Maybe I should just leave it inside the door here?"

She slipped between a drum table and an old wooden sewing machine cabinet, onto an ottoman, and into a clearing, brushing dust from her jeans and straightening her ponytail. "I'll take it. No bills right?"

"I'm just the messenger. I only take credit for the checks. Post office policy." The man just inside the doorway was twenty years her senior. The sun had just begun to line his face and his frame told the story of a man who walked for a living. He was dressed in a traditional postal uniform, dusty blue with a messenger bag, but in his arms he carried a brown paper bag, like the one she brought back from the market.

She lifted a plastic bag overflowing with My Little Pony and Strawberry Shortcake dolls from next to the register and dropped it behind the counter, making room for the bag of mail.

Riley dropped it on the counter. "There's a lot of mail here. Been holding on to it for a while now." He waved a hand to the door. "What's all that out there?"

Penny wiped her arm against her forehead. She grabbed a bundle from the top and riffled through the envelopes. A lot of junk. "I put a bunch of stuff out for a sidewalk sale. Spread the word? I'm selling everything, and I'm very motivated."

Penny ripped the rubber band from another stack of mail. Electric bill. Trash bill. She shoved her hand in the bag and scanned the contents. There weren't even any magazines.

"Hey. I remember this." Riley reached his hand into an old crate and pulled out a small wooden frame. Behind the glass, postage stamps that had once been glued to the burlap backing had quit adhering. Over the years, the glue had given way, and they'd slid to one corner. "What are you doing with this?"

"Trash? It's pretty beat. It's not a high-ticket item, and I didn't think anyone would want it."

Riley brushed his hand across the glass, wiping away yellow dust. "This used to be in the newsstand. Way before Warren took over. God, I was just a little kid. Funny I liked stamps back then and ended up doing this, huh? I had no idea whether these were special or important, but it hung behind the counter, and I always wanted to play with these stamps. I guess because they were such bright colors. The guy's name was Sam. The guy who ran the place. I haven't thought about him in years. He kept candy behind the counter for us kids. Little taffies and Swedish Fish and Tootsie Rolls. You'd give him your dollar and point at what you wanted. He'd run down the total on the paper bag and send you home with a treasure. God, I saw him every day and haven't thought about him in years. All the kids in this town will be forgetting about me in forty years, that's for sure. You ever stop thinking about somebody who's been gone a long time and feel guilty when you remember them again?"

"God, do I ever. I lost my mom when I was fourteen. I think about her every day, and I want to tell her every time something good happens, but sometimes, something good happens and she's not the first person who comes to mind. I definitely feel the guilt."

Why was she telling this total stranger her life story? She tossed the bundle of mail back in the bag.

Riley clutched the frame. "Sorry about your mom."

"It's okay. It was more than half my life ago. Anyway, you can have that if you want it."

"Are you sure? All of this stuff was for sale."

She shook her head. It was worth more to him than it was to her. "Tell you what. You can pay me back by spreading the word. A lot of this stuff is free with the purchase of another item. I really just want it all to go to good homes. Everybody here says they'll miss the place. They should all come by and collect their memories. She left me with a lot of debt. I have to wrap this up, so I can pay it off and get back to my life."

"Thanks. It's a deal." He tucked the frame inside his bag. "I'll definitely fix it up and put it in the post office. Maybe it'll bring some other kid some joy, huh?"

Penny saw him out, waved goodbye, and closed the door behind him, so she could hear the bell ring if someone came by. She carried the bag of bills and magazines to the little office under the stairs and sorted through it. An old milk crate made a perfect recycling bin, where she tossed the junk mail, envelopes, and bill inserts. Anything of value she left in a pile on the desk. A new phone bill came, so she threw the old ones into the crate. A new electric bill with a comma in the price tag showed up. There were a few past due notices in pink and yellow. Three credit cards that were over their limit. Sewer and water bills. Maybe she should have taken the mailman up on his offer to buy that picture.

She had never seen so many letters from angry institutions, but she'd never been lucky enough to have a house and that many bills, either. It didn't help much that they weren't hers, that it wasn't her irresponsibility that caused them all to pile up. Not that she'd have done much better if they had been hers. Along with a cat and a store full of debris, she'd inherited her grandmother's organizational competency.

She folded up the empty bag and shoved it in the recycling crate. No one had taught her how to deal with any of this. How many more bills would show up? How many more creditors? Would any of them work with her, absolve the debt, and let her off the hook? Fat chance.

Seeing all the bills arrive at once, spread out on a desk like evidence photos or family pictures hurt worse than being stabbed in the chest. Gunshot wounds were one thing. Stab wounds and severe burns, patients in agony and distraught family members. She could deal with that. All of those things were external problems to break down into tiny pieces and solve. But this was personal. She couldn't afford to pay these bills. All this damage was her whole life unraveling in front of her. A future of bills and not enough money to pay them.

She pulled all the papers into a pile and stacked them. They took up less space that way.

She knew from experience that staring at a problem wouldn't solve it, and neither would looking the other way. Lunch. She should have lunch and go to the bank and get access to her grandmother's accounts. She knew from the statements there wasn't much in there, but she needed every cent. Then come back to the store and call all the creditors. Cancel the services, ask for final bills. Just thinking about making those calls and seeing the final numbers made her sweat even more.

Penny dropped the letter opener back in the old beer stein her grandmother used to hold pens. The clang it made was satisfying. How could her grandmother be so disorganized? How could she care more for other people's things than for her own affairs?

But Penny's own life wasn't in much better shape. She didn't even own a filing cabinet. Everything too important to throw away sat on the floor of her closet until it was too old to remember what it was for. This was just a taste of things to come if she didn't get her own life squared away. But she was entirely too angry with her grandmother to give her any credit.

She shivered at the thought of dying alone in a hospital bed with no one to leave all her stuff to. Nothing planned. Her clothes and papers and the fodder of life all piled on the floor of her apartment for some maintenance guy to throw in the dumpster.

Jake mewed at her feet and rubbed her calf with his chin. "As soon as I get back to the city, I am organizing all that mess."

Penny left the office, wishing it had a door to slam, with Jake at her heels.

"Look at all this stuff. It's like she was running a furniture orphanage. All those lives are gone. The people who wrote at that desk and the clothes they put in that dresser. The woman who sat at that sewing machine. The people who cared about that hideous picture of a dirty street. They're all gone. No one wants this stuff anymore. Maybe Riley liked that one thing, but if people really wanted this stuff, they'd have come for it already."

Her grandmother wasn't running a museum or building a time capsule. It was a graveyard. Maybe the woman couldn't accept that those times and those people were gone, but it was way too much for Penny not to notice.

She grabbed her keys off the little white kitchen table. "Coffee and lunch, then the bank. I'll be back, Jake. I gotta get access to her bank account so I can pay the people she wouldn't pay. Don't do anything crazy or spend any money."

She slammed the back door and stomped to the Jeep, taking an angry drive through the roundabout and down Main Street. She parked across from Marissa's bakery and crossed the desolate road without looking.

From the sidewalk, the bakery looked like a fairy tale, nothing like the cafeteria at the hospital where she shoveled bland food into her stomach as fast as she could. Pinks and yellows and light blue accents covered the walls. The floor was an immaculate white tile. It was the kind of place that would have sent her into a sugar frenzy as a kid.

Inside smelled like fresh-baked cookies. It made her want to buy a cupcake or a dozen donuts or an entire sheet cake.

"Penny! It's nice to see you." Helen twisted in her seat.

A man at the counter turned. "So you're the new thrift shop girl, huh?"

Thrift shop girl? Hardly. She resisted the urge to lunge across the counter and squeeze cupcakes in her fists. "I'm actually a medical student. Future surgeon. I'm not staying. Definitely not a thrift shop girl. Except for shopping. I'm definitely a thrift shop shopper."

Helen turned toward the guy at the counter. "She's selling the place, Grey."

"That's a shame. Lots of—"

Penny cut him off. "History in that place. I know. My grandmother wouldn't have been bankrupt if people bought some of it instead of dropping it on her doorstep. I wish history paid the bills."

A woman who must have been Marissa passed a bag across the counter to him. "Enjoy," she said with a smile. "And good luck getting the truck fixed. Jaleesa drives a hard bargain."

He clutched the bag and adjusted his beanie cap. "She does. The only mechanic in town can afford to. Truth be told, though, I don't care if the door sticks. Nobody rides in it but me anyway."

Grey extended a hand to Penny. "I'm Grey. Plumber. Did a lot of work for your gran over the years. She wanted a bigger shower upstairs and that little sink in the kitchen leaked all the time."

Penny folded her purse in her arms. "I hope she didn't owe you any money."

"Nope. Paid me in cash. She tried to pay me with a new bedroom set one time, though. That was a little awkward. Thing was massive. I've got this little apartment, you know?" Brown curls swished beneath his cap when he shook his head. "Gotta run. Gotta try to bribe Jaleesa to fix my dang truck without charging me a fortune. You all have a good lunch."

Penny stepped up to the counter. It didn't seem possible that there were enough people in Ramsbolt to warrant all the bagels, donuts, muffins and croissants, the breads and cookies and cakes in the displays.

"I won't ask you if you're the new girl, 'cause I heard you say you're not gonna stay. Shame, though. That store's been there forever. It'll be missed. So what can I get for ya?" Marissa poised a pen over a green ordering pad.

"You have the world's best everything bagels. One of those, toasted with cream cheese? And a cup of coffee, please."

"You got it. Coming right up." Marissa made a note and tucked the pen behind her ear. She grabbed a paper cup from a stack and passed it across the counter. "Help yourself to the coffee on that dresser there."

"Care to join me?" Helen motioned to the empty seat at her table.

She needed to get to the bank, to get access to her grandmother's tiny checking account. To get back to the store and call all the creditors. To find a home for Jake and a buyer for the store. But a little idle gossip in a sunny bake shop wouldn't hurt. There'd be plenty of time for business after a little dirt on Adelle and a story or two about her cute, friendly neighbor Nate.

CHAPTER TWELVE

Penny left her Jeep at the curb, parked outside the hardware store between an old Buick and a green Saturn with a dented bumper. A small crowd flowed down the sidewalks toward the church. Girls in dresses and boys in dark pants, holding their parents' hands. Little ties and tiny purses. Everyone bundled in jackets against the autumn evening chill. For Penny, jeans and a button-up shirt would have to do. They were lucky she brought something more presentable than scrubs and yoga pants.

She picked a woman at random and trailed her up the stairs and through the arched double doors. Inside, a woman with short dark hair in a denim skirt handed her a program and tried to hug her. If she were planning to stay, she'd probably have found the scene charming.

"There's a casserole supper in the basement after. I hope you'll join us."

Penny slinked into the sanctuary and found a seat in the back. A free meal made by someone else was the most appealing offer she'd had in Ramsbolt so far.

The pews filled around her, faces she didn't recognize. There was no sign of Shauna or Dan from the bar. No Helen, who probably came on Sunday mornings if she went to church at all. Penny kept her head down, eager to avoid another round of *No, I'm not staying, please come buy your crap back.* She read the program instead.

A thunderous crash of cords rang out, and Penny jumped and stifled a yelp, her heart in her throat. No one around her flinched. They stood, some with hymnals, others with their hands resting on the pews in front of them, and began to sing. All of them in one tone, as if summoning some entity to rise up from the floor or descend upon them, depending upon which they subscribed to.

She flipped the program over in her hands to be sure. Methodist. Harmless.

When the hymn was through, the rustling of skirts and books being returned to their racks echoed through the vaulted room. Everyone seemed in on the plan, but that was the point of church, she supposed. Feeling like you're a part of something. A minister stood in a white robe with gold trim and rattled off the news. The casserole supper would last until eight. Volunteers were needed to set up for the Christmas Cantata. And then the announcements. Penny sat forward, on the hard edge of the pew. Should she raise her hand?

A woman stood. Without declaring herself, she proclaimed that the next bake sale to pay for new choir robes would be held after next Sunday's service. They were only short a few hundred dollars, and the more brownies they could sell, the sooner they'd be rid of their tattered old red ones. A smattering of applause said the new robes would be welcome. Penny could go for a brownie, but she'd be long gone by then.

A man near the front stood, his hand gripping a Bible. "I heard from the postman that someone's moved in to take over Eliza's shop."

Penny started to raise her hand, to counter his claim, but confused chatter rose up from the congregation, silencing her initiative.

The man's face flushed, and he raised his voice. "I heard she's moving everything in there out of state."

"I heard she's putting the cat down." A woman in a long-sleeved floral dress waved her program in the air.

I never suggested any such thing. Why would I just put down Jake? Who would do that? And I'm a medical professional!

"Adelle said she had a fit and threw a bunch of stuff on the sidewalk."

"I saw a Jeep fly through town so fast you'd think there was a fire." A woman with curly gray hair and a dead mink wrapped around her shoulders cried out. "It must have been her. Not many Jeeps in this part. When I saw it, I said to Ray, I bet there's somebody new in town. Ray didn't believe me, though. He said it was a tourist passing through, but I knew. I knew it was somebody new."

She looked to the minister for a sign of reason, but he made no motion at all. His eyes seemed fixed on the back wall, as if he took his official break during the announcements. A man in the back row, across the aisle from her, banged his fist on the back of the pew to get the crowd's attention. "Someone said to me that she's sending it all to the dump."

The church erupted with gossip and innuendo. A man shouted, "But all our old stuff is there." A woman burst into tears, exclaiming that her grandmother's treasures deserved better treatment.

What a horrible, selfish town. Penny felt a vein throb in her neck. She cracked her knuckles and crumbled the program into a ball.

The minister came to and raised a hand. "That's a wonderful new development, Christopher. Thank you for sharing."

Penny's blood boiled.

"Does anyone else have any news to share?"

She shot to her feet. "I sure as hell…heck do."

Gasps flared throughout the chapel. The congregation spun in their pews, and all eyes fell on her.

I said heck in church. In front of sixty people. Half the town must be here. And I said heck. Her mother had raised her better than that, but under their scrutiny, she really didn't care. Committing one sin only made her want to commit another.

"I'm Penny. Eliza's granddaughter. I am *not* moving into the store. I'm selling everything, because she was in a lot of debt after taking in all your wayward furniture and not being able to sell any of it. And I'm not killing the cat. Jake is up for adoption, if anyone would like a sweet little kitty. And I would appreciate it very much if instead of spreading rumors you would all just show up at the store and buy back your old stuff, because I can't afford to carry her debt around with me forever."

It was as if someone hit the mute button. No gasps or deep breaths or sneezes or sighs. No shuffling shirts or crinkling candy wrappers. Just a deep impermeable silence. Even the children blinked, wide-eyed, at the alien in their midst.

At the end of her pew, an elderly woman who thought she was whispering leaned to her friend and said in a volume too loud for polite company, "I don't see why she doesn't just take on all that debt, because that's what good granddaughters do if you ask me."

Nobody asked her. Least of all Penny.

Penny threw her hands in the air. "Look, you don't even have a real estate agent in this town. I need to sell the building. It would make a lovely home for someone who wants to run a little store. I'm only here for a few days so stop by and make an offer. Please."

"But what about the antiques?" A woman in her thirties in a smart blazer asked. Finally a reasonable question. But it was hard to meet it with civility through the barbed wire defense mechanism she'd constructed.

"If you want them, come and make an offer. Otherwise, they're going to the closest dump."

Penny twisted the program in her hands. She didn't really mean it, that she'd throw it all away. But she had no choice if the town wouldn't buy it back.

She had no intention of sitting through a sermon about a plague of frogs. Not when she had her own disasters to deal with. The effort had been a failure, anyway. Anyone who didn't already hate her certainly did after that outburst.

She slipped out of the pew, out the door, into the hallway, and straight into Riley.

"Whoa there." He clutched brass trays to his chest. "You're gonna dent the collection plates."

"Sorry." She shoved the program into her pocket. "On my way out."

"I didn't take you for a church person."

She snorted when she laughed. "Definitely not. I'm too nice to be a church person by these standards. I'm not a Ramsbolt person either. This place is horrible, inefficient, unprofessional, disorganized, and I cannot wait to leave."

CHAPTER THIRTEEN

"If everything in life were as easy as dealing with Ramsbolt Savings and Loan, I could have healed the world with an aspirin and a Band-Aid."

Penny dumped the contents of the orange folder on the kitchen table. Jake hopped up to inspect her haul. She brushed aside a welcome letter, a thick booklet outlining her privacy rights, and a stern brochure about retirement planning. She slipped the new debit card into her wallet and clutched a book of starter checks. "Fifteen minutes, Jake. And look what I got. One little folder with everything. Checks, as if it isn't the twenty-first century. But now I have a bank account for your mom's estate with sixty-three dollars in it, so we can start paying some very small bills."

She pressed the button on the coffee maker and tapped the back window. Morning dew dripped away. Birds pecked at dormant coneflowers where the parking spots met the tree line. Jake hopped onto the windowsill to take in the view.

"I asked if they knew anyone who wanted to buy the store, but the manager guy didn't know anyone. He said he'd spread the word though. And no one at the bank wants a cat, so it's still you and me against the world, bud." Penny filled an old diner mug with coffee, tucked the checkbook in her back pocket, and grabbed the rest for recycling.

"Is that you, Penny?" A woman's voice called out from the store. She sought to place it. It wasn't Helen or Marissa. And it was more pleasant than Adelle's.

Penny rolled her eyes at Jake. She'd forgotten to lock the front door. Some poor woman had been in there shopping alone while she was at the bank. And just Penny's luck, she hadn't stolen anything.

She slipped from the kitchen into the shop, coffee in hand, and found the woman studying an end table. "Sorry. I ran out to the bank and forgot to change the sign."

"Zoe." She stuck out a hand. Penny set her coffee on the counter and shook it. "I drove by and saw all the stuff on the sidewalk. Then I remembered Helen saying Eliza's granddaughter was here to close the shop. I had to get down here before everything was sold to the highest bidder."

I wish.

Finally. A customer. Penny tightened her ponytail. She had no instinct for sales, but gave it a shot. "I saw you looking at this end table. It's…" What? Not too old? Not dinged by vacuums and scratched by keys? Heavy, clunky, and so 1970s that it may have starred in *The Brady Bunch*? "I love this piece. Very distinctive. There are no prices here, so feel free to make an offer on anything that catches your eye. Anything with a blue sticker is free with any purchase."

"Oh, not the table. I found a few baskets outside that are to die for, and I'm really curious about that little breakfast table back there."

Penny followed the woman's gesture to the sunny kitchenette. "You mean my grandmother's table?"

She liked that table. Sure, she banged her knee on the leg a few too many times, but that wasn't the table's fault. It was cheerful. She liked sitting there with Jake in the morning. She liked the notches and nicks in the surface as if memories had taken their toll. Maybe it was a medical thing, finding humanity in the scar tissue, but she liked it. It would be nice to sell some things, but did it have to be Jake's table?

"I feel weird even asking about it, but I heard you weren't staying, and everything had to go. I thought you might be willing to sell it. It's so cute, and I always admired it."

The woman's apologetic expression smoothed over the intrusion, but Penny folded her arms in defense anyway. "I couldn't possibly sell it. It was my grandmother's. I never knew her, but it feels like something she cherished, you know what I mean? I have no idea where I'm going to put it, but I feel like I oughta keep it."

What was she going to do with a table? She didn't have room for it in her apartment, but she couldn't stomach the idea of letting it go.

"What are you planning to do with the table?"

"I'm sprucing up a little corner of my kitchen. It's just this little void. I get home from work and just throw things there. It's just a pile of shoes and coats and mail. I thought I'd turn it into a cute breakfast nook."

"I have another super cute table back there, behind that hutch. The one with the lap desk on it. Would you consider that one?"

"Would you take seventy-five for it and these two baskets?" The woman held up one of the wicker baskets that had rested on an old bench out on the sidewalk.

"Sold! That sounds perfect." Seventy-five wouldn't cover that month's electric bill, but it would more than cover what she spent at the bar. Plus, if she accepted any offer that came her way, rumor might spread that stuff was moving fast. After so many years of turning away customers, it was high time the store became known for selling things. It might even smooth over the impression she gave at church the night before.

Her ears burned red, and her cheeks warmed at the memory of her outburst. She couldn't go back and undo what she'd said, how she'd reacted to all those rumors being tossed around in a church, but she could try to make it a happy place to shop and maybe people would spread the word that she wasn't trying to burn down the town and kick all its puppies.

The woman dug into her purse and pulled exact change from a pink leather wallet. "Before I get all sweaty hauling this thing to the door, here."

The cash sat in Penny's palm. She would have to do something with it. Deposit it. Pay taxes on it. She knew nothing about taxes or running a small business. She didn't even have cash to make change. It was as if each hurdle brought her no closer to the finish line, but added a dozen more hurdles on the horizon.

"Let me get you a receipt." She folded the cash and stepped over a tattered, rolled-up rug. The cash register was a confusing landscape of buttons and levers. She opted for a handwritten receipt from a little green pad she found tucked under the edge. "A breakfast nook sounds like a cozy idea. There's something wonderful about clearing way some clutter. I know all about that." Zoe had already made it to the door with the table. Penny put the receipt into her hand.

"Do you need a hand getting everything into your car?"

"Oh, no. I'm fine. Thank you for offering. I...I heard about what happened at church last night. I wasn't going to say anything because I wasn't there, and it's none of my business, but you seem really nice. Don't take Ramsbolt too seriously. Sometimes it feels like the rest of the world left us behind up here. We can't identify with reality TV and all those movies. We're a little distrustful of outsiders sometimes, especially the older generations who see a lot of it slipping away. Anyway, we don't all feel like that. This is a really nice town. It just had a bad day. I'll be sure to spread the word about your sale. Thanks for helping me spruce up the kitchen."

"You're welcome. And thanks. I got a little defensive last night. I'm under a lot of pressure to get this place off my plate. It's been scary and stressful. Thanks for the kind words."

The woman grasped the table and lifted it, her back arched, and carried through the door. She pushed it into the back of a pickup truck, slammed the tailgate, and waved goodbye. Penny's first customer was gone.

Jake inspected the vacant spot where the table once sat. "I swear you're part dog. What do you think? Should I change the sign to Not Everything Must Go?"

From his newly accessible spot on the floor, he leapt to a chair.

"Well, that was a surprise. I wonder if there's anything else in here worth setting aside." She stroked Jake's back, and he flexed out of reach. He hopped from the chair to a china cabinet. "Did Grandmom love any of this stuff? Is there anything here I'll regret selling or giving away someday?"

Jake peered down from the top of the cabinet and surveyed his domain. She reached up and scratched his chin. Behind her the door chimed.

"You forget something?" Penny turned, expecting Zoe. Instead, she found a man with wiry gray hair and a lanky frame, his head peeking in the door and his feet firmly planted on the sidewalk outside.

"You've been kicking up the dust in here, haven't you?" he asked.

"I sure have. I'm starting to make a dent in this massive pile of stuff she left me with."

He nodded to the far wall. "There's stuff hidden back there I haven't seen in thirty years. I'm Warren. I run the newsstand." The door closed behind him, and he sneezed.

"Bless you." Penny hopped down from the table she was standing on. "Sorry about all this dust. Every time it starts to settle, I move things around again."

"Think nothing of it." He wiped at his nose with a handkerchief. "I was an old friend of Eliza's. She and I went way back. Riley dropped the mail off and said she left you in a bit of a bind, and you're in a mad dash to get rid of this place. I'm always looking for new ideas for my window displays, so I thought I maybe could sell some of these things on consignment for you. Old pen collections, maybe, or newspapers or anything related to the newsstand? Even old toys, like this box of tin soldiers here."

Warren picked up a cardboard box with a faded label stuck to the side, its flaps ripped off, and its edges jagged. Penny's mother's name was written in thick, black marker on the side. *Poppy's men.*

"Tin soldiers? Can I see that?" Penny reached out for the box. It was cold from having sat by the window. Inside were two dozen or so little metal soldiers, their red and blue coats faded with the years. Penny recognized them from her mom's Christmas photographs. They'd been staged under the tree as protectors of a cardboard village dusted with glittery snow.

She plucked one from the box and held it in her palm, warming it with her hand. When was the last time her mother held these little soldiers? Funny to think that sometime, many years ago, her mom lived in this space, under this roof. And there was a day, just like any other, when a little Poppy set down her tin soldiers and never picked them up again. To Penny, it had always seemed like a giant brick wall stood between her and everything before she was born, keeping her distant from her mother's memories and photographs. It took a very small army to start knocking it down.

Penny owned those soldiers now. She flipped the little man over in her hand. It weighed more than she thought it would.

"I'm sorry. I can't." Penny wrapped her arms around the box. "These were my mom's."

Warren gave her a knowing smile tinged with sadness. "Not those, then. But something else, perhaps. That old doll house would be great in my window. I bet I could sell it for you."

What dollhouse? In all her reorganizing and untangling, she hadn't noticed the ornate dollhouse up against the wall. White with green shutters and two fireplaces, their stone chimneys rising above the gray mansard roof. The front door stood open, an invitation to every bug and spider that roamed the shop seeking shelter from Jake.

She never pictured the shutters green. In the black and white photograph tucked in a sleeve of her mom's album, it had sat on a table under a window, and Penny had always imagined those shutters to be blue. Her mother would run her hand over the picture. And she would say, "I always imagined I'd live in a house that looked like that someday. With a giant chandelier hanging over my bathtub. I wonder where it is now?" And the dollhouse meant so little to her grandmother that she buried it beneath the discarded rubble of an entire town.

Warren moved through the store, talking about the newsstand perhaps, or the town or the window display. Pointing out things he thought he could sell or display or burn in the town park, for all she knew. His words couldn't pierce the ringing in her ears. Her mother's childhood didn't deserve to be treated with such disregard.

"The dollhouse was hers, too. My mom's. It's not for sale." The place could be full of things that belonged to her mother. She fought her voice to keep it steady.

Warren stepped further into the mess. "No problem. It was just an idea. Offer stands, though, if you stumble upon some things you'd like to bring down to the shop. Can I buy a few things before I go?"

Penny gnawed at the hangnail on her thumb. "I'm sorry. I didn't mean to be so...I don't know. This is more emotional than I thought it would be, going through all this stuff." The town's and hers and what could have been her mom's all thrown on the floor, scattered on the sidewalk because the building couldn't hold it anymore, and it was getting hard to breathe.

"There's a little metal lantern out front that I would really love to have. Your gran used to put a candle in it, and we'd eat out back there, on the porch, in the summer. She loved to watch the fireflies." His eyes grew red as he talked about the past. She knew that look, someone thumbing through the postcards of their life. She took shallow breaths, afraid to disturb the air, and let him spill it out, as she had so many others who had lost a part of themselves. But it was personal this time, and she clung to every word.

"She loved wine, your gran. White. As cold as she could get it. She'd put it in ice, in a tin bucket, and we'd sit back there and watch the stars.

Mosquitoes never bothered her, but they eat the hell out of me, I tell ya. I never complained. Sitting outside with her was some of the best days. She had a way of making you feel like you were the only one she wanted to talk to."

He paused and picked at a string on his sleeve, his eyes growing redder. The silence burrowed into Penny's chest, digging a hole and planting a sorrow for what she never knew, for all that he had lost.

But what he remembered was still at odds with the damage her mother sustained. The buckshot of living in all this stuff had embedded itself in her mother's life and found its way to Penny in the shape of a giant hassle and a lot of debt. Maybe her grandmother did have a lot of friends and a happy life, but there wasn't a lot of room for her redemption in Penny's.

She lowered her eyes to her sneakers, their white stitching brown with dirt and dust. "You can have the lantern, if you want. For free. If it meant something to you. Something to remember her by."

"I couldn't. I know you want to get back to school. It's gotta be expensive, trying to be a surgeon. Your grandmother said you were passionate about it, and now you're left with all this."

Amid all that rubble, someone finally saw her. Someone in that town got it. That she didn't ask for this, she wasn't trying to change things or take anything away. She just wanted to do as little harm as she could, get past it, and move on.

"I have to do this on my own. I've done everything on my own." Finding her mom in the wreckage changed things. It wasn't that she couldn't trust him to sell a few things. It was that memories she never got to have could be scattered all over the store, and she needed to find them before someone took them away.

"I know you've done it all on your own. After losing your mom."

"It might take a while, but I have to do this right. I have to go through everything and figure out if any of it was Mom's."

"Eliza kept a lot of personal stuff upstairs in the attic. And that chandelier was hers, too." Warren pointed up. Hanging in the center of the room was a black iron chandelier. It wasn't the grandest or shiniest, but it looked like it would have fit perfect in their old farmhouse. A dozen or so candles leaned in cups around a wood spindle. The whole thing dangled from a rafter by a rusted chain.

"That was in the farmhouse? Before they moved here? I think it was in a picture." The way her mom told it, the farmhouse was situated outside Ramsbolt. Her grandfather died while tending a potato crop, and they moved to town and opened the shop shortly after. "Do you know if the farmhouse is still there?"

"Been gone a long time, now. Some people from outta town bought it and abandoned it. Fell down one winter. Roof caved in." Warren put his hands in his pockets, and his body sagged beneath the weight of his memories. Penny had seen it in the emergency room, the way people sink into themselves like they're protecting bits of the past that might escape. Things they'd rather keep to themselves.

"Were the two of you close? You don't have to say, if it's too personal."

"No, not like that. I was too young, and she was too wise, but we were good friends. She had a gift for placing objects with people."

It wasn't worth arguing with him, telling him that he was clearly wrong. The town was wrong. It was the other way around. Her grandmother worked hard to keep people from having things. The woman left so much debt and risked her granddaughter's future because no one was good enough for all that garbage. Maybe she wasn't a hoarder like her mom said, but she'd stood between people and what they wanted for too long.

Penny hugged the box of tin soldiers. "Well, I'm sorry for your loss."

"You, too. Let me pay you for the lantern?"

"Not a chance. It's yours. Belongs to you."

CHAPTER FOURTEEN

Penny peeked in on her mom. It was hard to tell without going all the way into the room, but her breathing was steady and deeper than usual. Definitely asleep. The coast was clear. She tucked her laptop under her arm, the charging cable in her pocket, and slipped into the hall, closing the apartment door as quietly as she could.

Brenda's apartment was just down the hall. As godmothers go, Brenda was better than the ones in the fairy tales. She was kind, generous with her dial-up internet access, and she was a great cook. She didn't make a lot of money working at the grocery store, but it was enough to put food on the table. And she'd made more than enough room for Penny, who sought refuge there when her mom wanted to be alone. She'd be spending a lot of time there once cancer finally took her mom, but she tried not to think about that.

Penny knocked, and Brenda let her in.

"You need to go online, Bug?" It had never been an issue to hear her mom's nickname for her come from Brenda, but sometimes she wondered if she'd still feel the same when her mom was gone.

Penny knocked the laptop against her hip. She hoped Brenda

wouldn't ask why. "If you don't mind."

"Help yourself." Brenda nodded her mound of blond hair and motioned down the hall.

Penny slipped into the room that would be hers one day. She'd already moved some of her out-of-season clothes and a few boxes of books to make things easier when the time came. When the inevitable came. It was an ebb and flow between preparing for it and denying it would happen at all.

She sat on the floor next to a stack of winter sweaters and connected her laptop to the phone line. The modem whirred and beeped as she connected to the internet. She found her grandmother's phone number on the phone directory website, scrawled it on a scrap of paper, disconnected, closed her laptop, and stepped into the living room.

"Thanks, Brenda."

"Any time. You want me to make you guys dinner tomorrow? I can bring something good from the store."

"Sure. Can you bring cookies? The soft ones with the raisins? She likes those. She hasn't been eating much lately, but she nibbles at that."

Brenda chewed on her lower lip. Her nod was almost imperceptible. "Yeah. I'll bring a rotisserie chicken home for us."

"Thanks."

Penny scampered home before Brenda asked too many questions. She could only manage one person's emotional well-being at a time, and her own had already taken a back seat to her mother's fretting about the future.

Back at their apartment, Penny slid the laptop onto the table. She stretched the phone into the hall, and pulled the door shut. She sat on the floor with her knees tucked under her chin and dialed the number, tangling her finger in the cord. On the seventh ring, a woman answered, her voice cracked with age and exertion.

"You don't know me, but I'm Penny. Poppy is my mom. She's dying. She has breast cancer. If this is her mother, I just want you to know."

Air moved past the other end of the phone, a breath drawn in and another escaping. Penny didn't give the woman time for objection or comment. She didn't need to hear the condolences, and she didn't need to manage anyone else's grief. She had enough of her own to bear.

"I don't want anything from you. I'm just letting you know, in case you have anything to say to her that she ought to hear. We live in Otley. There's a bus stop right out front. You don't have long if you want to come see her." She had to put it into words, the deadline. She had to drag it up from the deep well of her vocabulary where words all swam without meaning until she put them together and said them out loud, and they became real. But that's all they were, words. It kept the tears in to think of them that way. "She only has a few days, I think."

Penny twisted and sat on her knees, picking at a stray thread where it met the baseboard.

"You can't call here. If you decided to come I have a number you can call and leave a message with the date and time. It's my godmother. She'll give me the message."

She gave her grandmother their address and Brenda's phone number. And she hung up without waiting for a reply.

Brenda didn't understand the message when it came, but she did what the woman said, writing a date and time on a slip of paper, and handing it to Penny before work the next day.

By the time Penny's grandmother was set to arrive on a bus from Ramsbolt, Penny's mom slept through most of her days. It was close, the visiting doctor had said. Too close to continue with chemo and pills. They changed up her medicines with a goal of keeping her comfortable. A nurse showed up from time to time, to say nice things and frown a lot, to give Mom some drugs. Penny accepted the gift of a pamphlet about end of life care, and she skimmed it at the kitchen table with one eye on the clock while she waited for her grandmother to arrive. Not that she absorbed any of it.

Penny tapped her foot on the linoleum and hummed the chorus of a Dixie Chicks song while it all played out in her head. She didn't really want the woman there, dragging in the dirt and filth she lived in. God knows what germs she'd introduce to the house. Her mom was never all that happy when she spoke of her mother. What if this was a bad idea? What if it backfired and upset her mom? It could make her angry and cost them valuable time. But it was too late to turn back. No, her gut had said that it was the right thing to do, letting them make peace with the past.

She let the events unfold in her head, preparing what she would say. There'd be a knock at the door. She'd open it and let the woman in. No niceties. No hugs or sympathy. This visit was only for her mother, to make amends and lift her spirits. Should she make sure her grandmother was on the same page? Maybe she should be firm and clear. The point of the visit was to reconnect with the past and bridge some differences, to buy Mom a few more days and let her worry less about the past.

Penny barely heard the knock at the door, a tiny fist against the metal entry. She stood and hid the pamphlet under her chemistry book, bumping into the red candle in a mason jar she borrowed from Brenda to cover up the smell of sickness. Red wax sloshed in the glass, and the candle went out. A stream of black smoke rose from the jar. She filled her lungs with the scent of apple cobbler and opened the door.

A tiny woman, thin as a rail, in a long denim skirt and floral knit top. A large tan handbag dangled from one arm, cracked and grayed from years of use. Her shoes made no sound as she shuffled into the apartment and let her bag fall onto the kitchen table with a soundless settling. Penny held back a cringe at the site of it. All that dirt from bus floors and who knew where else, on her clean kitchen table. She worked so hard to keep her mom safe from germs.

Her grandmother waved her hands, as if fanning herself. "Come in for a hug, dear."

Penny broke her vow and obliged. She didn't want to know the woman. Definitely didn't want to like her. Not without her mom's consent. Not until they'd repaired what stood between them, if at all.

"She still doesn't know I'm coming?" The voice cracked with age.

"No." Penny twisted the hem of her No Doubt T-shirt in her hands. "I didn't tell her."

Her grandmother nodded, a silent understanding.

"There are rules. No yelling. No fighting. If she gets upset, you have to leave. This is happy and positive. You're making amends. Or it's nothing at all." She would never pull down the protective barrier she'd built around her mother. Not for anyone.

"I promise. No fighting." Her grandmother patted her arm. "Do you want to go first? Let her know that I'm here?"

No, she didn't want to go first. She didn't want to be the one to tell her mom that she'd brought the one person she hated most to see her when she was at her weakest. She didn't want to face the wrath or sorrow of it all going wrong. She didn't even want to hear about it if it all went well. She was barely capable of handling her own shifting emotions. But she moved to the bedroom anyway.

"Mom?" Her mother was awake. Eyes fixed on the nothingness that existed beyond the bedroom walls. It was cruel that it all went on without her, she'd said on a stronger day.

"Mom, your…your mom is here. Don't be mad. I called her. I wanted you to have a chance to say…" Penny couldn't say the word. Not goodbye. She'd removed goodbye from her vocabulary the day the doctor suggested an expensive therapist to help them face the notion. It was cheaper and easier not to say it at all. "Anything you want to say. I don't know. Maybe you want to take a stroll down memory lane or something."

Poppy nodded her head. Her sunken eyes didn't give away emotion anymore. Penny waved her grandmother in, a little relieved her mother wasn't vague and didn't scream at her.

"I'll stay in the kitchen. So you two can talk." To her grandmother she said, "She speaks softly. And slow. And it makes her tired. You have to be patient. And she gets mad if you try to fill it in for her so let her get around to it. There's a trash can under the edge of the bed in case she has to throw up."

Penny left them alone. She moved her grandmother's bag to a chair and pulled out a math textbook. Polynomials. Something to pass the time.

"I'll take Penny," her grandmother said. "I'll take good care of her."

The woman hadn't paid one bit of attention to the rules, had she. Penny tapped her pen in the trough where the open pages met. Her gaze went fuzzy with the adrenaline rush, and she tried to focus on the rebound of the pen against the paper, but all she was doing was scratching the page. This wasn't why she'd called her grandmother. She was not moving from Otley. Not away from her friends and Brenda and into the same mess her mother hated so much. The woman was a witch, and Penny was not moving anywhere with her. She wanted her mother lively and happy, dancing and singing in the kitchen with a wooden spoon as a microphone again. She squeezed her hand into a fist so tight the skin of her knuckles turned white.

Her mother's protest came through soft and broken sentences. "She will not go to Ramsbolt."

"Isn't it better if she's with family? A girl should grow up with her family."

"Is it still a mess? Did you get rid of anything?"

"It's not a mess. It's a store. I keep it clean. You never liked that store, but it put food on the table."

"Not enough. You didn't answer my question. She will not go there. Won't live in that garbage. No place for a girl to grow up. School is here. A great education here."

"She can get a great education in Ramsbolt. You went to a great school."

"In a house. Not a school. She's happy here. You'll ruin it."

In the silence, Penny heard the swish of a tissue pulled from a box. A blowing nose that wasn't her mother's. Down the hall a child cried, and a door closed.

"You come here and say this, and now I'm supposed to die in peace. Knowing all the plans I made for her would be torn apart? I didn't ask you here. Butting into my life. I did it all by myself. I raised her to think for herself and won't let you cage her in that hell."

"I know you did." Her grandmother's voice was soft but strong. "You didn't have to do it all alone, though. You chose to leave. You never returned my letters."

"You loved stuff more than me. She can be a doctor. Anything she wants. She's smart. Smarter than me. You want to take her from school and her teachers and send her to a one-room schoolhouse."

"You don't even have furniture here. I can give her a life that's better than any tiny apartment. Children don't thrive in cities like this. Where will she go? What did you plan for her?"

"Brenda. Her godmother. She lives in this building. I had things. I gave it all away so Penny doesn't have to." The bed creaked. From the corner of her eye, Penny could see her mother's hand reach out for her grandmother's wrist. "You won't drag her off to that town. No. No."

"What was so horrid about your childhood that you can't bear to let your daughter grow up with her own family?" Her grandmother's voice shot up an octave.

"I never had a childhood. I was lonely and sad and trapped." Her mother coughed a wet, phlegmy hack.

"I think you should go." Penny spoke loud enough to be heard but not so loud she'd startle her mom. She closed her book and stood from the table, letting her chair bang against the counter on purpose. Her grandmother padded on silent shoes into the kitchen and slipped her arm through the handles of her bag.

"I assume you don't need a taxi." At fourteen, she towered over her grandmother and found joy in outstaring her. The woman's eyes fell to the floor. A swell of something rose within Penny. Maybe it was pride. Later, she would be ashamed at the satisfaction she got from dominating her grandmother, but she would not let her mother be disturbed. She would not let this woman ruin her mother's last days, like she'd ruined the first.

"I hoped it wouldn't go like this. I won't take you from your school or your friends."

"Not against my mother's wishes. Or mine." Penny stepped forward, inching her to the door, but the divide between them widened. "I didn't invite you here for that. I invited you here to talk about the past, and all it did was give her another reason to hate the future. Now she's going to worry, and I'll be the one who has to clean up your mess."

"I didn't mean it. I'm sorry. I'll write to you. I'll send letters. To keep in touch."

"Leave her alone." Her mother's voice was stronger than it had been in days, but her assertion took its toll. "Don't come here or write a single letter. Never again." The bed creaked as she lurched and vomited into the bucket.

It was hard not to admire the steel expression the woman wore when she slipped out the door and out of their lives. Penny closed and locked it behind her. It turned with a satisfying click.

"Tissues, Mom." Penny put the box on the bed. The woman didn't even care enough to put the tissues back within reach. "I'm sorry. It's all my fault. I thought it would be good. A chance to say whatever needed to be said."

Her mother pulled a tissue from the box and wiped her lips. "It's okay, Bug. I said what I needed to say. Not what you expected, huh?"

"She was bad for you. She tore your family apart. Our family, I guess."

Her mom squeezed her hand. Her skin was cold and papery. Her fingernails broken by chemotherapy treatments. "Sometimes the past just belongs there."

It was another wish of her mom's, a promise she'd keep forever. She would never speak to that woman again.

CHAPTER FIFTEEN

Penny carried her morning coffee from the kitchen through the store and up the stairs, eager to find more of her past hidden in the shadows. She left the cup on the dresser, next to the box of tin soldiers and her grandmother's brush. Warren said there was an attic where she kept her prized possessions, and there had to be access somewhere. If her mom's things or family history were scattered about, she needed to find them before she accidentally sold them off. She searched the unfinished ceiling, the underside of the floorboards between the raw wood joists, and found a pull cord dangling in a shadowed corner. With a tug on the thin rope, a panel released and a set of stairs descended. Bits of wood and insulation rained down on the area rug.

She sneezed and swatted debris from her hair. The last thing she needed was insulation stuck in her curls. The stairs looked sturdy enough to hold her weight. She tested the first step and scampered up the rest.

Slabs of plywood ran from one end of the attic to the other. It smelled musty and hot. Like old leather and damp cardboard. Sunlight struggled against the grime that covered the tiny triangle windows, streaking the floor with ribbons of yellow. She tugged a thin cord overhead, and a light shined on all the things her grandmother deemed too precious to store downstairs. Behind her, Jake thumped up the steps.

File boxes with writing too small to read were stacked along the walls from one dark end to the other. Small sets of shelves rested among them, holding books and shapes she couldn't make out.

"It's dusty up here, kitty."

Jake sat and licked a paw.

"Don't get splinters in your little toe beans."

She pulled the neckline of her T-shirt over her nose to keep from breathing in the dust and walked through her grandmother's inner sanctum. Ramsbolt School yearbooks that could be her mother's, marbled gray and silver covers with neon swooshes. An entire shelf of photo albums, sepia memories taken all over town. The pages stuck together by the warmth and humidity. From another shelf dripped a folded stack of yellowed fabric, thin and dry. She touched the lace that edged a cloth, brittle and frail. Old tablecloths, perhaps, stained from a thousand family gatherings.

"Why do people save these things, Jake?" She ran a hand beneath whatever topped the stack and lifted it gently, glad her grandmother did. She'd take any history lesson the woman left behind. The fabric was brittle, thin at the folds, and she unfurled it gently on the floor. A giant, stained oval with a lace edge. "Holding onto all those family dinner memories, I guess."

She folded it back into its square and returned it to where it came from.

"All these things meant something to somebody, and the meaning left when they did. It's kind of sad."

She crept along the wall, careful not to kick up dust as she followed the collection of relics. Half a dozen paintings leaned against a stack of file boxes. She thumbed through, resting them against her knee. One was of ships painted by some guy named Degory Howland, who scrawled his name in red ink, lower left. A little green cottage surrounded by purple lupine and marigolds. Penny had never been one for art. She rested them back against the boxes, careful not to ding the frames.

On a makeshift shelf, nothing more than a two-by-four wedged between the studs, sat an old cookie tin with rusty edges. On the lid, a scratched and scraped Victorian Santa in a red wizard robe with a beard to his knees. She pried off the lid. Inside, a few black and white photos of a man in a military uniform. Army, perhaps. Penny never could keep the uniforms straight. Beneath them were a two-dollar bill and a few silver dollars. She put the tin back on the shelf, in the dustless ring where she had found it. Next to the tin was a small lacquered box with painted flowers on the lid. Inside, were necklaces, bracelets, and thin rings with small stones. Pearls, probably faux. Rhinestones in silver.

"Probably not very valuable, but they're really pretty. What do you think, Jake?" She tried on an elaborate rhinestone necklace and smoothed it over the T-shirt she'd slept in. "Too elegant for my jammies, huh?"

Jake flicked a foot and sashayed across the plywood floor.

"What a critic. You wouldn't know good fashion if it landed in your food bowl."

She placed it back in the box.

A stack of old wooden crates, their paper labels and stamped logos peeling and faded, stood in one corner, their corners askew in a rickety tower. The top crate was full of more photo albums. She opened the cover top box gently, so dust wouldn't fly into the air, and carried it to the window.

JENNIFER M. LANE

The orange-tinted photos couldn't be that old. A man in a dark, baggy suit stood on a porch next to a woman in a printed dress, flowers or leaves perhaps.

"Is this granddad?" A man in a field with a blur of a dog. A woman, her eyes shadowed by a bonnet, holding a child in one arm and the reins of a workhorse in another.

A man pulling a girl in a wagon, and on the back in pencil was written *Poppy and Frank.* Her mom and her grandfather.

Eliza and Poppy in white Easter bonnets, carrying bright shiny purses that could be patent leather.

The shape of his nose. The curve of her jawline. These things looked familiar. She knew them from her own bathroom mirror, but here they were in black and white, the history of her own expression. She'd never had a chance to see it before. Why had her mother left all of this behind?

The photos got older as she dug through the crate. In an old leather book with gold lettering, the cover unattached, she found pictures of a man who could have been her great-grandfather, standing next to the family's first car, primitive compared to her Jeep parked out back. Had her grandmother remembered what that old car smelled like? Penny would never be able to ask.

She'd always thought the three albums of her mother's were all there was to her family's pictorial history. Just baby pictures of her mother, like she sprouted from the floorboards of an old farmhouse, clad in the off-color Kodachrome dresses. But here it was, the whole story. One she would know if her mother hadn't kept it to herself for all those years. Those two-dimensional pictures were a major omission from her three-dimensional life, and it wasn't fair of her mother to keep it all from her. It was hers, too, and she shouldn't have had to wait for someone to die to

142

learn about what was rightfully hers.

She placed the album back in the crate with the rest. Someday she'd sit down and go through them.

"What do you have there, Jake?" In the center of the attic was an old trunk. The kind people stuffed with corsets and bulky dresses and dragged onto ships for a trip across the Atlantic. It was made of wood with bands of metal holding it together and thick leather handles on the sides. Jake perched on the curved top and scanned the room for signs of life. Penny shooed him away, and an envelope fluttered to the floor.

"What's this?" She collected it from the floor, turned it over, and brushed the dust away.

Penny.

Her name, in tight little letters in the center of the envelope. Its corners were faded and bent.

How long ago did her grandmother know? How long ago did she pick up a pen and write on that envelope, knowing that she would leave that mess downstairs to her granddaughter and not do anything about cleaning it up? Long enough ago for thick dust to settle on the envelope, that much was obvious.

And why not leave the store and the junk to someone in town? Warren liked her. So did Helen. She could have left all this to someone who cared for it, for her. Maybe she thought Penny would swoop in and clean it up, just like she did for her own mother when the end came.

Penny lifted the flap and pulled out an index card. A little white card with blue lines.

The trunk is from an ancestor's voyage to the new world. Your story is inside. The wedding dress was mine. I intended it for Poppy, but you know that story all too well, I'm sure. I kept two promises to you: I wrote you letters, and I never sent them. You'll find them all inside. Keep what you will, discard the rest. Much love, Eliza.

Penny crouched on the plywood and pressed the lever on the latch. The closure fell, and a metallic clang echoed in the attic, sending Jake scurrying. Lifting the lid would betray her mother. The mom who fed her carrots and peanut butter for an afternoon snack. The carefree mom who'd lived like the worst of her days were behind her, like she'd chosen her path and had no regrets. The mom who wanted more than anything to shield her from the things she'd run away from. Penny was exactly where her mother never wanted her to be. Away from school, away from her dreams and her goals, away from the education she'd worked so hard for, and drowning in the fodder of her grandmother's life. Drowning in meaningless cast-off items that nobody wanted enough to keep.

She placed her hands on the lid.

Mom said her grandmother never deserved to have them in her life. She'd made her choices and pushed away her family. But nobody else saw it in that light. They said she was kind. Generous. Warren's eyes filled with tears when he talked about his friend. Nate liked her company and missed his old neighbor. Helen used to sit and talk with her, two women mourning the loves they lost. Was it all polite discourse? A beatification of the woman who lived among them? People tended to do that with the deceased, wax poetic about the life they lived, as if only the good was magnified in the passing.

Maybe all of it was true.

The lid gave way with a creak of its hinges, and dust scattered into the air like fragments of diamonds in the light. A cigar box of pictures from when Penny was small. Tottering on the sidewalk outside the store. Bundled in a blue coat, her nose pink in the cold. Christmas, perhaps, when she was about a year old. Penny had no memory of having been to Ramsbolt prior to her grandmother's funeral. Why hadn't her mom ever said that she'd been there? She'd asked about her grandmother, and Mom never said.

She shifted her weight and sat on the floor, dust sticking to her sweaty palm that she wiped onto her knee. There was a physical discomfort to digging through everything, as if she intruded on her own life. On her mother's excuses and her grandmother's absence.

She returned the pictures to the cigar box and set it aside. A white box and inside, an old wedding dress, its lace yellowed with age, stiff and brittle to the touch. Wedding dresses and tablecloths all come out the same in the end. Another note card was tucked in the neckline. *This was mine. Made by my mother and my aunt, who ran a dressmaker's shop on Main Street.*

She could picture a shop like that, with hats and dresses in the window. Across from the market, perhaps. She'd have to ask around. Maybe Warren would know where it stood.

A shoe box full of letters, folded and creased, but never sent, rested at the bottom of the trunk. They weren't tucked in envelopes. Lined up like thoughts jotted down and filed away.

Penny unfolded a tightly creased letter written in black ink on faded notebook paper.

Eliza had spent a rainy summer afternoon writing letters at the little white table. Penny was nearly four. Her grandmother knew better than to mail a gift, so the happy thoughts would have to do. The warmth of the day had sparked a memory of playing with Poppy out in the yard. Making stew out of pebbles and mud in a puddle at the edge of the fields. Eliza missed those carefree times, when the land was in charge. It sounded good to Penny, too, owing time and energy to the land instead of to reams of paper. She'd take the sound of birds and walking through a field any day over beeping machines and running down slippery halls with doctors screaming at her.

Christmas Day and Penny was ten. How tall was she then? Did she have her mom's red hair? Her father had been a redhead, too. He'd lived in a house on the east side of town. His father worked on a farm, and his mother tended the church office. Poppy and her beau left town and ran to the city as soon as she turned eighteen. They split up soon after, and he moved to Europe to follow some vagabond dream. Poppy, headstrong as she was, wouldn't take help of any kind. She hoped Penny was happy and doing well in school.

Penny had never heard that story, that her dad went to Europe. She never thought of him at all. Her mother had raised her in a self-reliant us-against-the-world dream, and she'd never given thought to living it any other way. Any question she'd ever had about her father, her mother had cast aside, the same way she had brushed off Penny's questions about her grandmother. Penny chewed at the inside of her lip. It was stupid of her never to question her mother's telling of it all.

A lump formed in her throat. "Is it dusty up here, or am I just starting to lose it, Jake?"

He rubbed his chin on her knee. "Europe, huh? Maybe when all this is done, I'll look him up. Maybe it's time to sign up for one of those genealogy websites. I wonder if my other grandparents still live here. How weird would that be? I could have walked right past them."

She unfolded the next letter, dated the day of her high school graduation. The memory of the cake Brenda brought back from the grocery store with its plastic graduation cap decoration and that whipped icing she loved so much. In the letter, her grandmother imagined her driving off to college, like her mother had sworn she would. Was her godmother good to her? Did she feel loved? Her other grandparents retired and moved way. Off to sunny Florida to ease his arthritis and her hatred of shoveling snow.

"I guess I haven't run into them in the bakery, then."

She let the letter refold itself along its creases. It wasn't just a grandmother and a father her mother had shielded her from. It was more than the heartache her mother had suffered that the isolation kept at bay. It was other grandparents and a whole other town that would have thought of her as one of its own and maybe still did in some ways. And she'd missed a chance to grow up with that. Her chin trembled with the threat of tears. She filled her lungs with musty air to guard against them.

Another letter from August. The week Penny started medical school. The letter dripped with disappointment.

I always hoped you'd show up one day, walk through the door, and sit at the table with me. We could drink coffee and look at old pictures. I'm very proud that you made it to medical school. You were so good with Poppy that day I visited. You're every bit the natural healer your mother said you were. Ramsbolt could use a good doctor. Hint, hint. But it's foolish of me to think that you will want to return to your roots and certainly not to run an antique store. But dreams come and go of their own accord, and time will march on. You must be true to your own path. Not many people even have one. I didn't.

Penny folded the final letter and put it back in the shoe box, with the others. She'd always assumed that her mother was right to isolate her from Ramsbolt, that her mother knew best. It had been an unquestionable truth that Poppy's childhood was horrid, but was it really? Was it selfish to keep Penny from her family? It wasn't her grandmother who had refused her to visit, it was her mom. And it wasn't just her grandmother she'd kept her from, either. It was her father and her other grandparents and anyone else she might be related to.

A tear landed on the plywood floor, and Penny wiped her nose on her sleeve. It was so unfair to miss the chance to know someone. She returned the letters to the shoe box and spread out the pictures. So many people she never met. So many lives she never touched. Her mom was an only child, as was her grandmother. Her grandfather had wound his way from Europe and landed in America as a fully formed adult. She'd been robbed of any chance to share a history with her people.

All she had to show for it was a building full of meaningless furniture and a boat load of debt.

CHAPTER SIXTEEN

Penny chewed the end of an old ink pen and studied the scenes of the past spread before her on the glass display counter. A farm in black and white. Her mother playing with the dollhouse on the stairs. Her elbows ached from leaning on the counter, sitting on a bar stool that was too high, hunched over the pictures with her chin in her hands.

"Costs more to keep the lights on some days, doesn't it?" A woman in a T-shirt and jeans entered through the open door. Her gray shirt was stained with splotches of oil, and her jeans were worn thin, tan in places. As if she'd sat on the ground and leaned on dirt all day.

Penny pulled the pen from her mouth and dropped it by the register. "I don't think I can argue with that."

"Jaleesa." The woman stuck her hand across the counter, and Penny accepted it without prejudice to the grime beneath her nails. "I run the garage in town. I'm over on Levering if you ever need anything. Heard you got a Jeep?"

"Penny. Nice to meet you. I do have a Jeep. Poor thing is ancient, but it keeps on ticking. It's moved me to and from a few apartments now. It's a workhorse."

"That they are." Jaleesa would her way through the furniture, hands in her pockets.

"You looking for some furniture? Better yet, do you want to buy a store?"

"A bigger garage maybe, but I'm all set with a store. It's a shame you're not staying. Jeeps are fun to work on. They get rusty up here. Always need something. Anyway, Helen's old Pinto needed some shocks. She likes to hang out with me while I work on her car. She said you were selling everything off, and I thought I'd take a look around. Maybe there's something here I can use in the waiting room." Jaleesa shot disinterested glances at the furniture she passed.

"There are shelves back there." Penny aimed her pen at the farthest corner. "The kind you nail to the wall. And a bunch of pictures of town from a long time ago. There might be some old cars in some of them. You need any little tables or anything?"

"Nah. No tables. Some pictures maybe. That'd be neat. I feel bad that I've never been in here before?"

"A lot of people say that." From most, it sounded like an apology. Sometimes it sounded like an excuse. They all loved Eliza, though. It was hard not to take their disinterest personally when Eliza's problems had become her own. "Browse around. Everything's negotiable. I'm giving big discounts for everything with a sticker. Blue items are free with the purchase of anything else."

"Good to know." Jaleesa flipped through a box of metal signs, none of which had looked all that old to Penny. Just a bunch of fake marketing signs. Girls in fifties-style dresses sipping drinks at soda counters with made-up soda logos. "Got any old tools or anything like that?"

Penny rubbed a spot on her temple. "I don't think I've seen anything like that. Though my grandmother had some tools I probably won't need once I'm done with this place. If I find anything, I can bring it over to you on my way out of town. Levering, you said?"

Jaleesa moved to the door. A gust of unseasonably warm air rushed in from the sidewalk. "That'd be great. Thanks. It was nice to meet you." She nodded and was gone. The browsers did that. They walked softly and pushed through the door with no more than a wave, as if not buying something made them ashamed. At least she was nice.

Outside, the pink sky was just beginning its fade to orange, bringing the sour day to an end. She'd sold nothing. Four people came in. They leaned on tables. Two women tried to guess who had donated what. They snickered at an ornamental lawn statue of the Virgin Mary, gossiped about the woman who had owned it, and declared the woman who left it on her grandmother's doorstep as anything but religious.

Penny pulled the empty shoe box onto her lap and took one last glance at the photos, lined up like a lifeline on the counter, lives lived flat. She'd done her best to put them in order, so winters faded into springs. Her grandmother wearing a stiff cotton sack dress hanging wet clothes on a line behind a farmhouse in a world where there was time for clothes to air dry. Sowing seeds and growing fields in a land where nature set the schedule instead of an overbearing advisor who wouldn't let her sleep past four. Over and over, summer faded to autumn. Harvesting potatoes. Pulling the greenery from the land. Birthdays and Easters and Christmas dinners all spread out with no hint of the passion or drama that propelled life forward. But it was there in every picture. No hint of slog or exhaustion or routine.

She studied the counters, the horizons, and tiny details searching for clues and mysteries to solve. Penny had a solid mental picture of a large farm in black and white with its tight rows of potato plants and a farmhouse with a wide front porch. Not a hint of paperwork or nagging computers. There was no hint of it in Ramsbolt at all, come to think of it.

Sometime when her grandmother was young, between Independence Day and an autumn harvest, someone moved a soup tureen from the sideboard in the dining room and put a candelabra in its place. Such a simple gesture, frozen in time. It meant nothing to them, but now Penny wondered why. Had they served soup? What kind? Was the recipe lying around in some box or folder and could she make it with stuff from the market? She never cooked food in Otley. She hadn't had a hearty meal since—she couldn't recall when. There was never time or energy enough for all that.

Later pictures placed her grandmother in the store. In an empty space with brick walls and hardwood floors. Standing among furniture scattered erratically, like a dinner party for one decorated by the Mad Hatter. A dining room table surrounded by desks and beds. The photos were fewer and further between and a sorrow seemed to bleed from them. A loneliness captured by the lens that hadn't been there a generation before. Few signs of her mother. But she knew where those photos had gone. They were in her apartment in Otley.

Penny swept the pictures into the shoe box. It was a shame it wasn't there anymore, that she couldn't drive a few miles outside of town and park on the shoulder to imagine the views from the windows. The way Warren spoke of it, no one even knew exactly where the house once stood. But maybe someone would remember. Someone at the bar.

She sifted through the photographs and selected one with a view of the house and closed the box.

"Jake, I'm gonna go out for a bit."

The floorboards creaked under his light steps, but he remained hidden, slinking through chair legs and pouncing on the shadows.

She sealed the photograph inside a plastic sandwich bag to keep it safe from beer and spills, locked the doors, and drove to Helen's Tavern. The parking lot was full, so she squeezed her Jeep between a rusted Subaru and the dumpster. There were no lines in the gravel lot, yet the town seemed to be in agreement, circling the bar like campers around a fire, waiting for stories beneath the churn of constellations.

This time, she knew her way around. Without hesitation, she breezed through the mud room and into the bar with a gentle tug on the door.

There was an empty seat next to Nate.

"Mind if I join you?"

"Come on in. Plenty of room." He leaned back and motioned to the empty chair. "How's the store going?"

"It's not, unfortunately." She slung her purse over the back of the chair and scooted closer to the bar. "A few people came in and browsed around because they heard it was closing, but nobody bought anything."

"I can't believe in this little town, where no one's a millionaire, and everybody loves the history, you can't find people to buy that stuff." Nate pushed his sweating beer around on the bar, leaving concentric wet rings. "Maybe they think Eliza turned them down from buying something once already, so there's no sense asking again."

Penny pulled a napkin from the stack. Not like her drink would be coming any time soon, but it was good to be prepared. "You might be onto something. I pulled a lot of stuff out onto the sidewalk and tried to make it more obvious that stuff was for sale."

"I heard you and Adelle going at it out there. I opted to keep my nose clean and stay inside."

"Smart move. At least I can move around in there now. But it still seems like everyone who walks in there is overwhelmed by the scale of it all."

"You want a whiskey again?" Helen called over to her, hand poised over a glass.

"That's perfect. Thanks." Penny nodded. "Maybe if I knew how to market it better. I'm a healer, not a junk dealer."

She winced when she said it. It wasn't really junk.

"It's a special kind of mindset, that's for sure." Helen placed the glass on her folded napkin and dropped ice in a second cup for her. "Ice on the side."

"Your grandmother had a way with...*things*." Warren slid from a seat in the shadows and made his way to the chair next to Penny. "Wasn't that she didn't want someone to have something. She just could read the meanings in things, and she knew if it wasn't a good fit. Like how a librarian won't steer you to the wrong kind of book 'cause she knows you won't be happy with it."

A woman Penny's age with brown hair pulled back in a high ponytail leaned and peered down the bar. Her eyes lit up, and her ponytail bobbed when she nodded. "I can attest to that. I went in for a bed frame. I wanted something better than a creaky metal thing that came with the mattress. I'm Sandy, by the way. I run the library. There's not much money in working at a library. Anyway, your grandmother showed me this gorgeous headboard. It was carved with these ornate flowers, and I fell in love with it. I asked her how much because, she doesn't have prices on anything. She wanted almost a thousand dollars for it. Well, there was no way I could afford that. So I kept looking, but nothing jumped out at me. I wasn't even upset about it. But she started asking me about the library and my life, and, get this, the next day when I got home from work, that bed frame—headboard and all—was sitting outside my apartment door."

That didn't sound like the grandmother she'd heard about at all. Penny swallowed hard, choking back a laugh. Whiskey stung her throat. "She had it delivered to you? For free?"

Sandy nodded, and the ponytail wagged. "It's my most cherished possession."

"She had so many sides I never got to see." Penny had been more than willing to accept that everyone who walked through the emergency room doors was worthy of repair, even a drunk driver who killed half a family was worthy of redemption. But she'd been unable to give that same grace to her grandmother until it was too late.

Penny turned in her seat and pulled the photo from her purse. "Do you know where this farm is? Or was?"

She dangled the picture across the bar. Helen braced herself on the cooler, squinting at the photo. "I remember about where it was." She plucked a tattered mop from where it rested by the office door and sopped a puddle oozing from under the cooler. "I can tell you a story about your grandmother you might not have heard. I used to babysit for her. For your mom. I knew *of* your family. Everybody did. But they lived outside town, so I didn't get to know you all until after your grandpa died."

"You babysat my mom?"

Helen wrinkled her nose when she smiled. "I did. She was an energetic child, your mother. Always into something. And fiercely independent. You couldn't tell her no for anything."

"Sounds like Mom."

"She fell in love with your father and that was that. She was moving out of this town and nothing was gonna stop her. Said there was nothing here for her, and she wasn't wrong. Jobs dried up. No one was out shopping. It was all those big box stores springing up out of the ground, taking up jobs and sending people out of town to do their shopping. Made sense at the time, it was a new thing. But your grandmother lost a lot of business and your mom, well, she had nowhere to work. So she and your father made a run for it."

"He went to Europe. That's what my mom said."

"Eventually. That's what we heard. His parents were long gone from here by then. Money don't buy you love or happiness, but when it leaves, it takes as much of both as it can. They split and moved on. Nothing your gran could do to make anybody stay. It was around that time that my husband and I split, and I sat at that little white table with her one night drinking white wine, and talking about that, why we can't make things stay as they are. I'll never forget her saying to me that was why she cared so much about things ending up with the right people. She had to leave so much behind when your grandpa died, and she had to sell a lot of what was left to get by. She could only bring what the horses could haul. Which turned out to be quite a bit, but not everything that meant something to her."

The photo of her grandmother standing alone in a store full of furniture came to life. "Oh, God. She lost her husband and had this tiny kid and had no way of making a living. She sold what she had to survive."

"She rented that place. Turned it into a used furniture store. She worked hard and bought the building and raised her daughter there. And one Christmas when you were too small to walk, your mom brought you back here. She sat down at the end of the bar there, not far from where

Arvil's sitting. Had you lying right on the bar. She said to me that she had no regrets, and her ma shouldn't either. Said we make the choices we have to make based on where we are at the time. Sometimes others get hurt in the process, and you can't go back and fix it. It's too late. You just gotta keep on."

"Too late. She said it was too late? You only say that if you think there's room or you wish you could—" But even when Penny gave her the chance to make those amends, her mom didn't take it.

"Sometimes you just gotta keep on and let go."

* * *

Penny drove around the circle, under the watchful gaze of the sailor. There was no rhyme or reason to him, a sailor out here in a landlocked town. There was no rhyme or reason to why her mother had to flee, why she refused to let her daughter know a grandmother. Penny couldn't reason with her mom any more than she could argue with the statue. Neither of them were inherently bad for denying her the clarity. As circumstances go, it simply was what it was. Penny had healed enough scrapes and bruises to know that you can only focus on the stuff you can change.

She parked her Jeep behind the store and stood in the rutted parking lot, taking in the autumn air. It was warm for an autumn night, and fireflies did their nightly dance along the tree line. She wondered if they knew it would all come to an end soon, that the nights would grow colder. It was almost time to burrow into the trees and into the ground. And the stars—so many stars. She felt small beneath them, head tilted to the sky beneath pinpoints of light from so far away. She'd never been so arrogant as to believe that earth held the only intelligent life, and sometimes, looking up at those twinkling planets made the passage of time and all it took with it seem less significant. It gave her comfort.

Headlights flashed up the narrow alley. Nate maybe. Or one of the neighbors coming home from the bar or a trip out of town. She dug her key from her pocket and let herself in, feeling along the wall for the light switch. Jake hopped from the table and circled her legs, crying for a second dinner.

"You ate already." But she grabbed the bag of food from the counter anyway. Kibble clattered into his bowl on the table. "Bottomless pit. But I like your little kitty voice." Through the doorless kitchen entry, she could see a red light blinking from the office under the stairs. A voice mail.

"Did you get a robocall from the kitty scammers? What are they trying to get out of you? *Give us all your kitty treats, and we'll sign you up for an insurance scam.*" She crunched the bag closed, sealed it with a clothespin, and ran her hand down Jake's orange back. He purred at her touch. "You're such an affectionate kitty sometimes. I expected more ankle biting, to be honest. I'm going up for my jammies. You enjoy the late-night snack."

She dropped his empty food bowl in the sink. "You really should learn to do your own dishes."

Blink... Blink... The red light flashed in the cubby beneath the stairs. It would only keep her up, blinking in the darkness. She slipped beneath the stairs and pressed the message button. The caller's voice filled the shop.

"Anderson here. From Rockland. Down by Owls Head. I ran into Cheryl from Bar Harbor at an estate sale, and she said she missed out on picking through all of Eliza's stuff. Terrible news about Eliza. She was such a talker, your grandmother. Cheryl said it all must go, and she doesn't have room for it. Shocker the way she buys estates. She's cheap, anyway. Never pays what anything is worth. Don't tell her I said that. Anyway, last time I was there the place was packed to the gills. I'll be by first thing tomorrow morning to value everything. And I won't undercut you the way Cheryl would. If it's as packed as it used to be, it'll take a good part of the day to look through it all. Call me if this doesn't work for ya or send me a text. I'll swing by first thing."

The man rattled off a number and hung up. She jotted it down on the back of an old envelope.

Did she hear that right or was it the whiskey talking? Everything? He would value everything? Even if he didn't take it all, anything would be better than nothing. If he was taking the time to look at it all, he must be interested. Penny's heart raced. It was the kind of adrenaline rush she loved, like she got when a flat-lined patient came to after a minute of stressful chest compressions.

"Did you hear that Jake? Someone's coming by tomorrow morning. We'll have to put on our best outfits."

Jake scrambled through the darkness, his paws pounding on the hardwood floor, chasing invisible prey. He found a length of twine dangling from a broken chair and swatted it.

"This could be our best chance to preserve your mom's legacy, Jake. To save Ramsbolt's treasures. We'd better get a good night's sleep."

Her footsteps rattled china on shelves, and wood clattered against metal. She grabbed the railing and headed up the stairs. Once raw wood, a treated branch from some felled tree, it was smooth from years of hands. Her foot barely skimmed the bottom stair when a banging on the back door jiggled the panes of glass in the window.

Maybe she left the headlights on in her Jeep.

No, it had been dark out when she looked up at the stars.

"Penny? You still up?" Nate's voice drifted through the door and into the shop.

Jake lifted his head as she passed on her way to the door. She pressed the latch and pulled the door open. "Is everything okay? What's wrong?"

He held out a half-full bottle of wine. "I'm not really tired. It's probably all this warm air. Global warming messing up my sleep schedule. Anyway, I thought I'd sit out here and polish this off, but the little table Eliza put out here is long gone, and it's not that much fun drinking wine by yourself. Saw your lights still on, so I thought I'd see if you'd like some wine."

Penny held the door open and waved him in. "I like the sound of that. We can celebrate. I have good news to tell you. And we have our pick of tables, that's for sure. You need an opener?"

He pulled one from the pocket of his poofy green vest. "I come prepared. You don't even need a glass. Just a table, two chairs, and yourself."

Penny slipped past a ravenous Jake who didn't lift his head from the bowl. Just inside the shop, on the left, behind an old wooden office chair on broken wheels and beneath the headless, armless torso of a battered mannequin stood a small marble table on a cast iron base.

"This should work. I've moved this thing a dozen times, and it's not as heavy as it looks. I've got wood bench seats over there by the counter." She nodded in the direction of the antique cash register. "They're not as heavy as they look either."

Nate crammed the wine bottle into the other vest pocket and lifted one seat in each hand. "After you."

Penny twisted and turned, hoisting the table around Jake and his second dinner, around the cabinets and out the door, down the short flight of steps and into the back parking lot. She dropped the table away from the cars and not too close to the trees, so as not to disturb the fireflies.

Nate dropped a bench on either side of the table and pried the wine bottle from his vest. He jammed the bottle opener into the cork and fought it out of the bottle. It gave way with a pop.

"That was a pretty cool photo you brought to the bar. You found a lot like that?"

"Yeah. Gran had a bunch of albums and boxes of pictures up in the attic. I can't remember if it was you or Warren who told me about the attic. Was it you?"

"Wasn't me." He dropped a full glass of something red in front of her.

"Thanks. I found a lot of neat stuff up there. Lots of old tablecloths, her old wedding dress, yearbooks. Nothing fancy."

"Wouldn't expect fancy out of Eliza." He perched on the bench like a parrot, his back straight, shifting his weight. Penny regretted the choice of seating. Made of raw wood and shiny varnish, they looked great outside, but they weren't very comfortable as chairs went.

The wine warmed her insides and left her mouth dry. Maybe it was a merlot. "There was a box of letters up there that she wrote to me but never sent. I came here expecting to get rid of things, not find things to take home with me. Speaking of, I might be out of here tomorrow."

Nate took a quick swallow from his glass. "Really? That fast. You got a nibble?"

"More like a giant chomp. At least I hope so. A guy who owns an antique place heard about it, and he's coming by in the morning to look at everything."

A drop of wine had traveled down the bottle, finally making it to the marble top. Nate brushed it away with his finger and wiped it on his jeans. "That's great news. I'll miss having a neighbor, but I'm happy to hear that all this stuff might find a home."

"Me, too. Fingers crossed it happens fast."

"What about Jake?"

"I haven't even tried to find a home for him. I could make up a story and say he's good at pest control or I figured someone would walk in and want to take him home, but I like his company, to be honest. Never saw myself as a cat person, but for Jake I could make an exception." Penny took a sip of wine. It was definitely merlot. "I'm a little bummed. I don't really wanna go yet."

"After all that *I'm not staying* stuff? Ramsbolt wore off on ya, huh?"

She tilted her head back to look at the stars. "A little. It's quiet here. You can see all that up there, which you can't see in the city. And nobody's in a rush to do anything."

"A nice change of pace from a hospital, I bet."

"You got that right. Everything is life and death, and the things that matter the most are the things they appreciate the least." Penny slung back the rest of her glass, and Nate refilled it. "Hey, can I ask you something?"

Nate set the empty bottle on the table a little too hard, and the scraping sound of glass on marble echoed off the trees. "Sure. Shoot."

"How did she get those chairs to hang from the ceiling? Do you know?"

"She had some might, your grandmother. She threw a rope over the ceiling joists and pulled the chairs up one at a time. Then she fastened the rope to something on the floor and tied the chair up with another rope. She didn't do it all in one day. It happened over the years. I guess she was trying to get them out of the way."

"Pretty smart."

"She was resourceful, that's for sure. You need help getting them down tomorrow before that guy gets here? I can come over first thing and help you with it?"

Penny waved a hand. "Nah. I was just curious. Nothing in there's that urgent. Thanks, though"

"Any time." Nate finished his glass and rubbed his eyes with the heels of his hands. "Fall pollen always makes me sleepy, and this hit the spot. You want help carrying these back inside?"

"I can get it. Or maybe I'll just leave them out here for another time. Sorry I prattled on about my problems." Penny threw her head back and gulped the last of her wine. She held out the empty glass.

The corners of Nate's eyes crinkled when he smiled. "You didn't have to finish it that fast."

"Nah. Every drink should be finished with passion."

He turned for his door. "Good night. And good luck tomorrow. Come over and find me if you need help pulling those chairs down. And if it all works out, don't leave without saying goodbye."

The light from the kitchen window caught the strokes of gray in his hair. He was sweet. There was no regret in him, no rush, no making up for lost time. His kindness was slow and placid in a way that made the stressed and hectic men in her life at home seem abrasive. She fumbled over her words, searching for the right ones to say she'd like to keep in touch, but all she could find were clauses and phrases that would make her sound foolish or drunk.

"I won't. Thanks for the wine."

Nate disappeared behind the door of the toy shop, the twin to her own. Lights came on and went off from his kitchen up to his second-floor residence. She pictured it cozy inside. Normal. A sofa and some artwork. A dresser covered with pictures and his wallet. Someday, she'd have a cozy house like that and not some cold, impersonal apartment shell.

Tired and world-weary, she had no energy left to carry the benches and table back inside. She checked the weather on her phone. No chance of rain. She left them where they were.

CHAPTER SEVENTEEN

The sun hadn't risen yet, but Penny couldn't sleep. She wound through the furniture with glass cleaner in one hand, a roll of paper towels tucked under her arm. Wads of wet, black and brown towels were in little piles all over the store. Cleaning had never been her forte, but it sure beat standing idle, waiting for that Anderson guy to show up. Jake thought the whole thing was a game for his benefit, hiding in the shadows and jumping out to attack her ankles when she passed by.

"I was kidding when I said I expected more ankle biting." She bent and released his claw from her sock, and he scampered off beneath a desk. "I'm trying to clean. It's not like I expect the guy to be offended by some dirt. He *is* an antique dealer. Why am I telling this to a cat?"

The more comfortable she could make the place, the more time Anderson was likely to spend inspecting everything. He would need a lot of time, considering everything that Ramsbolt had cast aside. And if he walked in while she was cleaning, at least it would look like someone valued it enough to make an effort.

While her back was turned, the sun came up and threw colors on the walls. Hints of pink and peach. Penny wiped a mirror and adjusted her hair. She didn't look the part of small business owner. Not like anyone who knew how to haggle over furniture prices. Who was she kidding? She couldn't fake it anyway. She'd have to bank on him being the understanding type.

The bell rang out, and a man entered the store. There was no doubt it was Anderson. No one in Ramsbolt seemed the type to sport a bowler hat with feathers on the side. Short, dark hair peeked from beneath. He wore a plain black sweater, tucked his skinny jeans deep into his Doc Martens and carried a big metal clipboard.

She twisted and turned, maneuvering around a dining room set covered with empty wood crates, the names of blueberry farms etched into them and worn away by hands and time, collecting dirty paper towels as she went.

"You must be Anderson." Penny declined the handshake when he offered, wrinkling her nose. "Dirt. Sorry. But you're probably used to it."

"I am. This is sterile compared to what I usually work with."

Not me, she thought. *I wouldn't dissect a frog in this wreckage.*

"Glad you got my message." His eyes didn't fall on hers. They wandered from the walls to the ceiling. There was no hint of judgment from him. Whether that was a good thing or not remained to be seen. "I was at an estate sale last weekend with Cheryl, and she said Eliza had passed and everything was for sale. Building and all."

"Did you know my grandmother? I mean, did you do business together?"

"Yes and no. We'd see each other at things. She never bought much. She sold *smalls*." He said the word not as if it were beneath him, but as if it were a distinction. As if you either dealt in one world or another. "Trinkets and dishes and tea sets. Old toys. That was her thing. She'd

166

bring everything to shows in these old wood crates. Like those, back there. She'd make a good amount of money at it, too. She was a hell of a chatterbox. I was across from her one year, and it was like watching a master at work. She'd start with these little questions. Compliment someone on their shoes or their bag. Then she'd pair them with an object she had for sale. I mean, it sounds like what salespeople do, but she had this way about her. Next thing you know, some guy who drives a truck for a living is walking away with a tea set he never knew he needed. But she knew. And he needed it."

He shaded his eyes and hovered over the glass display cabinet. Rhinestone jewelry sparkled yellow and gold in the early morning sun.

"Everyone here says the same thing. I never knew her, but it sounds like she was the humane society for cast-off furniture."

Anderson spun to face her and beamed. "That's my store. Cast-off Culture. Like, material culture that needs a home." He dug a card from his wallet. "Here. So you've got my email. Cheryl spoke highly of this place. Just glancing around, I can tell it's full of stuff that will sell. This town is really charming. I mean, it's a damn postcard. But it's gotta be tough to sell stuff in a place like this. In small towns, people want *smalls*. They want decor and cute stuff for the kitchen. I don't know how she expected to sell fifty dining room tables in a place like this. Boston or Portland or Bangor, sure. But not here."

His words washed over her like a stream rushing over rocks, carrying away some of her biggest fears.

She wanted to grab him by the sweater and beg him to take it all to anywhere but here. "I'm glad to hear you say that. It's been hard to get people to buy things. It's like they feel bad they never shopped here because they wanted to, but there's nothing they need."

167

"It's all about market. Just like anything else." Anderson opened his clipboard and tucked a pad of paper under the clip. "So here's what I'll do. I need to look at everything, if you don't mind. Look at how it's made, peek in the drawers at dovetail joints, and try to date everything. Do you have provenance on this stuff?"

"Provenance?" She didn't bother trying to mask it. She had no clue what he was talking about.

Anderson didn't seem to mind her lack of knowledge. "Do you know where anything is from. Who it belonged to. Makers and dates?"

"No. I've been through all her files, and there's nothing about the furniture."

"Okay. Nothing to worry about. It can only help, not hurt. Value is fluid, anyway. That's why the quotes I'll give you won't last very long. What people value today won't be what they want tomorrow."

"Is that why she didn't put prices on anything? Nate from next door said it was because she would outprice people she didn't think would take care of things."

He opened his clipboard and took out a pencil. "Well, both may be true. Thing is, the most beautiful jewelry in the world can have no value at all while the rattiest, dirtiest piece of wood can be priceless. Then aesthetics can fall out of favor. Sometimes it's easier to have no prices at all. Imagine changing price tags in a place like this."

Crouching on the floor, he peered at the underside of a table. "Objects evolve. Not because they change, because we do. We want something new and all the prestige and self-worth that come with buying something new. Then it ages and becomes outdated. It becomes a burden on our home, and it no longer says what we want it to about who we are. So we get rid of it. We donate it or sell it, and it sits in a place like this until the right buyer comes along. Who that buyer is, the meaning they apply to this table, is what sets the price. Is it an antique? Does the buyer find it valuable? Is it worth saving because it's rare or it evokes some nostalgia? Or is it only good enough to fill the room because your kids will destroy it with their shoes and their skateboards? That's where people like me come in. And your late grandmother."

Penny squatted next to him and tried to see what he could see. It just looked like a table to her.

"As a seller, if I sell too soon or too late, I miss a window to make more money. From the object's perspective, it wants to find a home that will care for it. But buyers want things they really need and *need* is subjective. It's funny, though. At some point, some items become priceless works of art. Then everybody wants it, but no one wants to pay enough."

"Sounds like healthcare. The more people want to have it and the better we get at providing it, the more expensive it gets."

"Is that what you do? Healthcare?" He flipped over a chair and shined a pen light at the underside of its seat.

She put her hands in her back pockets. "Yup. I'm a third-year medical student. Studying to be a surgeon."

"Good for you." He clicked off the light and made notes on his notepad. "Better you than me. I'll stick with furniture. Easier to repair and easier on the stomach."

He scanned the room, his clipboard in one hand, the other on his hip. His eyes caught on one object, then another. His soft smile said he was pleased. So was Penny. She felt a hundred pounds lighter. "You have a lot of really lovely things here. Do you have email? Of course you do. If you don't mind, I'll go through all this and write up a big report for you.

I'll need to go back to my shop and do some research, work up valuations on some of it. Then I can email you tomorrow morning with prices. You can take up to ten days to decide. I'll come back with a check and a truck. If anything sells in the meantime, that's fine. I don't want you to miss out on a sale." He rested his fingertips on a walnut dining room table. "But I'll fight them for this. It's exquisite."

How anything in that store could be considered exquisite was beyond her. It made her feel guilty for all the boxes and crates and scratchy metal things on every surface, though.

"How much of it do you think you'll be interested in?" *Please say all of it. Please.*

His eyes narrowed, and he surveyed the room. "Most of the big furniture. Probably a good amount of the medium size things, too. Like that ottoman over there and the end tables. Not as much of the small stuff. But that works out great for both of us."

The store would be empty. She'd be able to walk through it. A warmth grew inside her at the thought of cashing a check and paying off debts. Is this what being an adult was like? Being excited about paying bills?

"All of this is great news." A car swished by. Through the wall she could hear Nate beginning his day. Doors opening and closing. She wondered if he had a headache after all he had to drink between the bar and that wine. Across the street, Adelle swept the last of the night's debris from her tiled entry and stepped back inside. "I can leave you to it. You don't need me in your hair. I have the closed sign up so the shop's all yours. Take your time. I'm gonna go check in on my neighbor, so I'll be right next door if you need me. Oh, and ignore the cat. That's Jake. He's friendly. Just don't let him out."

Penny left Anderson alone and walked the ten steps to the door of the toy shop. She hesitated. There was no reason to bother Nate. She didn't need help with the chairs. She had no news to share. Really, she just wanted his company. She inched the door open and stuck her head in, wrinkling her nose to situate her glasses.

"Nate? You open?"

From behind the counter, he waved her in. "Just counting down a drawer. I was too lazy to do it last night."

"You survived the wine, I see."

"Barely. I'd had enough to drink before I started in on the wine. Some nights are like that. That guy is here already?"

"Yup. He says he may not want all of it, but he'll want some, and that's better than nothing. I probably shouldn't get my hopes up."

Nate smiled and zipped cash in a blue pouch. "Then what? What happens after he buys that stuff?"

"I don't know. Depends on how much is left, I guess. Rent a big box truck and take it to the county dump? Then I'll have to find a real estate person from outside town and sell the place, since no one here wants it. I can't wait for it all to go away so life can get back to normal." She sank into a giant red bean bag chair, and it poofed around her. She was never going to be able to get out. "On second thought, I might just sit here forever. I forgot how comfy bean bag chairs were."

"Throw in a big bowl of cereal, and some cartoons and it's like being a kid all over again." Nate swept together scattered piles of brown paper bags and stacked them on the short edge. A scrap of paper tumbled out and fluttered to the floor, and Penny reached out to grab it.

At eye level with the display counter, a figurine caught her eye. Among the trains and metal cars was, in bronze metallic plastic brushed with black paint, was a sailor, his eyes shaded by his cap, and his hands fixed on an immobile ships wheel. It was identical to the figurine in the window of the hospital gift shop.

"Where'd you get that? That little sailor statue."

Nate leaned forward and gazed down upon the sailor. "Had a batch of those made up for the tricentennial of the town. We were a town long before this was a state. Anyway, I didn't sell many. Wrote 'em off a long time ago. I keep 'em around, though, in case a tourist comes through who really wants one or some kid gets really enthusiastic about it. Happens once every few years. Why?"

"I saw one of these in the gift shop at the hospital where I work. It reminds me of someone." Of Lee. Who felt so far away. It seemed like months had passed since she bought two bagels, and he tried to overanalyze her decisions. Everything about Otley felt a million miles away. The hospital, her apartment, the schedule, the early morning alarm clocks.

"Take one." Nate pointed to the back of the store. "They're with the snow globes back there. So after you're rid of us, you'll have something to remember your adventures by."

"I'll take you up on that." She hopped to her feet and grabbed one from the shelf. "Hey, you wanna go get breakfast? My treat."

Without a word, he reached over and flipped the sign against the store window to say *Closed.* "How could I say no to an offer like that?"

* * *

Main Street was dead. One car parked outside the market, engine pinging from a dash for milk or eggs.

"Maybe there's an option other than throwing it all away. I just need to brainstorm. I think Ramsbolt would be happy if I could find happy homes for all that stuff," Penny said. "At least it would have a new lease on life, and I wouldn't have to go into debt to send it to the dump."

The smell of cinnamon and blueberries floated down the sidewalk, and Penny picked up the pace, as much to get out of the morning chill as to reach the food faster. Nate paused, his hand on Marissa's door pull.

"Wait to see what that guy says. Maybe he'll take more of it than you think, and this is the way it was meant to happen." He paused and squinted at the laminated list of the week's specials taped to the window.

"What is it today? I know yesterday it was blueberry donuts. What's today?"

"Says it's half-priced tea on Thursday." Nate pulled the door open and waved her in.

Penny wrinkled her nose. "I'm not much for tea. I'm more a coffee girl."

CHAPTER EIGHTEEN

Early evening sun warmed the attic, drawing from its wood a haunting ether. It smelled of places Penny never knew. Places like tabernacles and woodsheds. Places laid out in old photographs that she placed back in their boxes, back in the trunk. If she had to carry that old trunk down the stairs and to her Jeep in pieces, she would. At least she got something from Ramsbolt, and it wasn't a total waste.

Jake rubbed his chin against the trunk as she closed the lid, marking his territory in an unchallenged dispute.

"What do you say we climb down out of here and find a snack?" Penny stood. She dusted off her butt, and checked her phone. Still no email from Anderson. But he'd said it would take a while to research the furniture and put together a quote, and he'd spent most of the day going through everything. It could take a while.

The sound of the door chime sent Jake scurrying down the stairs, and Penny followed. The attic stairs creaked beneath her feet.

"Welcome!" She called down to her shopper. "Browse around. I'll be down in a bit."

"It's Nate. I hate to bother you, but I need help." His voice was high and frantic. It carried up the stairs on a lilt of pain that she knew well. She rushed down from the loft to the ground floor and found Nate just inside the door, holding his left hand close to his chest. There was no sign of blood, but his face was contorted with agony, his eyes were glazed with shock.

"What happened? Did you break something?" Penny pulled out a metal chair with a red vinyl seat and pushed him into it. "Let me see. Did you hit your head?"

She sat across from him. His eyes weren't dilated unevenly.

"No. Just my hand. I fell off a footstool."

"No risk of concussion?"

"No. Just two fingers, I think." He winced as she peeled his hands apart. "I was stocking shelves and slipped, and I landed wrong. I tried to catch myself, but my hand slipped, and I fell on my fingers."

She pulled his hand onto her knee.

"Ow, don't."

"It's a bone. Trust me. I've seen worse." When she lifted his hand, his ring and pinky fingers drooped. "They're a little pink. Not too swollen yet."

"Yet?"

"It'll swell. Just the body doing the hard work of healing you from the inside out." She rested his hand on his knee, his fingers straight. "You probably have some tendon damage. Is there an orthopedist in town?"

She knew the answer. Nothing but a pharmacist, a dentist, and a general practitioner. If the town had enough thermometers to assess a common cold epidemic, she'd have been shocked. Expecting an X-ray machine and a technician was asking too much.

"We just have the doctor on Elm Street." Nate's eyes were fixed on his fingers. His right hand squeezed his knee.

"They don't do broken bones do they? They can't make a decent splint?"

Nate shook his head. "Colds and flus and that kind of thing."

"What do you do in major emergencies? Like, a bone protruding through the skin or a stroke or a heart attack?" It was unfathomable that a town could survive without a hospital. That not a single resident wanted enough health security that they didn't lure some doctor to town with the promise of good bagels and a monopoly on emergency services.

"We call 911, and an ambulance or helicopter takes us to Saint John's."

Saint John's. Her first internship had been at a hospital called Saint John's. *Funny. There have to be a million of them.*

"How far is it by car? I can make you a quick splint, and we'll drive there."

Nate touched his pinky finger and winced. "About an hour. Out by Colby."

"Oh, I know Saint John's." Colby. With its eight red lights, four fast food restaurants and that little diner with the world's best lemon meringue pie. She hadn't been to that tiny metropolis since her first internship ended. At least she knew the fastest way to get to the emergency room parking lot, because the signage was a disaster, and the main entrance was nothing but potholes held together with some crumbly tar patches.

"Keep your fingers like this on your leg—straight and flat. I'll be right back with some ibuprofen and some stuff to make a temporary splint." She dug through the desk drawer in the little office for a roll of electrical tape and tugged some scraps of cardboard from a box of recycling. "We need to get you to a specialist who can make you a custom one. This will hold it until we get there."

Nate called after her. "How long will it take to heal? I've never broken a bone before."

"Couple of months. You may have a little bump when it heals. They'll take X-rays and tell you all about it."

She cut cardboard strips and slipped them under his fingers to keep them straight and tied them off with electrical tape. "There. Do you need to lock your store?"

He nodded and pulled his hand close to his chest. "I can run and do that now."

"I'm parked out back." *Duh. Of course you're parked out back.* "I'll pull the car around and meet you at the curb."

It was hard not to smile, despite Nate's sullen expression, remembering the day they met, and he yelled at her for parking on the street. She dropped pills in his hand. "Here. Take these and meet me at the Jeep."

He left through the front door, and she locked it behind him. All of her plans would have to wait. Paying bills and balancing her grandmother's checking account. Waiting for an email from Anderson. All of it forgotten when the instinct to care for a patient kicked in.

She grabbed a bag of frozen peas from the freezer and an old scarf from a hook by the door. From the dusty bookcase, she tugged a well-worn paperback to keep her company in the waiting room. Some steamy romance with a rancher on the cover. He held a rope loosely in one hand and a woman tight in the other. It wasn't Penny's scene, but it would pass the time. She locked the doors, shouted goodbye to Jake, and pulled the Jeep down the alley, parking in front of the toy store. Nate struggled into the seat and fought with his seatbelt.

She tossed the bag of frozen peas onto his lap. "To keep the swelling down. But I'm gonna make you a sling real quick. I have no idea how old this scarf is or if it's clean, but it'll keep you elevated so the swelling doesn't get too bad."

Once he settled with his hand tied to his chest above his heart, she pulled away from the curb and entered the roundabout faster than the locals.

"I don't understand the purpose of this circle. Aren't they supposed to control traffic? No one comes here."

Nate braced himself against the door, his hand held to his chest. "It's just the park. I dunno."

"But no one seems to use the park, and it's in the way."

"Been there as long as I can remember. Slows tourists down when they come through. Slows down most people, actually. Not you, but most people."

She threw him a grin and took the road halfway around, the road out of town and to the east.

"There's Riley." Nate pointed to a cross street. Riley stepped back onto the curb clutching a bundle of mail to his chest. "Must be almost done for the day, if he's already been through that part of town."

Riley waved when they got closer, a look of recognition lighting up his face. Penny pulled the car to the side of the road.

"What's the rush?" Riley leaned in Nate's car window. "Why you all bandaged up?"

Nate held up his left hand, his fingers taped to strips of cardboard. "Broke my hand when I fell off a step stool. Our resident doctor here is taking me to Saint John's."

Riley adjusted the strap of his postal bag. "You need somebody to watch the stores or anything? I can let some people know."

Nate shook his head. "It's okay. All locked up."

"You want me to tell anybody? I'll be by your sister's house within the hour. She'll be at work, though, it being Friday, but I can leave a note."

Friday?

It couldn't be. There was no way that many days had passed. Riley delivered mail six days and week and spent all his time in the sun. He must have lost track of the days. She'd arrived on a Sunday and painted the sign. Then she went to the bank on Monday. No, Tuesday. Then she spent a day in the attic going through her gran's stuff, so that was Wednesday. Yesterday, Anderson showed up.

"It's Friday." Penny's blood pressure shot through the roof of the Jeep. The deadline to register for next semester and declare her specialty had passed. The woman in the admissions office had talked to her as if she wasn't responsible enough to make it home to fulfill her academic obligations, and she'd pushed back. There was no way anything would stand in the way of school. And now it was Friday.

Heat rose from her chest to her face, and she broke out in a sweat. She rubbed her forehead, her hand coming away with wet dust from her time in the attic. How could she have lost track of time?

"Are you okay?" Riley's brow was furrowed. "Your face is all red."

Friday. She couldn't do anything about it, now. She'd have to call from the waiting room. They'd be cutting it close to get there by five, when all the university offices closed. Dammit. How could she be so careless? She got so sucked into Ramsbolt she completely lost track of time.

She leaned over the steering wheel to see past Nate. "Sorry, Riley. We gotta run. If I sit here too long, I'll cause a traffic jam."

None of them believed it. Riley gave them a smile and a wave, and she made off in the direction of Colby and the hospital.

She flipped on the radio and let Nate pick the station. Anything to drown out the sinking feeling of letting her future go to waste. A commercial in French Canadian faded into a song by Rush. It wasn't her favorite, but it reminded her of childhood, listening to the radio while her mom cleaned the apartment. Classic rock interrupted by commercials in French for trucks and snowplows. She focused on the memories to keep the ache of uncertainty at bay. She didn't want Nate to pick up on it, to make him worry or have it lead to her spilling her guts. He had enough to worry about, and no one wanted an uncertain doctor. Besides, the world ran on loopholes, and she could find one as soon as she could get them on the phone.

The trees and ponds gave way to the town of Colby. They whizzed past shopping centers and a bowling alley. A warehouse with an electronic sign promoted curling team sign-ups. Being long and straight, the hour drive was uneventful, but not fast enough for Penny. She needed to be on the phone, begging for mercy.

She took the shortcut through a shopping center, behind a grocery store, into the rear parking lot of the hospital, and edged the building. She parked in a spot near the emergency room door and pulled the key from the ignition. "Saved us a few minutes sitting at lights and stop signs. You good?"

Nate cradled his hand close to his chest. "I'm good. It doesn't hurt too bad. Just throbs a bit."

"Wait till it starts to swell and pushes against the splint. Fun times."

Penny pointed in the direction of the entrance and followed him up the sidewalk, her keys in one hand and a romance novel in the other. It was a selfish wish to rush inside and settle in some quiet corner so she could call the school and put a Band-Aid on whatever wound she'd opened up.

It had been ten years since she stepped foot in Saint John's. Inside, nothing had changed. The same blue plastic chairs on metal frames bolted to the same gray tile floor. A registration desk with new admissions staff, wearing the same exhausted look masked by a painted-on friendly façade. While Nate dug his wallet from his pocket and stepped up to the registration desk, Penny chose a chair near a vending machine, not too far from the doors to the patient rooms. Behind it, a million memories. Stepping out of the way for a crash cart the first time a patient coded in front of her. Her first early labor when a man rushed his wife in. She could smell their panic and fear. A few hours later, word came down that she delivered a healthy baby boy, and the father only fainted once. And her last day. They had a cake in the conference room, and everybody signed a card. Dr. Beall gave her a letter of recommendation, the nicest she'd ever read. They'd lost touch over the years, but she thought about him every time she used a defibrillator.

She unlocked her phone, and the clock lit up. It was almost five. The admissions counselors would soon head home for the day. The woman's number was on a business card lost in the shuffle somewhere. She scrolled through her contacts for the school's main number. The woman's name started with a J. Jessica, maybe? Jamie?

"Penny? Funny seeing you here."

Her eyes went first to the shoes. White sneakers with white laces. The blue hem of scrubs pants. A man in a white lab coat pushed quarters into a vending machine and extracted a bag of Fritos, but his eyes were fixed on her.

"Dr. Beall." Penny stood and extended a hand. Now, of all times, her favorite mentor. "It's nice to see you."

She'd never stopped thinking of him as her mentor. She concealed her surprise by closing the app on her phone. He must have had thousands of students since her.

His eyes narrowed. Once a scrutinizing teacher, always a scrutinizing teacher. "It's been at least a decade. What brings you back to Saint Jurassic?"

She'd long forgotten the nickname the staff had for the place. Judging by the state of the waiting room, the moniker still applied. "A friend, well someone I know, broke two fingers." She scanned the room, but there was no sign of Nate. He'd been whisked away already.

"It's a long drive from Otley." One eyebrow raised, he looked like her old mentor again, waiting for the answer to a question he posed only for her edification.

"I, um…I had to take a break for a few days. My grandmother lived in Ramsbolt, and I inherited her debt when she died. So I'm over there tying up loose ends." The ends weren't loose. Not at all. They were so frayed they were located in different zip codes. "Hey, thanks again for that recommendation letter. I ended up… Wait. How did you know I'm in Otley?"

"You're doing a residency at Otley Memorial. I've been good friends with Lunsford since we were both at Harvard. I was just talking to him this morning. He mentioned you."

"Lunsford." He was in charge of the residents. Hardly the mentor Beall had been. He was the polar opposite. Strict, addicted to the paper trail, and he found fault with everything. It annoyed the hell out of her, but she told herself she'd be a better surgeon for it. She nodded her recognition. "Yup. He's in charge of my program."

Beall ripped open the bag of Fritos and stuffed one in his mouth. "What made you go on hold?"

"What?" It had been ingrained in Penny as a student, not to let a patient know if she lacked an answer, to keep up a confident face, never to admit her faults unless it was to a mentor. Her pride wouldn't let her admit to Beall that she may have messed up, though. She was long past the days of looking for help from others.

But was Lunsford that much of a dick that he had the paperwork on standby, and he pulled the plug before the week was even up? She barely had a chance. And then he went bragging to his friends about it? As if this were a sport to them, ruining young doctors. She hadn't asked for any of this. She didn't deserve this. She felt the blood drain from her face and fell back in her seat.

"Lunsford said you didn't finish your hours for the semester." Beall dug into the bag for another chip which he pinched in his fingers and wagged at her. "Never took you for the type to go on academic hold."

No, no, no. It happened too fast. "I'll fix it. I'm sure they'll understand if I just call them and explain that my grandmother's affairs were messier than I thought." She squeezed the book and felt its cover bend in her hand.

Another rush of adrenaline washed over, making her warm and her heart race. Without school, she had no identity. Without a future as a surgeon, she had no future at all. She had no place in the world. She felt a surge of sympathy for the novel and released her grip.

"Maybe you heard it wrong?"

A smile crossed half his face. The kind of smile she'd give to a patient searching for hope where there was none. "But you did take time off?"

"Just a few days."

"Sorry to hear about your grandmother. Look, stay on the right path, okay? You're a natural at this. You were the one always screaming about the Hippocratic Oath, that our focus should be on the patients not on the red tape. Don't let the red tape get you down."

She rolled her eyes. "Tell me about it. It gets worse when you leave Saint Jurassic. They still generate all the same paperwork, but now you have to do it in triplicate and enter it into a computer under a ticking clock. And treat the patients in half the time." She'd always hated it, but she'd never complained as much as she had the last few months. "I shouldn't complain. I'm sure there's a reason for all the record keeping. Ramsbolt turned out to be more of a vacation than I thought it would be, I guess."

"That's the little town with the sailor statue and the circle, right? The red light in the middle of nowhere?"

"Yeah. That's where my grandmother had her antique store."

"It's adorable. I always mean to stop but never do."

"It is cute. Not a bad little town at all. There's a really good bakery on Main Street that puts hospital bagels to shame."

"I bet. An antique store, huh?" He waved another chip. "No paperwork. No obligations. Not a bad gig, if you can make enough money at it. Not much reward in it, though, for a natural doctor like you."

It felt good to hear him say it, that she was a natural, and that Ramsbolt wasn't the rathole she'd thought it was. Looking at the quaint photos, being immersed in its history as she crawled through the attic, and visiting its cozy shops, she couldn't tell if Ramsbolt had been wearing off on her or if it had been wearing her down. And she'd noticed something in her voice, the way she said her *O*s and *R*s. Ramsbolt was definitely making an imprint.

It felt good to hear him say it. Maybe she wasn't crazy for enjoying the quiet for a while.

His beeper went off. Down the hallway, people in lab coats and scrubs rushed, their figures distorted through the glass door. Wavy ghosts of doctors and nurses. She sure hadn't missed all the sirens and beeps and shouts in echoey tiled corridors. She hadn't missed the *rush, rush, rush* of it all.

"I gotta run. It's not your friend with the broken fingers. Promise." He held up the pager. *Code 99, Room 6* flashed on the screen.

"Enjoy your flat line." He turned and bolted for the door, the beeps and sirens roaring and fading as the door swished to a close behind him.

She could live without that sound. The discord of machines each with its own urgent need, belting out its line in a symphony of horrors. She felt the soft edges of the book's worn pages in her hand and smiled at the thought of reading every novel in that old secretary. Suddenly they didn't seem all that bad. She could almost picture herself selling smalls and trinkets in a little shop on the road out of town, kept company by Jake. Eating all her meals in that little yellow kitchen and splitting her drinks between the tavern and the table in the gravel parking lot. But that wasn't where she belonged.

She sank deeper into the chair and unlocked her phone. Six minutes after five. She called the main number for admissions, and it was just what she expected. Voicemail. "All offices are currently closed. Please call again during normal office hours or…"

It was slipping away. All of it. School and work. The dream she'd held so tightly was melting in her sweaty, sticky hands. How could her hands be that sweaty while her throat was so dry? She squeezed her phone, and it dug into her palm. It felt good, a hard burr on her phone case digging into her hand, keeping her rooted in the waiting room so she didn't float away like ash from a campfire. She felt like she was in a campfire, though, with the last of her dreams being eaten by embers that threatened to snuff it all out.

Behind the door the rushing ceased, and the corridor emptied. Everyone was focused on a patient, filling their role, and Penny didn't have one. She didn't even qualify to throw on scrubs and help a veterinarian.

Nate was back there somewhere. Someone would unravel the scarf, slice through the tape and throw away her cardboard splint. Send him down the hall for an X-ray. He'd sit on the edge of the bed and wait in a blend of pain and fear and concern for the bill. But it was nothing compared to what Penny was going through in her seat next to the vending machine. She was losing her place in the world. Everything she worked for was slipping away. Most students who end up on academic hold never get back into rotation. They never become doctors. They never reach the end of the game. Her hands shook, knowing she might never find happiness or become the person everyone said she was supposed to be along. That wouldn't be her. It couldn't be her.

She wanted to swallow the lump in her throat, but she couldn't. She opened the book to the first page, where a woman proclaimed she could never love again. *Yeah, right,* she said to herself. That woman would find love on page three, and that book was no match for the adrenaline coursing through her veins and the grief that pulsed in her chest.

A panicked mother rushed into the emergency room with a wailing child. Colic, maybe. Or teething. Two nurses who looked vaguely familiar stepped up to the registration desk. Penny hid beneath her hoodie, pushed her glasses higher on the bridge of her nose, tucking her red hair inside the cap, and pulling the cord tight. She pulled up a game of Sudoku on her phone to pass the time and quiet her nerves.

The mother and child were whisked to a registration office, leaving behind two nurses. "Beall said she's out," one of them said. "I heard she flunked."

"Can you imagine? Getting that far and finding out you can't hack it? What do you even do after that?"

"God, I guess you become a blogger or something. Give motivational speeches to kids about staying in school."

Penny shrank in her seat. What gave them the right to create a narrative and determine what her life had been and what it would become? If either of them knew the value of hard work they wouldn't be standing around gossiping while there were patients to treat. And didn't the one with the long black hair fail her nurse's exam twice?

Besides, they were wrong about her. She was a surgeon at heart. Her mom knew it, her grandmother knew it. It had been her fate from the day she was born. It couldn't be over just like that.

CHAPTER NINETEEN

Her pen had one of those pointy blue caps with a dimple in the end, but Penny had chewed it nearly flat. She squeezed between two molars, evening out the ridges. Perched on the old stool that wobbled when she shifted her weight, she rested her elbows on the cold glass display counter, and squinted at her laptop screen, hoping to find a miracle in Anderson's spreadsheet. The romance novel she had committed to read rested ignored, open and face down on the counter.

Anderson's quote was as comprehensive as he'd said it would be. For each piece he wanted, he included a photo, the estimated date it was made, the maker of the piece if he could determine one, and the price he was willing to pay. Most of the prose was meaningless to Penny. She couldn't tell the difference between Chippendale and Hepplewhite. She had no idea what block and shell styling was and had no intention of clicking the link to read about Townsend and Goddard, whoever they were.

He wanted forty items, mostly large pieces. A few tall secretary desks with their wavy glass doors. An old farm table, the one with thick wood pegs holding it all together was at the top of his list. It was enough to clear a large path through the store and make it easier to move.

She ran a sum on the column containing his quotes. It was a lot to the Penny who had to pay for medical school, but it wasn't enough to pay the debts.

Her elbows ached from leaning on the hard counter. She took off her glasses and tossed them aside, rested her elbows on her knees and rubbed her eyes with the heels of her hands. The dry, dusty air was no balm for the tightness in her chest. She ran her fingers through her tangled red curls. How was she supposed to accept an offer that was less than what she needed? She could say no. Send a quick and polite reply thanking him for his kindness and try to sell it some other way. But it hadn't gone well so far. And if she didn't get back to Otley, her entire life would consist of trying to offload used crap to people who didn't want or need it.

She pulled the manila folder containing her grandmother's debts from beneath the cash register and flipped back the cover. The balance of her grandmother's last credit card bill jumped off the page with a twenty before the comma. On a notepad, she did the math, a cumulative act she'd avoided. Water, sewer, utilities, debt. She knew her failure to take stock of the worst things in life was the crux of her own destruction, that what she put off for later grew more painful in the delay. This time, the truth hurt more than the mystery. These abstract real-world dangers couldn't be resolved with an amputation. The blood loss couldn't be stopped with a suture. She scribbled over the column of numbers, digging the pen deep like an angry child with a crayon at the breaking point. She threw the pen down, and it rolled away from her, onto the floor on the other side of the counter. Her teeth ground into the pen cap.

Jake jumped up beside her and settled next to the register, his eyes closed and chin lifted as he purred in a stripe of sun. She ran a hand over his soft fur. If only she'd done the math sooner. If only she'd called some distant real estate agent who could make a fancy marketing plan and put the place up for sale, as is, for the cost of the debt plus the junk removal, she could have been finished with all of this. She'd be at the hospital, treating patients and solving solvable problems, earning hours toward graduation. She'd be living the life she was supposed to live instead of sitting in a dusty store.

Her laptop pinged with a new email. A bold addition to her sparse inbox. From *Admissions*. There was an attachment.

"Jesus, Jake. When it rains."

She ran her finger across the trackpad and clicked. The email opened in an agonizing, slow load that wasn't worth the effort. She knew what it said.

This email follows the letter mailed to your permanent address. Due to your failure to complete the required hours for this semester, you have dropped to below half-time student status. And because of your failure to enroll and declare your specialty, you have been placed on Academic hold.

Based on our records, you should expect to hear from your student loan lender regarding loan repayment, which will begin in six months. Counseling is available in our financial aid office.

If you wish to reenroll, contact your advisor at your convenience to state your intention. After one calendar year has passed, you may apply for readmission to your program. At your convenience, if you intend to reenroll, you can use the link below to state your intention, and our office will contact you...

She clicked the link, entered her social security number and contact information. She liked to think, when she hit submit, that somewhere in Otley, her academic advisor's cell phone buzzed, and he had a panic attack that his star pupil had been dismissed. But the truth was, she was a great student who barely knew her advisor, and he wouldn't know her if he ran over her with a truck. Her expectation of hearing back from someone who would do anything other than read her a riot act and give her a list of deadlines was slim.

She slammed the lid to her laptop and a startled Jake shot off the counter. Her jaw ached from chomping on the pen cap. Though it kept her from screaming, she spit it in the trash can.

"Coming here was a huge mistake. I should have known I'm not good at keeping up with stupid deadlines and all these damn requirements. Now I have this impossible store with this impossible stuff and this impossible mess at school to clean up. I don't even have the right requirements to be a nurse or a general practitioner."

She pulled the plug from her laptop and tugged it from the wall. There was no sense staring at a bunch of stupid emails that wouldn't solve anything.

"What am I supposed to do? Drive four hours back to Otley and beg? That…that admissions woman said she can't make exceptions. She's got to be wrong. I need a second opinion. There are always exceptions, Jake. Always."

The keys to her Jeep rested on the little white table in the kitchen. Next to the milky vase of fake flowers. The urge to grab them and run was palpable. A bitter taste washed over her tongue. She could camp out at the admissions office until they opened on Monday morning. But giving up on the store and running home on a Saturday wouldn't solve anything either.

"I can't start repaying my loans in six months. I can barely pay my electric bill. Besides, I still have to pack all this stuff that was Gran's."

Jake slinked around the boxes on the stairs on his way to the loft. They were packed with letters and pictures, old tablecloths and tin soldiers. A waterfall of history spilled down the stairs, and it was all Penny had to show for spending days in Ramsbolt when she should have been at home.

"None of this would have happened if my mother hadn't been so damn stubborn and just stayed in touch with her mother like a normal person."

"Who ya talking to?"

Penny spun her head to the door, the stool wobbling beneath her. Nate's head peeked through the door, opened enough to permit him entry, but not enough to ring the bell that dangled overhead.

"I just stopped by to thank you for the help yesterday." He held up his hand, displaying his two broken fingers wrapped in custom splints of black plastic.

She hopped from the stool and straightened the legs of her jeans. "How is it? Does it hurt?"

"They told me to take some Advil. It's not bad. But they said same as you. That it'll swell, and that it will hurt a bit."

"You can put ice on your wrist, and that might help."

Nate bent and picked up the pen that rolled on the floor. He wiped dust from it onto his pant leg and dropped the pen on the counter.

"Hell of a note you made there." He lifted his eyes from her notepad with the scribbles and deep gouges and considered her through narrowed eyes. "How are things going?"

"Truth? I got kicked out of medical school yesterday."

"How?" Nate's brows furrowed. "Why? I can't imagine you're not a good student."

"No, it wasn't that. The semester ended like they all do, but instead of finishing my hours at the hospital, I came here to clean this up. In six months my student loans will go into repayment."

"There's nothing that can be done? I'm sure if you called them and explained everything—"

"Nope. I've exhausted all my options and loopholes." Penny shook her head. "My mother never prepared me for anything like this, cleaning up a financial mess and dealing with this stupid small town. I don't know if anyone's mother did, but mine sure as hell didn't. I'm really pissed at her—at both of them—for leaving me with this hell-scape. My entire future is at risk, and the only thing keeping me from setting this place on fire is the fact that it's attached to other buildings."

"Thanks...for that. Appreciate the not setting it on fire part."

"No problem." She threw her hands in the air and turned away from him. "I'm sorry. I shouldn't be unloading all my baggage here. It's my own damn fault. I should have taken care of things when they came up, not put them off until they were too big to manage. I always do that."

Nate pulled a metal chair from beneath a metal-edged table from the fifties. It scraped across the floor, and he fell into it, propping an elbow on the faux marble top. "Every time I procrastinate, I end up making the wrong decisions. But other times I move too fast, and that's not good either." He tapped the tip of his finger on the table for emphasis. "Don't beat yourself up about what could have been. You gotta deal with what is. What about that guy who was here?"

"He wants about forty things. It would make a big dent, but it won't pay off all her debt."

"It's better than nothing. Every penny matters, right?" He smiled at his feet.

She'd heard them all before. A Penny saved. Bad Penny. Penny for your thoughts. She ignored it. "I guess I keep hoping that fate will do its job. I'm supposed to be a surgeon." Her eyes widened as she spoke the fundamental truth of it. "My fate is there, at the hospital. Not here. I figured the answer would fall into my lap the way big answers do. I waited for a buyout, some grand gesture from the universe that would solve it with the wave of a magic wand. But that's not happening, and there isn't enough foot traffic in this town to sell enough stuff to make it all work. There's no real estate agent to hire to make it all go away. And I'm not prepared for any of this. I just need all this to end."

She ran a hand over her face and through her tangled hair. The walls drew closer, caving in on her. Dishes, animal heads mounted to the wall, leaning rows of prints and paintings. Boxes and crates of old toys and knickknacks. Chairs stacked, their legs jutting out their long wooden fingers, reaching for her, trying to drag her in and squeeze her to death.

"All of this needs to just disappear so I can get back to Otley. And I know it's not anyone's fault, that it is what it is, but it makes me so mad at my mom."

"What would she have done differently? If she were here, what would she have done?"

"Nothing. That's the problem. She ran off and disowned her mother. She did a terrible job of keeping up with her family. She could have prevented this disaster by keeping everyone in touch. If she hadn't separated us, I could have helped my grandmother downsize before it came to this."

The neglect was an avalanche. It started with one tiny pebble rolling downhill and turned into boulders while Penny stood at the bottom, holding out her hands and hoping for the one diamond to land in her palm like some kind of miracle. She slumped, her hands in her back pockets, and let numbness wash over her.

"I could have done it myself. Stayed in touch with Eliza all these years. I could have taken that Cheryl woman up on her offer to buy it all for two thousand dollars. If I had, this place could be for sale already. I could have accepted that there was debt and put it off until I was a surgeon and could pay for it. But I will not be stuck in this town. I need to go home. I'm gonna take Anderson up on his offer, then I'll call a junk truck to take the rest. That's it. No more of this."

Nate picked at the bent metal edge of the table. "Ramsbolt will be sad to see it go. And you."

Exasperated, she tugged her hair into a ponytail with the hair tie she kept around her wrist. "People keep saying that, but no one ever shops here. If they're that sad about it, they should have stopped dumping their shit here and bought something instead."

He stood and pushed the chair back beneath the table, a solemn and sympathetic look painted on his face. "I'll help spread the word, that people need to come and see what they want before it's all gone."

CHAPTER TWENTY

The little white table barely held it all, the laptop, Eliza's checkbook, Penny's phone, the folder of bills and Jake, who cut a stately figure as he peered over the laptop at her coffee. Jake pawed at the vase.

"I'm not giving you a treat. I locked that front door so I could have one uninterrupted hour to get it all together. Eat your crunchies."

He jumped to the floor and sauntered up the stairs.

Anderson, she typed. *Thank you for the quote. I am happy to accept your offer. Let me know what day/time is good for you, and I'll be here!*

His reply was swift. *Great! I'll be by on Monday afternoon at 1 with a check, a big truck, and some people to load it all up. See you then!*

She slouched in the rigid chair, relief dissolving some of the strain. With money on the way, some of the clouds parted, shedding light on a plan.

She opened a new browser tab and made a spreadsheet in her cloud account. Starting with the newest bill in her manila folder, she entered them one by one—the amounts and dates they were due, account numbers, and phone number. Once she had Anderson's money in the bank, she'd be able to pay some of them off and close the accounts forever. The utilities she needed to keep on, for now. But one small credit card she would be able to pay off. It was a small accomplishment, making a spreadsheet and getting a handle on the bills, but she felt like running a victory lap through the store.

Riding the high of achievement, she called the credit card companies. A kind woman explained the social security death index, how it notified her creditors and prompted the closing of her accounts. It was a relief to hear that interest was no longer being accrued, but they still expected a payment, as long as the estate still had funds. She could contest the debt with lengthy forms and documents, but after the building was sold, the credit card companies would expect their money. They could even send her to court to force her to sell the store to recoup it, but most of the time they were happy to make other arrangements, so she could retain the property she inherited. Penny wouldn't let it come to that. Once Anderson gave her a check and cleared out much of the clutter, she'd be able to figure out the rest. Find a way to clear out the store and put the building on the market. Someone, somewhere had to want it.

She called the utility companies and gave them what was left in her grandmother's checking account, keeping only enough funds in the bank for the account to remain open.

Knowing the answers to the big questions felt better than fearing them, better than having them wind their way through her chest and constrict her lungs like they had been doing. A lot of hurdles had stood in the way of grasping that financial picture. But having created the hurdles herself didn't make them any less gratifying to leap over. She grabbed her coffee cup with both hands and took a sip, savoring the vindication. In the place where her cup had been was the ghost of a letter etched into the table. P.

P for Poppy?

Had her mother sat here and done her homework, struggling with math and biology? How many cups of coffee had her grandmother had at that table with people from town? And what was that sound?

Penny leaned to the side, squinting through the dark shop at the front door. The form of a shopper lit by the sun, overexposed like a bad picture, appeared at the door.

"Shit. Someone's at the door. You should learn how to unlock it, Jake." She closed the manila folder and tucked it beneath her laptop, careful not to bump her knee on the table leg when she stood and scurried to the door.

"Don't leave! We're open." Penny fumbled the key into the lock. "I just have to unlock this door. The key sticks in the lock."

She swung the door wide, letting in the first crisp blast of autumn morning air. "I'm sorry. Time got away from me. Come on in. Sorry it's so dark in here. I'll get the light on in a second. I'm Penny. Enjoy the browse, and scream if I can help you find anything."

"Thanks." The woman stepped inside, hesitant. As if she were afraid she would break something. A few years Penny's junior, she had long brown hair and a look about her as if she didn't belong in Ramsbolt. Penny knew the feeling. She wove between tables and desks, her eyes peeled for something Penny couldn't interpret. "I wasn't even sure you'd be open."

"We get tourists through town who stop. Mostly for the bathroom, but a lot of them buy little trinkets and things." That's why Nate was open, anyway. Otherwise, what was the point?

Penny reached behind a tall desk, flipped a switch, and overhead lights flickered and warmed. The woman took a basket from the stack by the door. She wasn't there for furniture, she was there for smalls. She examined little objects that rested in pools of light, stacks of dishes, the pots and pans that covered shelves and tables, trinkets and long-forgotten toys.

That's a first, Penny thought. *And people who browse don't pick up baskets.*

She slid behind the counter, sat on an old trunk, far more comfortable than that old bar stool, and picked up the romance novel she'd neglected. She'd made it halfway. It deserved to be finished. The woman slinked through the furniture, combing through plates and dishes, adding one of each to her basket.

"Is it any good?" The woman approached the counter and rested her basket on the floor.

"Not really." Penny straightened her jeans and stood. "You furnishing a giant dollhouse?"

"A what?"

It was small talk. An ice breaker. Something to say to kill the silence, but she regretted saying anything at all. Despair came off the shopper like heat from a parking lot on a summer day. She had the look of someone starting over. Someone on the run. She did the woman a favor and charged her a dollar each for the items she chose. A plain white bowl and a gold rimmed plate with pink and yellow flowers.

"Just small talk. This place setting. It looks like it could be for a big dollhouse."

"Oh, no. I'm new here. Starting a whole new life, if you know what I mean. Just trying to get on my feet without spending a fortune."

Penny knew that feeling, too. Her first set of dishes had come from a discount store, some sort of thin plastic. Bright red. It wasn't a choice, it was what a college student with no support system could afford. But while washing it off and putting it on the shelf above the sink in her studio apartment, she removed a Made from Recycled Materials sticker that gave her one small thing to latch onto. She hadn't purchased something new that would just end up in the landfill when she could replace it with something better. Maybe her shopper would feel the same.

"I haven't been here that long myself. That's good of you, buying used instead of new. There's so much trash in the landfill. We keep buying plastic, throwing it away and replacing it. Stuff never disappears. Our grandkids'll be swimming in the stuff." Penny slipped the items into two plastic bags. She jotted the prices on her receipt pad, totaled them up, and dropped the price by ten percent. It only saved her a dollar fifty, but it was something. "First time customer discount."

"Thank you." The woman's eyes were fixed on the bag, and she gave off a vibe like she wanted to bolt. "This town is really nice. Everybody here."

"We take care of our own. We take care of newcomers, too. Not that we get a lot of 'em." She didn't know why she said it, why she staked her claim on the town and counted herself among them. It seemed the welcoming thing to say, but it burned inside her, like a lie she knew better than to tell. "It's a great place to live. Not a lot of jobs around here, but we all get by."

"Yeah, I... Yeah." The woman lifted the bags from the counter and returned the shopping basket to the stack by the door. "Thanks again for the discount. That was very kind of you."

"You got it. Come again."

"I will. I'll need the rest of this set one day."

The woman lifted her bags from the counter. The plates clinked through their wrapping paper, cutting through the silence. In the briefest look, Penny saw the kind of relief she knew from her patients. Still in the clutch of sadness, but there was a flicker of hope. Like a mother clutching the printed instructions on wound care for her broken son, knowing that in the short term, life had changed, but it would all heal in the end.

The woman turned and stepped through the door, out onto the street with her paper-wrapped dishes. This time, Penny had no paperwork to file, no obligation to an ungrateful administration. Just a lingering gratification of having offered a cure to a trauma, even if she never found the source of all the pain.

How many more of these items could heal? Was someone out there desperate to reconnect with a little plastic doggie whose ears wagged when you pulled his tail?

Penny left the novel on the counter, face down, marking a page she was determined to return to. She washed her hands, more out of habit than anything, and started a pot of coffee under Jake's watchful eye. Tapping her fingers on the old countertop, she waited for the black liquid to fall into the pot, spitting and sputtering, when the doorbell rang.

"Penny?"

She left the coffee to progress on its own.

Warren waved from just inside the door. "Nate said these are the last days, and you're selling off everything. I bet Adelle is having a right old fit."

She wiped her hands on her jeans. "Last days, indeed. Adelle comes out of the flower shop every once in a while, scowls, and goes back in. I don't know why she has it in for me so bad, but it's not worth asking her. She probably doesn't know either. Anyway, I was thinking of making some flyers, maybe taking them around to see if some of the stores downtown would put them in the windows. Going out of business sale, that kind of thing." Like she should have done for Jake, but never wanted to badly enough.

"I'd put one up. Sure." He shoved his hands in the pockets of his dark gray pants. "I figured I'd come by and see if there's anything I could use to spruce up my old window displays. Maybe some old magazines or newspapers or something. Stuff related to the newsstand. It gets stale, that window."

"What about pens? There's a whole crate back here." She slipped between a desk and an old radio cabinet, and pushed aside boxes of records and old oil cans. "I don't know if this is the kind of thing you're looking for, but you can use it if you want. Might make a neat display."

She found the crate. The wood was old, thick. The edges rounded by decades of hands and wear. She slid it across the fifties diner-style table, and Warren plucked out a blue pen with a chrome clip: Millie's Books. He unscrewed the barrel and let the chrome coupler fall into his palm. "They don't make pens like this anymore."

He screwed the pen back together and drew out another. It was opaque plastic, white aged to an ombre yellow, with a red button and red writing. "Jenkins Jeeps. No idea where that's from. But there are a lot of pens in here from places that are long gone. Lots of memories. I could make a neat display out of these."

Warren pulled out a chair and sat, spreading the pens across the table in a rainbow of forgotten times and long lost places.

"Oh! I have a lap desk." Penny scampered through the rubble. "One of those old wooden ones? It's somewhere around here. I know I've moved that thing a thousand times...I have to retrace my steps for a second. I found an old watering can, the banged-up metal kind, and I wanted to put it with some other gardening things, there were lengths of fence along that back wall. I stopped and looked at this ice chest because it has these pretty brass latches. That's it. I put it in the ice box."

She pressed down on the latch and opened the ice box door. Inside, resting on the metal wire shelf, was the lap desk on its side, held closed with a length of twine. She lifted it slowly so as not to scratch the wood on the shelf. Not that she'd been careless with things, but since seeing Anderson's admiration for a table, she thought better of accidentally destroying something of value.

"That's what I get for trying to protect delicate things by stashing them places." When she stood with it in her arms, she found Warren, tears in his eyes, clutching an old oil lamp. "What's wrong? What happened?"

"Do you know where Eliza got this from?"

She rested the lap desk on the table among the pens and stood next to him. His thumb brushed over initials carved into the pewter.

"I don't. I'm sorry. She didn't leave me any records of any kind. Do you know it?"

"I do. My great-grandmother lived in a house a block to the west there. Not far from the cemetery. It's gone now, but when I was small, and she was a billion years old, she'd light this to read by at night. My grandfather carved his initials into it when he was a kid, playing with a knife. Took a wicked switch for it, too. The way he told it, he couldn't walk for a week." Warren chuckled and turned the lamp over in his hand. "It ended up in my grandparents' house. Sat on their mantel. My parents were gone a lot, working the farms, and they'd light it when it stormed. There's not a storm that comes that I don't think about this pewter lamp."

"I have things like that. There's a blanket that was my mother's." Sometimes, when the sun came through a window and fell on the edge of her bed just so, when a crumpled tissue caught her eye, when a certain wet cough came through her apartment wall, she wanted to clutch the edge of it, touch her mother's hand beneath it. Penny brushed it aside. "I wonder how that lamp ended up here. Sounds like it should have been with you all along."

"My aunt is how it ended up here instead of with me. My dad's sister took it all. She had an eye for nice things and took everything she wanted when they died, everyone else be damned. If it turned out not to be worth nothing, she just threw it aside. She'd go into debt to buy an egg and throw it out the window if omelets went out of style. That's just the way she was. There was a rift between 'em, my dad and her. We never saw anything from that house that she took. She moved off to some big city, and we never heard from her again."

"So the lamp ended up here when she didn't want it anymore. It's a shame she didn't see what it meant to you and give it a proper home."

"I don't see how she could have known. And I never would have thought she'd have wanted this thing, but that's gotta be how it ended up here because my dad never had it. I loved this lamp so much. When I think about their house, growing up there, this is what I think of." He turned it over in his hand. "This dent. It fell off the mantel when I was horsing around. My granny was smart enough not to keep the glass with it or it woulda been in a million pieces on the hearth. I was in here so many times. How did I never see this?"

His features were sharpened by the red around his eyes. The puffy skin that came with age, tinged pink.

"You should have it." She gave it a gentle nudge.

"I need this. I know it's silly to want a thing so much."

"It can't be silly, or there wouldn't be so many antique stores."

He held it out to her. "How much? I have to pay you for it."

She shook her head. "No. I couldn't."

"I need to. It wouldn't be fair to take it from you when you're stuck with all Eliza's debt."

"Fine. Make an offer. Anything you want to pay. It all has to be gone as soon as possible, anyway. I'd rather see it go home, back where it belongs, than to a landfill." She'd rather see people lifted up by connecting with the past, by finding themselves reflected in things they discovered, than to pay someone to haul it all away.

He dug his wallet from his pocket. "I have twenty-five bucks. Is that good?"

"Twenty and let me hang a going out of business sign in your window?"

"Deal." He stuck out a hand, and she shook on it. "I'm gonna keep looking around, if that's okay? Especially now that I know you haggle down instead of up."

Penny couldn't help but laugh. "Of course. Just pile anything you want over there on the counter. I have something going on in the kitchen here. Take your time, and I'll be right back."

She wiggled through the furniture and past Jake in his spot on the table to pour coffee into an ancient mug. There wasn't any single reason for the tears to come. There was no deepened sadness for the loss of her education or gloom at the deepening debts. It was the whole broken cycle. Her grandmother taking in all these objects, refusing to let them find happy homes. The knowledge that her grandmother amassed all this hurt, keeping things from people. Maybe she didn't keep the lamp from

Warren on purpose, but what if she did? All of these things could have been out there, enriching people's lives. How many people were turned away from even the smallest pieces of history?

What if there were a way to reconnect the people of Ramsbolt with their past, the way Ramsbolt had connected her to the sinew of her family. If she could pair more of the things in this store with the people they belonged to, she could right her grandmother's wrongs.

Penny wiped her eyes on the back of her sleeve and checked herself in the tiny mirror taped inside a cabinet door.

"Warren," she called out. "Do you want a cup of coffee while you browse? I'd love to hear more of your stories about Eliza!"

CHAPTER TWENTY-ONE

A woman breezed through the antique store in a cloud of earthy perfume, picking up everything small enough to grasp. Penny recognized her from the bakery, though she hadn't caught her name. She'd been buying a dozen cupcakes piled high with pastel rainbow frosting, and Penny hoped to God she had a kids party to host or the woman was destined for a diabetic coma. She was dying to ask her how they were, but she tried not to pester people when they came in to shop. The more they browsed, the more likely they were to buy. Instead, she sat on the trunk behind the counter, reading through the romance novel she couldn't get into and couldn't put down out of obligation.

"How late are you open?" The woman looked at her through narrowed eyes, a tarnished silver teapot resting in her hands.

Penny set the book on the counter. "All night! Take your time. I'm not going anywhere."

"But it's Saturday night. You should be painting the town." She set the teapot down on its tray, next to the sugar bowl and creamer, and picked up a mantel clock, turning it over, and running her fingers along the back as if looking for a trap door.

Penny shook her head. Like there was anything to do in Ramsbolt on a Saturday night. "I've got nothing going on so feel free to shop." God knows she wasn't into the book she'd been reading so there was nothing to close up the shop for. "If that clock interests you, there are more like it. They're in that back corner…" Penny's phone rang, a shrill interruption. She pulled it from her back pocket.

The area code was Otley. It had to be the hospital. A sour taste washed over her mouth, and her stomach clenched. How could she have such steady hands when she sutured a patient but shake so much when the phone rang? She could end the call and send it to voicemail, but she'd still have to hear about it later. It was probably some administrator calling with a litany of ways she pathetically failed the administration and her fellow workers. It rang again, and her face flushed. She let out a slow breath to get it under control. It was as if all the good she'd done for patients wasn't enough for them. All those anxious parents of sick kids and the worried children of elderly parents, all of them battered by the fragility of the human experience, plucked from their lives and forced to face the shortcomings of the human form. No amount of paperwork could record the value of soothing the fears of people who love, facing their loss. And she just didn't want to hear the hospital tell her that she failed their system, when they weren't the ones that mattered.

Penny motioned to the little kitchen, excusing herself for the call, and slipped into a chair at the little white table.

"Hello? This is Penny."

"I'm Erica. Calling from the HR department at Otley Memorial."

Penny ran a hand over her forehead as her face grew hot, and her skin prickled with electric shame. Had she forgotten more paperwork?

"We know you've been pulled from rotation in the ER because of your school status, but I may have some good news for you. I am friends with Marnie, and she mentioned that you might be interested in some positions we have open. Do you have a second to talk about your situation?"

Her situation. Like she was pointed due north waiting for instructions. And leave it to Marnie to spread her business all over the hospital. Penny wasn't even there to defend herself. But she wasn't in a position to turn down a decent offer, either. "Yeah, I have a second."

"What are your long-term plans? I assume you'd like to get back to school eventually."

"I haven't talked to them yet, but worst-case scenario, I have to take a year off." She ran her finger along the routed edge of the table, expecting to find comfort in the ridges of old paint.

"We have a few positions open, and it's hard to get people to fill them. You might be a good fit, since you know your way around."

"What kind of positions are you talking about?"

"There are some entry level office positions like data entry and billing."

Paperwork. The punishment for not fulfilling her destiny was to spend the rest of her life doing paperwork?

"There's also a position open in the kitchen."

Penny held the phone away, so the uncontrollable snort wouldn't make her seem ungrateful. "I'm definitely underqualified to work in the kitchen. I'm barely proficient in microwaves."

"I hear that. It does require some certifications, though, so I doubted you would be interested. But how does central sterilization sound? We have a few positions open for techs to clean and pack instrument trays. And we have one vacancy for a tech to clean OR and ER rooms after patient discharge."

She snapped the hair tie around her wrist, a little bite to ground her to reality. The embarrassment of being talked about by the nurses at Saint Jurassic was hard enough. Working in it on purpose would be torture. But would she be willing to do any of them for a year, just until she could get back on her feet? Could she endure it for a year? She couldn't come up with a single reason to accept a condescending consolation prize for putting her dream on hold. But she didn't really mean that. It was unexpected and nice of Marnie and the hospital. For all her shortcomings, it may have been more than she deserved.

"Look, thank you *so* much for the call and the offer. I don't think any of those are a good fit for me. I really appreciate it."

Erica rambled through the rest of the call, thanking her for the time, offering to help if she changed her mind. Penny pretended to write down her number on her way back to the counter. She let her phone fall next to the register with a satisfying thud.

In the far corner of the store, the woman had abandoned her search for a mantel clock and seemed focused on a collection of glass Christmas ornaments.

"You have so many cute things," the woman said over her shoulder. "I can't decide what I want."

"I know just how you feel." Penny didn't know what she wanted either. At least the shopper wasn't making life or financial death decisions and rashly turning down job offers because they didn't suit her ego. Penny grabbed a pen and shoved it in her mouth, biting into the cap. What did she want? If she didn't want to be at the hospital, if just thinking about it caused her that much anguish and sent her into a tailspin of panic, what did she really want then?

She gripped the caulked edge of the glass counter, the palms of her hands so hot she could melt the glass.

"I'd love to have these two chairs here, the ones with the carved backs. And I'll take that nightstand. I wasn't even looking for them, but they're perfect for my bedroom. This clock, definitely." She held it up with one hand like the Statue of Liberty and spun her head. "And what I came for, all of those metal chairs from outside. Those fifties looking metal ones with the chipping paint. There's a table out there with them that I'll take. And is this rug for sale?"

Her eyes refused to focus on the rolled-up rug leaning against the brick wall that separated her store from Nate's. She blinked away the blur and swallowed hard, hoping her voice made her more steady than her insides felt. "Anything. It's all for sale. The floors, the ceiling. Name your price."

"Five hundred? I swear this is the cutest place. I don't know why I never came in here." The woman lugged the carpet from the wall, through the gauntlet of furniture, toward the counter. "Well, I never needed anything before, that's why. But I started on this whole thing to redecorate the porch after my husband left me. I want to enjoy these last few fall days. Then I realized how much I hate my nightstand. And this clock! Thank God he took his mother's ashes and that tacky urn off the mantel because I didn't like being under her thumb when she was alive. I sure as hell wasn't going to let her leer down at me a second longer. I wish I had room for that cute table and chairs, the marble-looking top? It's got this comforting feel. Like time was simpler then. That's what I want to live in. A simpler time. That's why I started with the porch. First thing you see when you get home. People stopping by to say hi. That kind of thing."

Penny *didn't* know. She'd never had a front porch or a simple life. She'd had one disaster after another. One failure of fragile human skin and bone after another failure of human spirit.

She scrawled the date and total on her green order pad. "Five hundred you said? Works for me." She decided not to negotiate down this time.

The woman gave her cash and declined the offer of help loading it all into her truck. It was an awkward wait, trying to get through another page of the novel while the woman chattered about her life as she wrestled the rug out the door. The sound of metal lawn furniture scraping in the truck bed bounced between the brick storefronts. Eventually, the tailgate slammed.

The woman poked her head in the door. "I just wanted to say thanks again. You have no idea what all this stuff means to me. I've been in that house with all our old things. Everything had a memory attached to it. I had the worst love-hate relationship with my bedroom because all the good times were wrapped up in that furniture. I remember shopping for it. Going out to dinner after and wondering how it would fit through the front door. It's just so hard to let go of stuff because it feels like letting it go means saying goodbye to the past. Then when I was ready, I wanted it gone. I was out for a drive and stumbled on this place. It just feels like you were here waiting for me. Sorry I interrupted your book. Just wanted to say thanks."

"Hey, it's no problem. Glad I could help. I didn't do much, but I'm really glad you found what you needed." *If I hadn't been so absorbed in my own misery, maybe I could have done more.* "Hope you enjoy that wine on your new porch. And come back when you're ready to work on the rest of the house." As if she'd still be there when the woman was ready to redecorate again.

The truck started, and the woman drove off to a new life. Just in time for the sunset to paint the store pink.

The book wasn't good enough to waste the sunset. She sat on the padded plastic seat at the fifties diner table and let the shadows grow long around her. Jake wound between her legs, his footprints soft in the stillness, and hopped onto the window ledge to stake nightly prey he couldn't catch.

"It's funny, what she said about her old furniture being tied to memories. I wonder if that's why my mom wanted to get rid of all that stuff. To keep me from toting around a two-hundred-pound dresser for the rest of my life because the emotional attachment weighs more than the wood."

Jake swished his tail in silent assent.

The obligation to text Marnie and say thanks pressed on her until it was too much to bear, too much to put off for another time. Like a sentence written without a period at the end, she had to bring it to a close, or it would haunt her.

The reply came quickly. *What are you gonna do now?*

She'd blown through options. If she had any beyond closing up the shop and going back to Otley to work at the grocery store for a year, she couldn't see them for all the fog. *Finish this mess, I guess. Head back to Ot. Get a job.*

What about school????

It was too much effort to type it all out. Having to wait and reapply and hope they had enough faith in her to let her operate on people after all her red-tape failures. Who was she kidding? She wouldn't want to be operated on by someone who couldn't keep track of the days of the week. In medicine, you have to accept your failures. You have to own the near misses you could have controlled and let go of the ones that you couldn't. You have to ask yourself if you could have avoided the mistake, what you could have done differently, and she'd failed to do that at every turn. She'd failed to learn from her mistakes, plowing blindly through the daily grind oblivious to the fact that she was her own worst enemy.

Don't know about school yet. She owed it to herself to figure it out, but she didn't have to justify it to Marnie. She would have to fill out that form at some point, though, to let the school know if she intended to reapply.

Keep me in the loop. Drinks when you get back?

Sure.

Drinks wouldn't happen. Neither would keeping Marnie in the loop. They were acquaintances out of convenience, that was all. If she did get back to school, she'd be assigned to another residency at some other hospital, and if she wasn't, she would beg for it.

She'd miss Dave though, and the folks at the bar.

And Lee.

Her finger hovered over his last text, and the screen picked up the heat from her hand, opening the thread without her touch. What would she say? That she blew it? It was over, and she wasn't coming back to school? Hoping for comfort would only lead to one of his psychoanalytical shakedowns, and she could do enough damage to her psyche by playing I-told-you-so on her own.

Jake hopped from the windowsill, and the thud echoed in the rafters. Somewhere, something metal rattled against wood, a tiny tremor from a mighty cat.

"This is it, huh? This is the end of the road. I couldn't do it. All those years, I aimed for just one goal." She ran a hand along Jake's tan coat. "What do you do if you can't achieve the only thing you were destined for?"

Brenda would call it the ultimate freedom, not to be tied down by the smallest of obligations. But that was just the way Brenda was. She had no larger goal, no driving force. She'd skipped from work to happy hour and home again, content to live in the moment. Maybe it was all a show, a mask she wore to give Penny a bright and shiny life until Penny went to college, Brenda moved to Los Angeles, and it boiled down to Christmas cards. But stripped of a sense of direction, with nothing on the horizon but a dark and endless sky, it gave Penny nothing to lean on. There was no one left to tell her where to go or what to do. No syllabus with a next book to read, test to prepare for. No professor with a demand or hospital administrator with a process to follow.

"It's up to me, isn't it Jake? No more ignoring things and assuming it will all work out."

Pleading the case, he jumped on a dresser and knocked over a tea set, sending a silver sugar bowl to the floor. It was a fulfilling clangor, gratifying in its shrillness, but Penny was too weakened by her sorrow to throw it and hear it again for the satisfaction.

She placed it back on the dresser without making a sound.

Around her, the sun threw all of its effort into making its longest shadows, a last gasp before the darkness. The elk on the wall, his life cut short, wove his antlers like snakes up to the ceiling and into the loft. What a way to die, being killed and stuffed and mounted on a wall.

"It was great, wasn't it? That life you lived? You knew exactly what you were supposed to do with your elk self the day you were born, and nobody tested you or you made you doubt yourself or forced you to pay taxes. You just did your elk thing until somebody took it all away. You never saw it coming, did you? If you had, you would have run. Not me, though. I saw it coming. And I let it happen anyway. What is wrong with me?"

Outside, a car sped by. Too fast for such a small town. Someone just passing through. The low sun glared off the windshield, caught in a mirror and bounced through the room. Her eyes chased it from one wall to another, past her grandmother's chandelier, and it all seemed different somehow. It all seemed as lost as she was. It wasn't a jumble of chair legs and outdated cast-offs held together by their own stale veneers. It was hope for a better future, aspirations they saved up to afford, manifestations of the lives that people wanted to make for themselves. It was what people wanted their lives to be amid the toil of making do and mending. Maybe it wasn't the best, the shiniest, the most perfect, though some of it was *quite perfect*, as Anderson said. It was what survived from the lives lived here.

Penny slipped to the floor, her back to the dresser, and hugged her knees. If she didn't do something about all this, it wouldn't live another life. It would waste away in this town or end up in a dump, lost forever. It would be another thing she hadn't accomplished. Another thing she'd failed to do right by.

Jake brushed against her leg and meowed for affection. Penny scooped him up, and he did happy feet on her lap.

"My mother would hate this. My failing at school and letting her down. But I wouldn't be in this situation if she hadn't let me down, too."

CHAPTER TWENTY-TWO

"You may have to get used to crappy food or start catching your own, buddy. We're about to be very poor." Penny scooped colorful bits of cat food into Jake's bowl. He settled before it and purred. "Six months. I have six months before student loans start knocking on the door. You and I are going to have to get rid of everything in here. And then we're gonna have to get a job, because even if we do make a tiny profit on this place, it won't be enough to feed both of us. Not the way you eat."

Feed the cat, drink the coffee, hawk the things, sell the store. For the foreseeable future, that was her goal. If she looked away, even for a second, she would drown under the weight of what she lost and who she wouldn't become.

When the coffee maker spit the last of its life-saving juice into the pot, she poured it into her old milky white diner mug and caught her reflection in the little mirror. The lines beneath her eyes made her look ten years older. For all the trying she'd done, she was worse off than she was the day she poured out her heart to her coworkers at the club, moaning about the inheritance. What choices did she have now that she didn't have then? Not much had changed. But if she could rewind life like a Netflix show and tell that girl at the bar to get her shit together, she'd shake her by the shoulders for added emphasis. She'd give a lot to be able to rewind. She'd give a lot to be able to drown her sorrow at the club. Just knock back a few with people who knew the same hustle and breathed the same shitty hospital air through the same papery surgical masks. There was a solace in knowing you weren't alone, and there was a comfort in being able to retreat to familiar places and routines. She needed that comfort. She needed a night at that bar where reality could slip away. A nice long drive wouldn't hurt, either.

She dumped more food in Jake's bowl and made for the stairs to the loft. "You keep an eye on things. I'll be back tomorrow morning."

Her suitcase, stuffed with the clothes she'd brought, banged down the stairs. She hauled in the sign, bumping it over the threshold, turned off the lights, and locked the doors. She dragged her suitcase through the kitchen, out the back door, and let the sound of her old Jeep, the gentle tapping of the soft top and the grind of the engine, soothe her back to Otley.

Moving through the city wasn't half as easy as getting around Ramsbolt. She sat at a light at Harding and Coolidge, a few blocks from the club, and her mind changed itself. She turned left and stopped at the curb, across from the apartment she'd shared with her mom.

The third window from the right on the fourth floor was dark. No one stirred behind it in the late afternoon. Behind that glass was the living room space where furniture left little dents in the carpet after the neighbors toted it away, piece by piece, while her mother laid dying and shedding it all like skin she'd outgrown. Beyond that, the kitchen where Brenda asked her if she wanted a second alone before they closed the door for the last time and walked down the hall, hand in hand, hearts in their throats. Neither knowing how to tell the other that it was all a convenience and there were no obligations. Brenda never knew anything about kids. She had no idea a fourteen-year-old could walk down the hall without holding someone's hand. She liked happy hour and makeup tutorials on the internet, and Penny had a medical degree to chase. Behind that window on the fourth floor, Penny had spent nearly a year preparing herself for a life without. Without parents. Without roots. Without a place to call home.

She mashed her foot against the brake pedal. How could she have sat behind that window and learned all that anatomy and medical knowledge and been so eager to cut into people to heal them yet still be so afraid of the reality of adulthood that she never learned to pay her bills on time? Was it because she never saw her mom do it? Because when her mom was dying, Brenda did it for her? Because Brenda was too afraid she was fragile? Or was she too confident in Penny's smarts to give any guidance. Penny had been far too stubborn to ask. Maybe it was all of those things. But the larger truth, the truth that Penny could never escape, was that her mom never had an adulthood. She lost her future. So why should Penny expect to have control of her own?

She waited for a gap in traffic and pulled away from the curb, aiming for downtown. Past the bakery where she'd ran into Lee, and they ate muffins by the window and talked about identifying opioid addiction in the emergency room and treating withdrawal. Taboo topics now. At least it felt that way. If she could go back to the in-service day, she'd have taken her own notes, filed her own paperwork, and run home to clean up her life instead of watching Netflix.

Buildings swelled, looming over her, and downtown Otley swallowed her whole.

The Jeep crunched to a halt around the corner from the club. It had only been a few days, but so much had changed that she was shocked to find the sidewalk still the same. Same uneven pavement with pebbles in the cracks. Same weeds jutting out from the soil in between. Music drained from the building like stormwater headed for the grates. The *thump, thump, thump* had somewhere to be, rushing past her and into the evening to dance beneath the streetlights.

The bouncer was different, but it was Sunday after all, and she rarely went to the bar on Sunday nights. Sunday was for sweatpants and chardonnay, if she wasn't working a double. At least it used to be. She gave him five bucks and slung her jacket over her arm.

Inside, no one looked familiar. It was a different crowd with a different energy. The usual drained professionals looking for a weekday refill had been replaced by people no younger than her, seeking connection in a world of frenzied heat. It was the same in the end, not feeling so alone. But it wasn't her scene. Her seat at the bar was taken by someone else, by a Sunday regular who leaned over a beer, flicking her false eyelashes at the woman next to her. Perfect makeup. Perfect hair. Everything was loud and fluorescent. She felt small and isolated, not pacified and subdued like she'd hoped she'd feel.

Penny fringed the bar and found an empty set by the taps. She ordered a glass of pinot noir from a bartender she'd never seen before, repeating her order twice to be heard over the *thump, thump, thump* of the music. It drove people to the dance floor, and Penny to the brink of panic. She checked her phone and bounced her foot on the rung of the barstool. It was far from being the solace she sought. She inhaled the scent of spilled beer as deep as she could and coughed.

"Water?" The guy next to her leaned close. Too close. His green polo shirt smelled like laundry detergent and cheap cologne. He raised a hand for the bartender.

"No." Penny leaned away. "I'm good. Thanks."

"You here alone? I mean, it's Otley so how unsafe could it be? But a pretty girl like you shouldn't be out alone at a bar like this without someone to look after you. Someone could spike your drink or—"

She crossed her legs and spun to face him. "Look. I'll allow for the slim possibility that you actually have someone else's best interest at heart, but there's a dark side to all the fear mongering about women not being allowed to leave their homes alone, and let me just be the next, if not the first, to tell you that women are going to be everywhere in your life. They will be at the grocery store, at the gas station, and they will treat you when you show up in the emergency room. And if you don't want to encounter them, even when your life is at stake, then you are the one who should just stay home."

"Whoa!" He raised both hands. "Triggered much?"

"No. Not unless someone brings another gunshot victim into my ER."

She dug a ten-dollar-bill from her wallet, tucked it under the edge of her full wine glass, and hopped down from her stool. She threw on her coat as she walked out the door, letting it slam behind her with a gratifying bang.

Who does he think he is? She kicked a pebble, and it bounced off the lamppost at the corner. *I'm so sick of people telling me what to do and who to be. Now they're telling me when to leave the house.*

She drove an angry six blocks to her apartment, yelled at a red light, jumped a green, and stomped up the stairs to release the bitterness.

There wasn't much of a home to return to. She wished someone were there to welcome her back. The soft release of falling into a comfy chair all her own. For a place full of things that made it feel like a home, not a box on loan. Not some other creature's comforts. The absence of a family, of a safe harbor, wasn't something she often yearned for, but in the absence of a future, a past to revisit would have been nice. No single place, no home with things, tied her to who she used to be.

She didn't plan on being there long anyway. She had to get back to Ramsbolt in the morning to feed Jake and meet Anderson. Too bad it was a four-hour drive that she was too tired to make again. She'd rather be there, with Jake, having a snack at the little white table. Listening to the rain on the windows.

A box of trash bags still sat on the arm of her sofa, where she left it the night she couldn't find her laptop and drank too much wine. Back when she should have known better than to waste a night on frivolous distraction when she should have been getting her life together. She unraveled a trash bag from the roll, and shook it open, satisfied at the snap when it unfurled like thunder.

She flipped the switch inside her bedroom door and white light radiated on the piles of clothes she'd left on the floor. She didn't need any of them. Not the fancy tops or the ten-year-old pencil skirts and definitely not the scrubs. It was worthless, except for a few pairs of jeans, comfy T-shirts, and a pair of yoga pants or two.

"What am I doing with all this crap? Who am I saving it for? Why am I talking to myself?" She grabbed at the clothes, clenched them in fist fulls and shoved them into bag after bag. Old sweaters and jeans that didn't fit, shirts with holes in the sleeves. She kept a small pile of things she liked wearing and everything else went into the trash, until more than a dozen black bags were stacked by the apartment door. All the mess and the clutter that had no meaning. The plastic tub from take-out soup that she kept sugar packets in. The three wooden spoons she never used. None of it had any meaning to her, and it wasn't worth holding onto.

The last trash bag fell onto the pile.

What is worth holding on to? Not much. A small pile on the sofa. A few pots and pans, photos and memories.

"That's it. That's all that holds meaning for me. It's all I need to live on. And I don't need to do it here."

There was no job for her in Otley. Nothing to wake up for or come home to. There was no reason to rush back to the tiny apartment after cleaning out the store in Ramsbolt. She had an entire year to do it before she could get back to school. If she let the apartment go, she could get her security deposit back. That thousand dollars could go toward paying some bills. And instead of paying rent, twelve hundred a month could be set aside to help pay student loans when the time came. Moving to Ramsbolt for a year wouldn't solve all her problems, but it would help.

Deep in the back of her bedroom closet, she still had the cardboard boxes she moved in with, flattened and pressed between the wall and her shoe rack. They'd been hard enough to find the first time around, so she'd kept them.

Cardboard boxes to pack away your life. That was worth holding onto?

She reassembled and filled them, one by one. The sweaters she liked and her warm winter coats. Snow boots and thick socks. The frame that held her bachelor's degree. Shampoo. Brush. Toothpaste.

She stacked four boxes in front of the television. All that was important took up so little space. Just four boxes the size of microwave ovens. Years of studying and hard work, all of her achievements and attempts at living, fit in four cardboard boxes. There were no pictures on the walls. Her furniture was the cheapest she could find in the charity shops, particle board and worn fabrics. Her TV stand was a broken table. All her efforts, all that work, and she'd achieved nothing. Acquired nothing. Pumping every penny into an education that left her with nothing.

Her phone rang from somewhere. She followed its beacon to the kitchen counter. Lee.

"Long time, no see." Penny scratched at a dried drop of wine on the counter. She never did buy those cleaning supplies.

"I thought you were supposed to be back last week, but I didn't see you around. Thought I saw your Jeep earlier at a light near the club, but I wasn't sure."

"That was me. I'm just back for the night."

"Can I see you?" His voice was carried on a sea of questions he wasn't asking. Questions Penny couldn't answer.

"Lee, I don't want..." She'd come too far, made something that felt too much like a plan, to let one night with Lee derail it.

"You don't need to know *what* you want to find out whether it's me or not." He didn't plead. A few months ago, the warmth of his voice would have melted her. In hindsight, she was surprised she hadn't caved by now, but something had changed. She couldn't put her finger on it, but something about school and the store and her grandmother's photographs and all that history had changed her.

"It's not you."

"You mean *it's not me* as in it's not my fault you're saying no, or *it's not me* as in I'm not your type?"

"Both." She opened a cabinet for a glass, but it was empty. What wasn't in a box was in a trash bag by the door. Wrapped in plastic.

"Okay. I'll leave you alone. I don't want to be that guy. The one who's all pushy and up in your shit. We work together and—"

"No we don't. We don't work together."

"Not directly, but at the hospital. We see each other all the time, and I don't want to miss out on our friendship and make it weird."

"I don't work there anymore."

Lee dropped silence between them. Processing perhaps. Or judging. "You quit?"

"I'm on academic hold. It's a long story, and I don't want to talk about it."

"Penn, that's terrible! It's like, the second worst thing that can happen, and you don't want to talk about it?" His therapist voice took hold. She was no longer talking to the Lee who could make her knees weak. "You need to get a good grip on this. Not the school stuff, but the emotional end. Remember we were talking about avoidance and how it—"

"Jesus Christ, Lee. I said I don't want to talk about it."

"But you always said this was your destiny. Your fate. Your whole identity is wrapped up in becoming a surgeon, and I'm concerned that—"

"What? What are you concerned about? That I'll spend fifteen seconds trying to figure out what I need to do all by myself instead of letting you analyze me and tell me how I don't measure up to expectations?"

"That's not what I'm saying at all. If you didn't measure up, you wouldn't be on my mind all the time."

"Really? What's so wrong with you that you need to fix everybody around you? Do you spend any time thinking about what all this unsolicited advice says about your grip on your own reality? Huh?"

Lee's gentle gnawing on a thumbnail bounced off a satellite and into her phone. But his silence wasn't going to make her feel bad for finally saying what she needed to say, even if she hadn't been able to put her finger on it before. She wished she didn't feel so bitchy about it, but she'd had enough.

"Penn. I'm sorry. This is just who I am. It's how I connect with the people I love. Like. Whatever. I get it. Not everybody thinks the same, and I'm sorry."

"See what I mean? We're not compatible. That's not what I need. I need someone who will listen to me. Just sit and listen and let me work things out. Not someone who tells me I'm not doing things their way."

"And I need someone who will analyze every wink and nudge with me because my brain is wired this way."

Had he finally convinced himself?

"No hard feelings, okay? I just don't think…Anyway, I don't work at the hospital anymore, and I probably won't again. So maybe I'll see ya around, okay? But for now, I'm going back to Ramsbolt. There's unfinished business."

"I'm glad to hear you say that. Surprised, but glad. And it's not weird between us. Thanks for the good times."

"You too. Stay sane." She ran her finger across the end button and tucked her phone in her pocket. Lee had been the one person rooting for her in Otley, and she didn't feel connected to him at all.

She grabbed her mom's blanket from the top of a box. The blanket her mother had loved more than any other. It was just thick enough and soft enough to fall asleep under, to feel comforted and loved under without it being too heavy or clingy. She opened the blinds so she could see what stars the city lights would allow and stretched beneath the blanket on the sofa.

CHAPTER TWENTY-THREE

Penny folded her mother's blanket into a square and nestled it into the last box. For all the time she'd wished for paintings or posters, for some color on the walls, the apartment finally felt right when it was empty. Ten years ago, the woman in the rental office had called it a blank slate. She'd signed her name to the contract with a blue pen and a broad smile and welcomed Penny to her new home. Like it was a destination. To Penny, it had never been anything more than a bland white box with no personality.

The sun had only just begun to glimpse over the horizon. The stairwell was as dark as it had been when she carried the first trash bags down the steps and threw them away. Morning frost covered the dumpster and the cars, and it crept up apartment windows not yet warmed by the sun. She moved without a sound, careful not to slam the tailgate of the Jeep when she put the last box inside. Her neighbors slept, but the city stirred with distant beeping trucks and car horns rousing the birds. A flock took off from a tree and dew rained down on a Camry.

She gave one last glance to the bags of trash, expecting to feel some hint of remorse for throwing it all away, but there was nothing. Not even a hint of loss over that rubber spatula with the snowman on it that she'd hoped would make her want to bake Christmas cookies. It wasn't even worth reselling in the store. It wouldn't fit in with anything there.

Everything in Ramsbolt had belonged to someone there, had been part of someone's life, and was destined to live on. Like Anderson said, there was a cycle. From an aspiration to an acquisition, from well-loved to well used, it was all destined to find its way back to someone who'd love it. But all that stuff in bags in the dumpster? Garbage. Funny, for someone who couldn't put a sweater away, it was really easy to throw it all out.

I guess it never mattered at all. None of it.

The first glowing rays of sun began to melt the dew. Water weeped onto the bags of her discarded life. Despite the chill and the damp, she felt warmer somehow. And lighter. As if the simple act of choosing what to keep and what to let go of unburdened her soul.

She dug her phone from her back pocket and opened her recent calls list. She pressed the little teal circle with an L and waited for Lee's voicemail, but it wasn't his professional voice that greeted her. It was groggy one.

"Penny? Is everything okay?"

"It's better than okay. Sorry I woke you. I just had to tell somebody, because I figured it out."

His bed creaked through the phone. She pictured him sitting up, shuffling pillows. "How to get back into school?"

"No. I'm not going back."

Lee sighed. Maybe it was a gasp. "That's the last thing I expected to hear. After last night I didn't expect to hear from you at all, but I really didn't expect this."

"I know. Me either. I came here last night looking for some kind of normal. I went to the bar, but it was loud, and no one I knew was there. It wasn't the same. So I came back to my apartment, and it just didn't feel right. I went on this major purge and threw everything away. All the clothes I don't wear and stupid kitchen shit I don't use. My whole life fits in four boxes. It fits in my Jeep with room to spare."

"Wait. Are you leaving?"

"I think I am. No, I know that I am. My whole life I've had a plan. I've had some major thing to strive for and a whole series of little plans to get there. And I don't really want it after all. I don't like doing what it takes to get there. I don't like the sense of urgency and that every little thing is life or death. I don't like all the beeping and rushing and yelling. I got exactly what I needed when they put me on hold. Life decided this for me."

"Are you sure? Are you thinking clearly? You've been at this for a long time, and it's a huge step to walk away from it all. I don't want to analyze you, because I know you hate that, but I don't want you to do something you might regret."

She didn't even care that he used his therapy voice. That he was trying to peel away her layers to get at the deeper mystery, even though he said he wasn't.

"Shouldn't I be upset about being on hold, Lee? Shouldn't I be heartbroken? I'm not."

"Okay. So if you're not going back to school, where do you go next? What do you turn to instead? A lot of people who lose direction end up in my office, addicted to something, striving to replace the passion in their life. I don't want that to be you, Penn."

"I know. I still have all that determination. I know what it feels like to help somebody feel better, to help them remember and pause for a moment in the middle of a crazy life and relive the past and dream. This woman came into the store and bought all this furniture after her husband left her, and it felt like healing a wound I'd never be able to reach in the emergency room. A different kind of healing. People come in and see these things they used to know, and it reminds them of places and people they'd long forgotten, and their whole day changes. They're different when they leave than they were when they walked in the store. There's none of the pressure, the paperwork, the anxiety either. And it's quiet. Deep down, I really believe I'm supposed to be in Ramsbolt. I'm supposed to save this store. It wasn't my plan, but it's the plan life gave me, and I'm gonna follow it through."

She could fail, but she'd made people happy. She hadn't denied anyone the right to buy anything like her grandmother had. And she'd made more profit than her grandmother did, judging by the books. Anderson had said that a town like hers was a better market for smalls. Once the furniture was gone, she'd be able to put more smalls on display. Besides, she'd never seen anyone admitted to the emergency room while suffering from a leap of faith. Not this kind of leap, anyway.

"I think it's great you want to follow your heart for a while," Lee said. "I just want to play devil's advocate and make sure you don't slam the door closed on being a surgeon until you're sure. You hate administrative tasks. There are a lot of them when you run a store. It's a huge learning curve."

"I may not know how to run a store, but I didn't know how to stitch a wound and pull a bullet out of a bicep either. I learned that. I can learn this, too."

Sun glinted off the drops of dew and beads like opalescent diamonds flashed on the trash bags that surrounded the dumpster.

None of this garbage was part of the plan. Just about everything that mattered to her was with her in Ramsbolt already.

"If you say so. It may not be easy."

"What ever is?" Penny picked a leaf from the roof of her Jeep. "I should get going. I have to be back in Ramsbolt by one. Anyway, thanks for listening."

"No problem. Glad it turned out to be Eden after all. Later, Penn."

This time, he hung up first. And she knew he'd closed the door on what could have been between them.

Two men skipped down the apartment stairs, their footsteps echoing off the brick buildings. They clutched water bottles, and ear buds dangled from their necks.

She waved to get their attention. "Hey. You guys going for a run?"

"Yeah. Good weather for it."

"You want to make a few bucks and get a workout at the same time? I have a few heavy things in an apartment I could use a hand getting down here. I'll give you fifty bucks total if you help me get it down to the dumpster."

They exchanged looks and shrugs. She handed her apartment key to the one closest, and he closed his fist around it.

"It's the second floor. On the right. Everything has to come down. It's not much. Sofa. Old mattress and bed frame. I'll be right up." She pulled her phone from her pocket and unlocked the screen. "I just have to do something real quick."

She leaned against the Jeep, and her jeans soaked up the mist that clung to the paint. She opened a blank email.

Hi! It's Penny from Building 5, Apartment 2A. I am currently month-

to-month and need to end my lease, so this is my thirty days' notice. I'll call you later today with a forwarding address for my security deposit, and the key will be in the drop box at the door. Thank you for everything!

Sending that email was some of the best therapy Lee would want her to have.

Through the window she could see the guys lift her sofa and push it through the door. She'd spent a lot of lonely nights behind that window. Afraid of the future. Afraid of dragging the past along with her. Putting one foot in front of the other without regard to her own happiness because the finish line of being a surgeon was all she'd ever raced toward.

She always thought she'd be happy if she could reach the next step. The next test, the next semester. She'd be happy when she got her residency. When she finally had some income. When she was finally a surgeon. When she found a hospital where she liked to work.

All that was left of her time in Otley was the TV, her bed frame and mattress, and that awful plaid sofa. Just a few more trips, and it would all be over.

She patted the side of her Jeep. "Why did I wait so long to be happy?"

CHAPTER TWENTY-FOUR

That sailor statue. With a few hours to spare before Anderson was due to show up with his truck, she could afford to make a proper introduction. She parked her Jeep on Main Street and crossed the road to face him.

"First time I saw you, you were in the window of a gift shop. Actually, that's not true. I saw you here, the day of my grandmother's funeral. I didn't give much thought to why a big statue of a sailor was so far from the water at the time, but now I'm kinda curious. Also, I might be a little crazy, standing here talking to a statue. If you ask Lee, I'm totally off my rocker. I mean, who leaves medical school this far along to sell used junk in a town so small one mailman can deliver all the mail each day. None of this makes any sense, does it? What am I doing? What's wrong with me?"

She admired him from the side. The figurine Nate gave her was a remarkable likeness.

"You mean something, don't you? Not in a memorial kind of way. No, the universe is trying to tell me something with you." A blue pickup truck sputtered around the circle, and she put her head down. No sense acquiring a reputation for talking to statues. She turned back to her Jeep. "I don't know what it is about you, but I'm gonna figure it out one of these days."

She parked behind the store. The little marble-topped table and wood benches were just as she left them after her bottle of wine with Nate. She should have stopped for one on her way back, to repay the generosity and share her news about sticking around. She'd have to do that soon. There had to be a place to buy alcohol somewhere around Ramsbolt. Her key stuck in the back-door lock, and she wrestled it free, pushing the door open with her hip. Jake waited just inside. He followed her through the kitchen, mewing his hello and weaving between her legs.

"I wasn't even gone a whole day." She scooped food into his bowl, though he had plenty. "Don't want you to think I'd let you starve."

But Jake stuck with her into the store, to the front counter. "I thought you were hungry. No?" He leapt to the counter, his dainty paws running the gauntlet of lanterns and perfume bottles. "Okay, then. If you're not gonna eat, you'll have to help me learn how to use this register today. No more of this paper mess."

She unlocked the front door and grasped the sign, but paused. "This isn't really true anymore, is it? It's not a going out of business sale. And not everything must go." She made for the kitchen, for the paint under the sink. She flipped the plywood panel over and painted a new sign: Penny's Loft.

"How about we make this a Grand Opening sign?" Her grandmother had a stack of colorful paper in a desk drawer in the office. She found a canary yellow sheet and cut a little starburst from it. In black marker, she wrote *Grand Opening* and taped it to the sign. With a small brush, she painted a little cat in the bottom corner.

"You get credit for your hard work, too, Jake." She stood back. "What do you think?"

Jake bumped her leg, and she picked him up and held him close. He rubbed against her ear and purred.

"My sweet kitty." Jake jumped from her arms to the counter. "Are we open on Mondays? I feel like we should be open on Mondays. Let's put it out, wet paint and all."

She grasped the sign and carried out the door, placed it on the sidewalk where no one tread, and crossed the street to admire her work.

The shop didn't need much. Her grandmother had taken better care of the building than she had the business within it. It was weather-beaten, and the windows were old, but that was part of its charm.

They could use a washing, though. There was a tall ladder in the store somewhere that she could probably use if she could stomach the height. Maybe she could paint the store name on the window. Some window displays would be nice. And an open house. She could get some baked goods and a big thing of coffee from Marissa's and let people come in for a browse. Have a big sale. Why hadn't she thought of that before?

With that bulky metal lawn furniture gone, the old wooden benches and metal buckets stood out. They framed the front door nicely. Somewhere in the back of the store were a pair of old cast iron garden seats that would look nice outside the window. And once Anderson took some of the tables away, she could get to the stack of old window boxes, bring them outside and fill them with flowers again. Once winter passed, she could fill them with plants and bring some life to the tired street. Or maybe not, in case Adelle would think she was competing. She would have to make nice with Adelle now. They were neighbors, after all.

The unmistakable sound of a truck bumping around the roundabout broke the silence. A big yellow truck with Anderson at the helm bounced down the rutted street.

He returned her wave and performed an expert U-turn at the corner, not that he needed precision. There was plenty of room on the empty street. The truck lurched to a stop at the curb, and Penny crossed to greet him without looking for traffic.

"You had no trouble getting here?" She extended a hand, and he shook it.

"None at all. I had more trouble convincing these two to leave Portland." He aimed a thumb over his shoulder at the two men in the truck. "I got a check here for you. Forty thousand."

He pulled it from the breast pocket of his coat and put it in her hand. It was still warm.

"This is too much. It's more than you said. It's more than twice what you said." She wanted to clutch it in her fist. Run away with it as fast as she could, straight down Main Street and into the bank. Throw it on the counter and demand they deposit it immediately, before anyone told her she didn't deserve it. It had to be a mistake. Nothing was ever that easy.

It won't pay all the bills, but it'll give me a really good head start. Please let this be real.

"I thought about it and did a little more research." He turned and tossed his sweater on the driver's seat before slamming the truck door. "A few of these things are very similar to items that outsold expectations at auction last week. I don't want to underpay, or I could lose your good business."

"Really? People are paying that much for stuff like this?" Penny folded the check and tucked it in her back pocket. If he was sure, she wouldn't argue.

"There's a very high market right now for handmade history. There'll always be a place for the varnished and polished furniture, because it represents the ideal. But there's a lot of appreciation for the everyday kind of things that survived. Things like that big table in there that were probably handmade by a farmer down the street. The antiques world is thinking differently about what represents American made these days, and the dollars are swinging in this direction." Anderson brushed his hands together. "Can we get started?"

"By all means. I'll stay out of your way. And thank you. This is generous."

She grabbed a small bench from beneath the window and crossed the street to sit outside the remains of a hair salon, giving Adelle's shop a wide berth. Anderson pointed and waved like a conductor, and the men moved furniture to get to his pieces. He was a master at work, and she had a lot to learn about barking orders.

Item after item came out of the shop and went into the truck, wrapped in moving blankets. It was nice to see them taking so much care with the furniture. Her gut twisted at the thought of all the negligence that came before. All those crates scraping on tabletops.

"This seat taken?"

Penny squinted up at Adelle, the sun in her eyes. She expected to be yelled at for sitting on the sidewalk or moving a piece of furniture or littering or some unknown offense. But Adelle stood with her arms hanging limp at her sides. Whatever she wanted, she wasn't indignant.

Penny scooted to the side. "Not at all. Sorry for all the ruckus. They'll be out of here soon."

"So this is it, huh? They're taking everything?" Adelle wound the cord of her green apron around one finger.

"Nope. A lot of it, but not everything. Enough to make room for me to sell some other things. Ramsbolt, as it turns out, is not the right market for large furniture. People in a town like this and tourists passing through are more inclined to buy small things to decorate with. At least that's what he says."

"So does this mean you're going to stay?" Adelle blinked down at her apron strings.

Penny nodded. It was a big admission. She was ready to live it. She just wasn't ready to say it. "Seems that way to me, at least."

Across the street, two men loaded a bed frame into the truck. "We don't get new people here very often. And when you said you weren't staying, I took it as an insult."

"I noticed that. I'm not sure why. I didn't intend to insult you."

"Everyone leaves. After graduation, most of my friends left. There were only thirty of us so it didn't take much for it to feel like a big loss. My high school sweetheart went to college and never came back. I couldn't have done that. My dad was the mayor at the time, before Morgan. I own this shop outright. The roots here are pretty deep."

"Don't take this the wrong way, but you could have left, too. It's a big world. You could go anywhere."

"Not really, though. It's a lot of work to try to sell a place."

"Tell me about it."

"Every day, I weigh the cost of staying open versus closing early. Every cent has to be spent wisely. Maybe this place isn't for everybody, but I'm holding on to what life was like, what it should be like here, because I like it this way. And here you come, ten years younger than me, sure of your plan and refusing to let anything stand in your way. You were making changes and taking charge like I could never do, and I'll be honest, I was just a little bit jealous."

Penny laughed. "I'm not in control of anything at all. When you said disorganization and chaos, you were pretty close. I'm good at medicine. I'm a great student. But when it comes to taking care of life, I'm lost. Maybe that's what I liked about working at the hospital. It had rules and tangible problems to fix. Broken bones? Easy. But my problems? None of them were tangible until Ramsbolt fell into my lap."

"I'm sorry I took it out on you. At some point, the jealousy kind of broke, and I started to see this place as something that deserves more than I've been giving it. I could paint the place, get a new sign. I don't have to be jealous."

"You can turn that place into anything you want. Except antiques. Trust me on that."

Adelle smiled. "Advice taken." She stood and smoothed her apron. "I gotta run. Roses don't dethorn themselves. Thanks for understanding. Coffee sometime?"

"You got it. I have this great little table that's perfect for it."

Adelle left, her slip-on shoes shuffling on the tile as she returned to her shop. *Maybe roses do dethorn themselves,* Penny thought. At the very least, that one tried.

Nate waved through the window of the toy store. He slipped around the counter and poked his head out the door.

"Whatcha doing sitting over there?" he yelled.

"That guy is here to buy a bunch of furniture."

Nate stepped onto the sidewalk, his eyes growing wide at the sight of the truck.

"He won't be here that long." Penny patted the bench.

He crossed the road and took a seat beside her. "I wish I'd never yelled at you about parking at the curb. You're never gonna let me live it down."

"I don't plan on it. Did you see the sign?"

"No. What sign?" He leaned forward and squinted. "Penny's Loft? Does that mean you're staying?"

Penny tilted her head back, taking in the cloudless sky. "I am. I'm gonna see what I can make of this place."

He bumped her shoulder with his. "That's great news! Did you put stuff upstairs to sell?"

"No. I was gonna sleep there. Why?"

He waved a hand toward the second floor. "Penny's Loft. It just sounds like there's two floors."

"I hadn't thought of it that way. I just gave the place a name. Is that misleading? Should I change it?"

He patted her knee. "No. I wouldn't change a thing. It's a great name. Sounds like you named your new home." Nate stood and wrapped his arms in his sweater. "I'm in the middle of inventory. It's chilly out here. If you want, come over and warm up with a cup of coffee when you're done."

"I'll do that. Can I give you a hand? Maybe you can teach me how to do this inventory thing."

"That sounds not fun at all. But it's a deal." He smiled down at her, his voice almost a whisper. "Hey, what was up with Adelle?"

"She was just saying how life gets hard, how people leave, and you hold on really hard to the best of what's left. And sometimes someone comes along who makes you see things different and maybe that's not as bad as it sounds."

"I don't know what all that means, but I'm glad you're gonna stay."

Nate made his way across the street. He didn't look when he crossed either. "See ya in a bit, neighbor."

She hadn't expected to name her home. She was only trying to rebrand the store and make it her own, but it was pretty cool that it worked out that way. And with the money from Anderson, she was halfway to paying off her grandmother's debt. If she could increase sales and get on a payment plan, she could keep the store. The credit card companies wouldn't be able to force her to sell it to pay off the debt. And it really would be hers.

Penny shivered in the cool breeze. Helping Nate with inventory sounded much better than sitting in the cold. With one last glance at the store window, she made a promise to herself; someday she would make enough money to afford a little house of her own. Then she'd fill that lofted space with things that people would want to buy.

CHAPTER TWENTY-FIVE

"You're all set. Fastest internet you can get." The guy from the phone company zipped his tool bag closed and emerged from the office beneath the stairs. He put a little white box in her hand with an aux jack protruding from the side. "Here's the payment method thing that came with your installation. I can set it up for you if you want, but it's super simple. All you have to do is download the app, plug that into your phone, follow the prompts to connect it to your bank account, and you're set."

"Ain't technology grand?" The little square was no bigger than her thumbprint. The small cost they took for each transaction was well worth the time it saved, and it was less than the bank wanted to charge for their point-of-sale system. By connecting it to the old tablet she never used, she'd be able to put the antique cash register out to pasture. She couldn't bear to get rid of it, though, even if she could lift it.

"Last thing and I'll be out of your hair. Initial this form showing I installed your router and gave you the dongle thingy there."

She scrawled her initials on the bottom line and held the door for him while he struggled with his bag and hauled empty cardboard boxes out to his truck.

The second her laptop connected to Wi-Fi, it started downloading updates, bogging down her search for business plans. Her plan would have to wait. It was nearly lunchtime anyway, and the fridge was empty. She bundled into her autumn coat and let the computer catch up with the times.

Past the toy store, the bike shop, and the small engine repair store, Penny crunched over scattered leaves. Swept up by little tornados, they crashed against the buildings and scraped along the sidewalk. She crossed the street to the park and climbed the small berm to reach the statue.

"What is your deal, anyway?" Penny lifted her face to the sailor. The autumn sun warmed her cheeks, but she kept her hands in the pocket of her hoodie, out of the cool air that pushed across the park. "Did you live here or was there some organization for retired sailors that put you here?"

A frosty gale, the coldest yet, swept across the circle. It picked up scattered leaves and pushed them into piles—at the feet of the weather-worn benches and around the base of the statue. She turned her face against the wind and saw the woman, the one who bought the mismatched dishes, rush past her, a phone to her ear. No coat, thin sneakers. Distress rustled the air around her like static. Penny waved out of kindness, but the woman was too agitated, her eyes on her feet, and her mind on her call.

"At least she didn't see me standing here talking to you like I'm some kind of crazy person." Penny kicked at a blue plastic cap that skittered to a halt at her feet, litter from passing cars or someone passing through town. "Does anyone ever come here just to sit? Probably not, huh? As statues go, you're probably pretty lonely. Even as a sailor, out on the water all the time, you had a job to do, a place to go, a mission, some coworkers. It looks all peaceful and calm out there on the water, little boats floating on the horizon, going nowhere at all, but you've always got a plan. Now you're just...there."

She squeezed her hands into fists in her hoodie pocket and felt her nails cut into her palms. What was the point in standing in the cold when she should be getting her shit together? But being alone in the store made her feel small. Weak. Like she wasn't strong enough to hold up the walls and keep the ceiling from caving in. Every corner held some catastrophe in the making. The plumbing could leak. Pipes could freeze and shatter and flood the whole place. Black mold could take over. She could die of an upper respiratory infection without health insurance. Sure, she'd figured out how the cash register worked, but at some point, the IRS would want this stupid store to be a business entity, and she'd have to learn to manage a bank account and file taxes and all of it made it fairly hard to breathe.

"How can you have your shit together more than me? No offense or anything. You're allowed to have your shit together, and I shouldn't compare myself to you. You've got this whole stoic *I'm a sailor* thing going on. It's a whole lifestyle. I was supposed to have that. Now I have to figure out how to save this store and make a living at it. So what would you do, Mr. Stoic Sailor Man, if you had bills to pay and a cat to feed?"

He sent his answer on the wind. It pushed through her hoodie and rustled her hair.

"Fine. Don't tell me then." She picked up the blue bottle cap. The least she could do was be productive and throw it out. She studied the park. A foil bag from someone's snack wrapped itself around the leg of a bench. An empty paper cup skipped across the brick path and patches of weeds grew between the stones that made up the circular walk. The wood benches that dotted the lawn were grayed by the sun, held together with rusted frames.

"Someone should really clean this place up. If it were a little nicer, people might actually come here. Maybe you wouldn't be so lonely." In a break between gusts, she tossed the cap in the air and caught it. "We could have a picnic or a concert or something."

A car rumbled past, an older woman behind the wheel, her white hair in tight curls and her car packed to the gills. Penny turned to watch her path, as she rounded the circle and made for the Canadian border.

"What about her? All the leaf peepers and the people headed to vacations and to the coast. Everybody says they're always going back and forth through here in the summer. What if there were a reason to stop? Something to make them stay? Nate could sell more of your figurines, and the town could make some money."

Inspiration hit her. "A festival. With some fancy marketing, this could be a bustling town for a long weekend. Visitors would spend money at the stores. At my store." She fumbled the bottle cap, and it rolled into the grass. "Oh my God. This could work."

She grabbed the cap from the ground and ran, tossing it in the trash can at the corner. She crossed the street and headed up Main. It could take some convincing to get people on board, and a few apologies to the people she insulted by being so quick to say she wouldn't stay. But Marissa was a safe place to start.

Penny threw herself into the bakery door and across the room. She leaned across the counter.

"Marissa? You back there?"

Drying her hands on a pink-striped towel, Marissa appeared behind the counter, in the doorway to the bakery.

"You look out of breath? Is everything okay? Do you need to sit?"

"No. I mean, yes. I'll take a coffee. But that's not why I'm here. I have an idea."

Marissa pulled a cup from the stack, passed it across the counter, and motioned toward the coffee carafes.

"Thanks." Penny dug a dollar from her pocket and put it in Marissa's palm. "Has Ramsbolt ever had a festival?"

"A festival? Like one of those giant music things where the girls wear flowers in their hair and dance like they're swatting at fungus gnats?"

"Maybe not that specific, but something like that. Like a boat festival or a lobster festival. There's no water anywhere around here, but you know what I mean. There's not much to celebrate here, but there has to be something. Potatoes, maybe?"

Marissa counted through her bagel bin. "No one wants cinnamon today. We've never had a festival or anything like that, no. The people who live here are already here, and the people who come through don't stop."

"But I had this idea that maybe we could fix up the park." Penny rocked her weight against the counter. "We could get rid of the weeds and paint the benches. Put up some tables and sell things. Sometime in the spring, when all the tourists start moving through town."

Marissa raised her eyebrows and twisted a towel in her hands. Was it inspiration or trepidation? "It does sound fun. There are some pretty busy weekends with people heading all directions. People would have to know it's here, so they know to stop. And it wouldn't be that hard to sell stuff from a table for a few days. It would take a little prep, making sure I have enough. Little sheep cookies would be fun. Get it? Ramsbolt? White fluffy cupcakes with little pink ears and jellybean noses."

"It could be a great boost for businesses. The town could use it." A small voice floated from behind her, and she spun to face it. It was the librarian she met at the bar.

"Sandy! I was in such a rush, I ran right past you. You really think the town would support it?"

Sandy nodded and brushed crumbs from her hands onto a muffin wrapper. "Sure. I could do a children's reading or a puppet show or something. Maybe tie it into the summer reading program I do for the kids."

"Yes! This is exactly what I mean. We need tons of ideas. People who are willing to join a team and come up with ways to draw people here and work together to make it happen. The stores could have sidewalk sales, and we could have a little concert in the circle. There needs to be more to it, and some kind of theme. But this is a great start."

"So you're staying?" Marissa grinned. "Because people who are only here for a few days don't usually get a wild idea to throw a town festival."

"Yeah, I am." Penny lifted her chin and smiled. She'd been quick, too quick, to set the record straight, to let the town know they were no match for each other, and she had no use for Ramsbolt. But maybe they needed each other after all. "I need to make it count. I have to save that store and make it profitable, so I'm all in."

"What about art as a festival theme?" Sandy gripped her tea in both hands, her eyes narrowed, deep in thought. "We could sell table registrations to artists. I mean, if you're trying to save the antique shop, having an arts festival would totally fit. It would look great in the town circle."

"It would." Penny nodded. "So how do we make it happen, the festival?"

"We'd have to get Morgan on board." Sandy swirled the last of her tea in the cup and peered into it, as if reading the leaves. "Once he approves it, I guess we'd have to organize it and promote it. It can't be that hard."

Red tape. My favorite.

"Morgan, for all his jittering around, can be a little lazy and gets overwhelmed pretty easy." Marissa dove into the display to arrange macarons. "You may need a lot of support to get him into it. I would say to start at the bar. Everything in this town that needs done happens at the bar."

"That's a good idea. Helen seems to know everybody. And I bet a bunch of drunk people could come up with a lot of ideas. Thanks!" Penny paused with one hand on the doorknob and her coffee in the other. "Do you guys really think this will work?"

Saving the store would take more than a festival. It would still take a lot of hard work to clear out the store, and make room for things that people really wanted to buy. And it would take a lot of effort to learn how to run a business. She couldn't afford to make a fool of herself or waste her time on a losing proposition.

Marissa bit into a lemon macaron. "Nothing worth doing is ever easy, and you never know until you try."

CHAPTER TWENTY-SIX

The headstones at Ramsbolt Memorial Cemetery were painted gold by the sunset. Penny stood among them, her grandmother's name etched into the reddish stone at her feet. The stone was flush with the ground, but it wasn't hard to find. Hers was still the freshest plot in the field. Whether she'd come to offer forgiveness or in search of her own absolution, Penny didn't know. Forgiveness wasn't hers to seek for what her mother went through, for growing up amid all that clutter and feeling like she mattered less than the mess. She wasn't sorry, though, for calling her grandmother in her mom's final days, though she sometimes felt like she should be. She knew even back then, at fourteen years of age, that she'd be the only one left to carry the regret.

"I sold a lot of what was in the store. I'm not criticizing you or…well, I am. I'm a little frustrated by the whole thing, but there's no use getting into it with a rock."

Under the sun's last pulse, she left a wild black-eyed Susan she'd found by the roadway It's jagged stem a testament to the effort she put into it.

"You wouldn't recognize the place. I sold a lot of the big stuff to a guy from out of town. You can see parts of the floor that haven't been visible since you bought the place, I'd imagine. You can move around in there now. I drove out to that big home improvement store outside of town earlier today. The one you probably would have hated. I bought some shelves. I can display things in there. And people have been coming in more, buying things. I guess that's what happens when you don't tell the shoppers they can't shop. Anyway, now I can sell other stuff, too. Not just furniture. I don't know what, yet. Housewares? Decorations? Something. I skimmed a few books you had in the office about running an antique store. I think some of it is starting to sink in. Would have been nice if you'd left a little more info lying around, but it is what it is."

The sun dipped below the horizon. The cemetery was only a few blocks from the store, but Penny had no intention of becoming a regular. The setting sun felt like a last call from a burly bartender. It was time to hit the road. "Anyway, Jake is good. Just wanted to stop by, because it seemed the thing to do. You're not *here*. I know that. You're energy, gone off to become something else, I guess. But I felt like I owed it to the past to say that there's gonna be a future."

The earth was soft beneath her feet. It threatened to ooze up around her shoes if she walked too slow. She reached the sidewalk and followed it past the houses on the west side of the empty town, back to the store where Jake was probably waiting for dinner as if his bowl weren't still full.

The first stars of the night leapt into the sky, reflected in the window of the shop as she passed. Jake was curled up on the sixth stair, where he liked to sleep when he wasn't begging. The lights were out in the toy store. Nate was probably done for the night, relaxing in his upstairs apartment. In the park, leaves collected at the base of the sailor statue. Thanksgiving was coming, and people would be tied up with their families. It wouldn't be easy to get them to help while their minds were fixed on the holidays. She would have to move fast to get them on board.

She turned right and passed the last of the year's blueberry shrubs that bordered yards, the broken driveways, and unkempt lawns that marked the south end of town. Gravel crunched beneath her feet as she took a shortcut through the parking lot at the bar. It threatened to twist her ankle, so she slowed her pace, reaching the cement slab in front of the bar's door grateful and thirsty.

The window rattled in its frame when she pushed her way inside.

Behind the bar, the woman who bought the mismatched plates, the one too distracted by her phone call to wave, looked down at her phone.

Penny slid into a seat near Dan. "What happened to Helen?"

Dan ducked his head and furrowed his brow, sharing a secret. "That's a sore subject. Best to order an easy drink, if she comes by at all."

"I'll save you the trouble." From two seats down, Bern snapped his fingers. "Logan."

The woman spun and slipped her phone into her back pocket, her glare softening.

Bern pointed down the bar to Penny. "She'll have a…"

Last time, she opted for whiskey. This time, she tried her luck. "White wine?" Penny asked.

Bern shook his head. "Nope. It won't be cold."

"Red wine? Pinot noir?"

The woman behind the bar shook her head. "No wine here. Sorry. I'm Logan, by the way."

"Penny. I run the antique shop. You came in and bought a few things.

Nice to see you again." Penny reached a hand across the bar. "How about just whiskey then. With some ice in a cup on the side?"

"You got it."

Dan leaned back in his chair. "I thought you weren't staying."

"I wasn't. Until I was."

Sandy waved from across the bar. She slipped from her barstool, wrapped a thin napkin around her sweating beer, and flopped into the stool beside Penny.

"Any progress on the festival?" Sandy wiped the condensation from her beer and left the napkin in a tiny wet wad on the bar. The chair squeaked and groaned as she shifted, settling into place.

"No progress yet. I took your advice, though. I came to see if anyone's interested in helping out."

"What's it?" Dan pushed away from the bar and pulled a new beer from a brown paper bag at his feet. Penny knew better than to ask. She'd seen enough of Ramsbolt's quirks to know they were harmless and better left unquestioned.

"I had this idea that we could all benefit from a little tourism. If we can get the attention of some of the people who go through town in the spring and summer, we could sell some things. I know *I* need something to boost business. I couldn't be the only one who would benefit from a boost in sales."

"Like, a carnival?" Bern raised one eyebrow, the corner of his mouth curled.

Sandy leaned down and peered at Bern. "Not a carnival. An art festival. With sidewalk sales and that kind of thing."

Penny nodded. "Maybe an evening concert in the park."

"I know some guys who got a band," Bern said. "They're older. They play bluegrass. Might not be what you're looking for."

"Bluegrass sounds great!" Penny shared a smile with Sandy. "I'm not sure if the gig would pay or how much money we could offer, and I hate to ask an artist to work for free. Would they be willing to negotiate?"

Bern snapped his fingers again, trying to get Logan's attention. "Might. I can ask." He sat forward and tossed his empty bottle in the trash can behind the bar. The smash of breaking glass got everyone's attention.

"It's a good idea to ask around here." Dan ripped the cap off his beer with his bare hand and pointed across the bar. "Just don't ask Arvil over there. He's never up for anything fun."

After her first encounter with the curmudgeon, she didn't doubt it.

Cold air wafted in with Grey. The plumber pulled off his beanie cap and curly hair fell into his eyes. "Talking about Arvil, huh?" he asked. "It's that kind of night?" He shrugged out of his coat and draped it over his arm.

Penny turned in her seat. "We're talking about an arts festival. Maybe get local artists and some from outside town to put up tables in the park. Have a concert at night. Sidewalk sales all over town. Things for kids to do. We could close off Main Street and make it like a street party."

Logan approached the bar, ready to take Grey's order. "The usual?"

He nodded at her and leaned toward Penny once Logan's back was turned. "It won't be what I want, but it's nice of her to try. Anyway, a festival sounds like it would be fun. There's no big profit in it for a plumber, but it'd be good to bring some people in. Snag 'em on their way through for a change. I could volunteer to do something."

"It won't just be good for the artists." Sandy clutched her beer in both hands. "The shops, too. Like Penny's store. For the whole town. If we could rent out tables in the park to the artists, the town could use the money to fix up the park. We could make it prettier so people might want to stop even when there isn't a festival."

"What's so wrong with the park?" Arvil shouted from across the bar. "Why are you trying to mess with the park?"

The bar fell silent, and all eyes turned to Penny. She hadn't been the one to suggest it, but everyone looked to her to defend it. The festival was her idea, after all. And if Arvil was the biggest objector to the idea, she might as well meet him head on.

"The park is hideous. It's full of crabgrass and dying shrubs." Adelle spoke up from her seat at the corner of the bar. "It needs some life. It needs fall and spring bulbs, a few native plants. Paint for the benches." She sipped her drink, something the color of cotton candy in a martini glass, and centered it on a napkin. "I'll tell you what, Penny. If the festival makes enough money to pay for the plants at cost, and if we can get a few volunteers to help with planting, I'll plan it out and get all the supplies."

"What's wrong with you?" Arvil rattled his newspaper into shape, his ears reddening. "Aren't you even trying to make a profit? If you did, you could paint that damn flower pile of yours."

Penny turned to Dan. "What is this guy's deal?"

Dan shrugged. "We'd all like to know."

"Don't listen to him, Penny. He's been bitter since before I was born." Adelle leaned down to see past Dan and Bern and smiled. "I mean it. I'll help."

"That's really nice of you, Adelle. I don't know anything about planting things, but I'd be happy to help." It could even be fun to dig her hands in the dirt.

Warren sat a few seats down from Arvil, in the shadow of the beer taps. He sat up straight and peered over them. "I could put some ads in the papers. If that would help."

"I can put a notice in the church bulletin." A woman in a floral shirt with pale pink lipstick offered. "We can mention it during announcements on Sunday, if you tell me what I oughta say."

"I don't even know." Penny glanced at Sandy for ideas and shrugged. "I guess that it's just an idea so far, and if anyone wants to volunteer to help, to come by my store on Ridge. It's all just ideas and definitely needs Morgan's permission before we can do anything. So maybe it's not the right time to mention it in church? I doubt we can just do this without the town's approval."

"Oh. No, you need a fully formed idea before you can go to Morgan." The woman in the floral shirt shook her hair and gray curls swayed like a treetop in a storm. "Best to mention it and get the ball rolling first."

"We could put a sign up out here. Once you get it approved and all that." Logan stabbed a mop at the puddle of water that seeped from beneath a cooler. "A banner, maybe. And you should talk to the state tourism people. They put out guides that promote events and large venues. They could get it on the calendar. And don't forget the arts alliances."

"Nate's a really good artist." Grey pulled a stool next to Bern. "He doesn't flaunt it, but he's really good. I bet he'd make signs."

"See?" Sandy nudged Penny's knee. "It's a great idea. Marissa said she'd sell cookies and cupcakes. Maybe she would make a huge cake and sell pieces of it in the evening. Like, a birthday cake for Degory."

"Degory?" Bern scowled. "Who the hell's Degory?"

"Degory Howland." Sandy rolled her eyes. "The statue in the park."

261

"It has a name? Why'd you want a birthday cake for the sailor guy?"

"He was an artist. If we do it in May, over Memorial Day weekend, it would fall on Degory Howland's birthday. And if it's an arts festival, it all makes sense."

"Nothing about that statue makes sense." Penny shook her head.

Logan dropped a beer in front of Grey, who shook his head but drank it anyway. "I don't get it either. That statue creeps me out," she said. "His eyes follow you."

Grey's phone chirped. He sipped his beer, wiped his lip on his sleeve, and checked his notification. "I texted Morgan and told him you had a great idea to raise money to fix up the park. He says he'll be right down, and he's been wanting to fix the park." He lifted his phone. "Also says he's glad to hear you're gonna stay and wants to know if you're gonna use those coupons. Whatever that means."

CHAPTER TWENTY-SEVEN

Outside the antique store, a November snow coated every surface, clinging to the trees and the street. Sunlight bounced off every surface and glared through the window. It would be a quiet day in the store. Quieter than usual. And cold.

Penny dragged a ladder across the floor and paused, letting it rest against her side when her phone buzzed with a text from Dan. In weeks of planning, she'd lined up local artists, painters and potters, a wooden spoon maker. There was a guy who made bowls from salvaged wood. The festival was still in its early stages, and it wouldn't be held until May, but there was plenty of interest. And Dan had convinced the bluegrass band to take charge of the music and coordinate a whole day of it in the park, and headline that night for free.

She replied. *That's so nice of them! Yes, I can meet them at the bar on Friday to swap info.*

It would give her something to look forward to.

She dragged a ladder across the floor of the shop, a length of twine knotted to the bottom rung wafting in her wake. Jake scampered after it.

She opened the ladder in a patch of light. "Couldn't do this a month ago, could we?"

Jake rolled onto his side, his paws batting at the frayed twine.

The ladder scraped against the floor as she pushed it into place beneath the rafters, where dangling chairs were affixed to large eye hooks, baskets were tied to the joists with rope, and chandeliers of brass and iron dripped from the ceiling. Penny climbed the ladder with a rope in her hand, intent on clearing as much of the ceiling as she had of the floor.

"Just picture this place, Jake. Soon, we'll be able to set up the furniture so you can actually see it. I can put the leaf in that round table and put the dishes with the blue flowers on it. It'll be so cute. People will stop on their way through town and buy little cozy Maine-made trinkets to take home with them."

Climbing ladders had never been her thing, but it was a lesser occupational hazard than violent patients, the risk of being stuck with a virus-laden needle, and the feeling of an impending heart attack if she failed to meet a deadline. She took a deep breath and climbed, one rung at a time, then tossed a rope over a rafter. She tied one end to the ladder, another to a chandelier, detached it from the ceiling, and slowly, gently lowered it to the floor.

Penny peered down at the chandelier. Conquering the crap on the floor had been one thing. Moving on to the ceiling amid the dust and spiders was something else. "Not so hard, huh Jake? One down, a billion more to go."

Jake rolled onto his back, the twine caught between his paws. He bounced to his feet and scampered when the bell rang out, and the door opened. Penny grasped the ladder, her heart in her throat.

"I'll be right down. Ladders aren't my thing so feel free to browse while I take my time."

"It's me. Morgan."

Penny peeked under her elbow to see him twisting his hat in his hands at the door.

"I have bad news."

What had she done, or not done, to deserve a visit from the town manager? She hopped off the last rung, grateful to be on solid ground, and carried the chandelier to the counter. Dust clung to cobwebs like thick morning dew. She wiped her hand on her jeans. She'd rather talk to Morgan and figure out how bad the news was than clean that old iron chandelier and find a spider.

Morgan hovered in the doorway, fresh snow clinging to his boots, hat, and gloves twisted into a rope in his hands. "How are you spending Thanksgiving next week?"

Was the news that bad, that he didn't want to say it? "No plans for me. I've never really had plans for Thanksgiving. I eat junk food, watch bad movies. Sometimes I read." She used to volunteer for shifts at the hospital, too, but those days were gone.

Why won't he just spit it out?

"You're settling in then?" His eyes were fixed on the floor.

"Yeah. I'm settling in fine. Thanks. I used that coupon from the welcome basket after all."

Morgan chewed his lower lip.

Oh my God. What is it? "Morgan, I don't mean to rush you along, but I have a lot of stuff to pull down from the rafters. You probably don't wanna stand in my doorway all day, either. Did I do something? Or not do something? Did I miss some kind of bill? A tax? If there's some kind of debt that my gran didn't pay, just let me know, and I'll figure it out."

"It's not that." He shook his head and beads of water dripped from the ear flaps of his hat.

"I know people pull up and park out here sometimes to load stuff in their cars, but it's only for a second. If it's a parking thing..."

"No. It's not that. There's been a setback with the festival. I'm so sorry." He shook his head. It looked a lot like a weary no.

"We can't have the festival? So many people are working on it. Jaleesa and Carol are trying to get electric out to the park, and Denise has been scraping all the stickers off the church's tables. I just heard from Dan that music is lined up. Why not?"

Morgan deflated with a sigh. "I've been trying to get Adelle to help with some of this town code stuff, but she's...she won't. It's hard to understand all the rules. I was going through it all, trying to figure out the money end, like we were talking about. If we're going to charge people money to rent a table, we have to have rules for managing it, remember?"

"Yeah." Penny shrugged. "Can't we just get a bank account and put it in there?"

"Yeah, that's it exactly. We just have to keep track of it. But that's not the problem. While I was digging through the town code, I found a law on the books that says any gathering needs to have a permit."

Penny's patience ran out. She rolled her eyes. "Then can't you just issue a permit?" She turned back to the lamp, wiping it down with an old white rag. "I'm not seeing what the problem is here."

"The law says that only a board of officers can issue permits."

"Why can't we ask the board? Who are they? When do they meet?"

"There isn't one. The town has no board."

"Why am I not surprised?" Everything in Ramsbolt was backward. But that was part of its charm, as long as it wasn't infringing on her ability to get things done. The simplicity that made for a simple life also made for some complicated realities. "There has to be something we can do about it. I'm not willing to just give up because Ramsbolt doesn't have a board."

Telling the story seemed to take the last bit of energy Morgan had. He fell into a cast iron garden chair, threw his hat over his knee, and ran a hand through his hair.

"It's not the end. It can't be." Penny sat across from him. "Why can't we make a board?"

"You can't just make a board of officers. Not just like that." He snapped his fingers.

"Yeah, we can. That's your job right? To make sure we're following the town rules? If we need a board, we need to go get one."

"But the board has to be independent. It can't be appointed by the town manager." His voice rose an octave, as if it should all be obvious to Penny. He shook his head, and water flew off the tips of his hair.

"Then I'll make a board."

"What? You can't just do that."

She threw her hands up. "Somebody has to. If you're not allowed, someone needs to do it. Do the rules say that the antique store owner can't find people to be on the board? Does the task specifically fall to the guy who delivers the cantaloupes to the market?"

His lips curled in a sarcastic grin. "No. But people need to vote. We need a whole election, and there's no time for that."

"The festival is in May. It's the middle of November. All we have to do is make a board and get them to vote to issue a permit. This can't be that hard." She held out her hands, as if presenting the solution on an invisible tray, but Morgan didn't bite.

"The permits have to be issued six months before the event. I don't even know what happens if we default on our own rules. Give me a break here. I'm barely old enough to drink. My biggest life challenge was taking my driver's license test in Helen's Pinto the day after an ice storm. I'm gonna let you in on a secret here. It's a little embarrassing, but I don't know what I'm doing. I know you think we're slow, compared to the city. We don't have a real estate agent or a big city doctor. Every kid born here wants to move out the second they're big enough to run. But people here don't like to get involved. That's how I ended up with this gig to begin with. Even the guy they elected to the task didn't want to do it."

"I'm not ready to believe that just yet. Every store on Main Street is on board for this festival. People are volunteering to set up tables and clean up after. Carol found a bunch of old ceiling tiles in the back of the hardware store and donated them to the high school kids. They're using construction paper to remake old album covers from the '80s. How cute is that? Everyone's excited and really engaged over this festival. I can't imagine they wouldn't want to help."

Hope glimmered in Morgan's eyes. "You really think you can get them involved?"

"They already are."

"We need nine board members. Do you think we can find *nine* people?" His eyes creased with worry, and he ran a hand across his forehead. "It's just that if we start this and don't finish, people will think we failed."

"If you never try at all, you fail before you start. And I can't afford to fail." Penny stood. "Okay. I'm on it. I'll get nine volunteers willing to be on a board."

"We need the town to vote, though."

"So we'll have a town meeting. It's supposed to be warm tomorrow. In the fifties. You tell everyone you see to meet at the park at sundown for a quick vote." She patted him on the back when he stood. "See? Nothing is insurmountable."

CHAPTER TWENTY-EIGHT

Penny ran a hand down Jake's back, and he arched, settling in the front window of the shop, his eyes fixed on the thaw and the water rushing down the street. She zipped up her puffy coat and wiggled her toes in her wool socks. She'd thrown away a lot of useless, out-of-style clothing when she left Otley, and she'd done it in a rush. Considering all the absent-minded bad decisions of the past, she was proud of herself for holding onto the practical things.

"You hold down the fort, okay? And don't eat too many crunchies. I have to convince nine people to become a board so we can have a festival." She slipped out the front door, locked it, and walked to the toy shop. She peeked through the window into the store. No sign of Nate. No sign of Adelle across the street either. But it was lunch time, after all.

She paused at the circle where the sailor stood, glazed by snow that melted from his cap and shoulders. It ran down his rain slicker and into the earth. The pavement was clear and dry for the most part, but islands of slush covered the grass. The park could be beautiful in the spring, covered in crocus and daffodils, if it weren't so neglected. And it would be inviting, strung with lights between the trees, tables with food and music in the air.

I hope the rest of the town can see the same thing. Nine of them, at least.

Penny turned down Main Street. At the end of the road, snow clung to the church steeple and dripped from its copper gutters. The post office was empty. She was either too early to catch Riley for lunch or he was moving faster than usual.

The smell of cinnamon buns rolled down the sidewalk, drawing Penny in. Inside the bakery, a line had formed. Tables were packed with people and coats. Penny cut to the front of the line and leaned over the counter.

"Marissa? You back there?"

"Is that you, Penny?"

"Yeah. I don't need anything. Just a question. Morgan needs a town board to approve a permit, and we have no time to do it."

"That's dumb." Marissa emerged from the back with a tray of muffins. "Why doesn't he just do it himself?"

"Stupid town rules. Can you be on the board?"

"I guess." The tray clattered to the counter. She dropped two muffins into a paper bag and passed them across the counter to a customer. "What do I have to do?"

"Be at the park tomorrow night at sunset."

"Sounds easy. I'll do it." Marissa nodded and took another customer's order. Bacon and egg on an everything bagel. Penny's stomach growled, but there was no time for bagels and coffee. She had a committee to make.

She turned for the door and spotted Arvil, his dark gray coat and sullen air a contrast to the sugar-coated pastel walls of the bakery.

"I want on it." With a fork, he carved into a yellow cupcake with blue frosting. Maybe he wasn't as rough around the edges as she thought.

"You want on the board?" Penny's eyebrows shot up. Being used to a hectic emergency room, she didn't lose composure often, but Arvil wanting to be on the board threw her for a tailspin. "I thought you hated the whole idea."

"I do." His tongue was painted blue with frosting.

"Fine." She couldn't deny him the right to a seat on the board, especially when she knew he stood in opposition. She'd just have to make sure the other eight were more open minded.

He waved his plastic fork at her. "What do I have to do?"

"You have to show up at the park tomorrow night at sunset. The whole town has to vote on it."

His eyes clouded over, their corners twisting in a scowl. "I don't wanna go out in the cold. And this isn't enough notice."

"It's plenty of notice for a town that doesn't know how to operate by its own rules." Penny propped one hand on her hip. "If you want to be on the board, you gotta be at the park at sundown. It would be lovely to have you."

"So you're running the town now?"

"Don't make her regret leaving the house today, Arvil." Marissa grabbed cookies from the display with tongs. "This is your chance to vote against something that will bring joy to the whole town."

Penny balled her hands into fists and propped them on her hips. "I'm gonna wish I hadn't seen you today, aren't I? Is this what I get for giving you the benefit of the doubt?" At the very least, no one could accuse her of being partisan. Getting Arvil on the board was the easiest way to ensure it was objective.

He folded the cupcake wrapper on his plate. "I'm gonna do your stupid thing. But only because I want to know what's up your sleeve."

Penny patted the table. "That sounds wonderful, Arvil. See you tomorrow."

She turned to the door and paused, her hand on the cold handle. "Everybody! It's a town emergency." Heads spun to her and silence fell over the tables. "We need everyone to come to the park tomorrow at sunset for a big vote. It's really important. Spread the word. Thank you!"

Chatter erupted behind her. She let the door close gently, leaving the town to generate its own buzz. Across the street, Grey stepped from his truck outside the hardware store.

"Grey!" She waved a hand and scampered across the street, careful not to slip in the sludge at the curb. "I have a strange question for you. Would you like to be on the town board?"

He considered her with narrowed eyes. "The town doesn't have a board. Does it? Is this a coup?"

She shook her head. "No coup. Long story short, the town needs a board to approve the festival so Morgan can issue a permit, and we don't end up violating our own laws."

"Man, this place is weird. Am I the only one who thinks this place is weird?" He took off his hat and ran a hand through his hair.

"Trust me. You're not the only one. Can you be at the park tomorrow before sunset?"

"I guess so. Unless there's some emergency."

"Okay, can you please not have an emergency and be at the town park tomorrow?" She clasped her hands and pretended to beg. "This is really super important."

"Fine. I'll be on the town board. Want me to ask Helen? I'm headed up to the bar in a bit."

"Perfect. We need nine people, and Helen makes four. Know anyone else who would do it?"

Grey aimed a thumb behind him, at the hardware store. "Carol."

"Carol! Great idea! She's already helping Jaleesa get electric to the park for the band and the lights. She's perfect. Thanks."

"It doesn't take much to get her involved in something. Tell her one thing you need, and she'll come up with ten more. I bet she'll be able to wrangle all kinds of supplies for ya, too."

"That's exactly the kind of spirit we need."

Penny lunged toward the hardware store. She clutched the brass handle of the giant door, solid wood with an old, wavy-glass window. Dark green paint flecked from the trim. She pushed the door open and stepped into a magical shop of cans and jars and spray bottles in a rainbow of colors for purposes she couldn't fathom. Snow shovels and bags of salt were stacked by the door. Aisles of things she'd never needed unfurled before her. The whole place smelled of old wood, varnishes, paint, and rubber.

"Can I help you find something?" Carol smiled from behind the counter. Next to her, a woman leaned against the wall, her fleeting look of interrupted gossip faded to an amiable grin.

"Hi, Carol." Penny stuck her hand out. "We haven't met. I'm Penny. Sorry to interrupt you guys. Grey said you might be interested in being on the town board? Morgan needs a board to approve the event before he can issue a permit for the festival, and we're short on time before we start violating our own laws."

"I heard about this." Carol tucked her hands in the pockets of her muslin apron. "Morgan's dad mentioned it to Shauna at the pet store. I was going to ask Morgan about it, but his dad said the town rules state he can't be involved."

"It makes sense, though." Carol's friend waved a hand, dismissing the confusion. "If you think about it, you'd want to have a board that's independent of its manager. Separation of powers and oversight and all that." She lifted her chin. "I'm Diane."

Diane. Penny had heard the name before. "You run the tea shop, right?"

"Yup. Next to the church. I've been meaning to come by Eliza's old store, but the tea place keeps me busy. It's open all day, and I can never tear myself away from it. I have so many things in the basement I need to get rid of. I thought I'd see if you could sell them on consignment. And I'd love to see if you have anything I could use to spruce up the tearoom. Little vases, maybe? Decorations? I could even put price tags on 'em and sell them through the tea shop if you want."

"That's a really neat idea. I was hoping to have an open house, once I straighten up a little more. I'll definitely stop by before I do. Maybe I could incorporate some tea from you and some baked goods from Marissa."

Was there competition between Diane's tea and Marissa's coffee? It seemed the kind of thing that could divide a town like Ramsbolt. If there was a rivalry, it didn't show in Diane's broad grin.

"She makes all our desserts. And a different fresh scone every day of the week." Diane tugged on hem of her linen shirt, smoothing it over her jeans. "So you need help with a town board in order to make the festival happen?"

"Yeah. Do you want to join?"

"All I have to do is show up at the park tomorrow night?" Diane tilted her head, her eyes narrowed. "No meetings or email chains or group texts about government stuff?"

Penny knew the drill. People were all for improvement, as long as it didn't cut into their schedule. "I promise. I will personally make Morgan swear that he will never start a group text."

Diane stuck out a hand. "Consider it done. That festival is a great idea. This town needs a little life."

"Thanks. I only came up with the idea. It's going to take a whole town to pull it off. I'm glad people are up for it. It's do or die for me. If I can't find a way to make the antique store profitable…" She'd what? Have to go back to medical school? "I don't know what I'd do. Anyway, thanks for everything. I gotta run and find a few more people."

Penny waved and pushed through the door, back into the crisp air. She rushed three doors down, past the pet store and the pharmacy. If anyone would grant her the favor, it was Warren. She hopped into the newsstand, and the bell above the door rang out, startling him as he stocked magazines on a shelf.

"Goodness, woman. Scare an old man half to death." He put a hand on his chest in mock terror. "What brings you down here in such a hurry?"

"I am here to offer you a coveted seat on the new town board if you can show up at the park at dusk tomorrow."

He tapped a stack of magazines on the shelf, lining up the edges. "Won't it be a muddy mess?"

"It might. Wear sensible shoes."

He shrugged one shoulder. "I suppose I owe you one. And Eliza. All I have to do is be at the park? I don't want to get involved in politics and government. I got enough to contend with keeping the envelopes with the right greeting cards."

"You don't have to do anything. I promise. We'll take a vote on the board, then the board will vote on the festival. I gotta run. I need three more people. See you tomorrow!" Penny waved as she dashed out of the newsstand.

Three more people. All they have to do is show up. It can't be that hard to find three people.

Across the street stood the market. Someone had painted a basket of sweet potatoes on the window and, in big yellow and red letters, declared a potato sale. Between the letters, she could make out the shape of Sean, bagging someone's groceries. She crossed the street without looking, skipping over puddles, and waited for the automatic door to let her in.

"Hey, Sean?"

He looked up from the bag of apples with a convincing look of terror. "What'd I do?"

"Nothing. Yet. Are you eighteen?"

"I just turned. Why? What's wrong with being eighteen?"

"Nothing, as far as I can remember. It's just...Do you think Ramsbolt is boring? I mean, all the kids grow up and leave, and what if we had a festival? Wouldn't that liven things up around here?"

His eyes grew wide. He placed a loaf of fluffy white bread on the top of a bag of vegetables. "Like a music festival? With those mist tents and college girls?"

"I was thinking more like art as a place to start."

His nose wrinkled. He might take some convincing.

"Forget that. Are you going to college?"

"Not this year. I gotta save some money for tuition. My mom said—"

"That's great. I have the perfect thing for your application, and you only have to do one thing."

Sean fit boxes of pasta into a brown paper bag. "What's that?"

"Be on the town board. Come to the park before sundown tomorrow. Everyone will vote on the board. Then the board will vote, so we can have the festival in May."

"Wait. This art festival thing. Is this what my girlfriend is making a bunch of little clay animals for? She said she's getting a table at a fair or something in May."

"That's it! And we can't have the festival unless we have a vote tomorrow night. It'll be good for your résumé." Penny did a little dance and tried to make it look like fun, but he was a teenage boy, after all. Nothing was fun to him but video games and his girlfriend. "And think what a supportive boyfriend you'd be for joining the board and voting yes so she can sell her art at the festival. Imaging all the brownie points you'd get."

Sean blushed. "Sundown tomorrow?"

"Yes. Be early? Thank you!"

The automatic door opened, and Penny spilled out onto the street. She counted her effort. Marissa. Arvil. Grey and Helen. Carol and Diane. Warren. Sean.

"Riley!"

Penny took long strides to reach him, avoiding patches of ice on the sidewalk, before he jaunted into the street.

"Riley. Wait up. I have a question."

A heavy bag hung from his shoulder. He turned to her. He wasn't in his usual good mood when she reached him. Not half as friendly as he was when he delivered the mail. "I only have a second. All the snow melt slows me down, and I still have half the town to do."

The last time she talked to him, she hadn't been so friendly herself. She'd slammed the town and run off in a huff. "I'm sorry. I know that I said the town was terrible, but I didn't mean it. I just didn't know it the way I do now. I couldn't see all the good in it because I brought too much bad with me. I didn't understand that all those people were just trying to protect something they like. I am too, though. I want to make it better."

"You wanna change it."

"I want to give back to it. Help it be the best version of itself. The festival isn't going to break anything. It's gonna bring money in."

Riley folded his arms. "What do you need from me?"

"I need you to forgive me. It's not going to be easy living in this town if the most likable guy in it hates me."

His arms fell to his sides. "I never said I hated you. I thought you were maybe a little ungrateful, that's all."

Penny shoved her hands in her coat pockets. "Well, you're not wrong. All I can do is ask for forgiveness. And a small favor. Can you spread the word around town that there's a town meeting at the park tomorrow night at sunset? We need as many people there as we can get."

"Is this about the festival?"

She took in a deep breath of damp air, full of thaw and melt. "It is. Look, I'll admit it's partly selfish. If I don't save that store, both it and me will drown. I have no other place to live, no source of income. Ramsbolt is all I have. I have to do something to boost sales and clear out more of that stuff so I can rehab the store and make it a viable business. And if a festival helps everybody else, too, then what could be so bad about it?"

Riley peered down at her, his six-foot-seven frame lacking its typical wilt. He seemed to stand in opposition.

"Please.-

A broad smile filled his face, and he slapped her arm. "I'm joshin' ya. I'll tell 'em. So there's a meeting at the park at sunset tomorrow?"

Penny sank with relief. "Yes. Thank you. I owe you one. I really do."

He walked backward toward the curb. "I'll get 'em there, hell or high water. Can't have Eliza's store or one of Ramsbolt's own falling apart on us. We had too much of that back in the day. That's how all that clutter ended up there in the first place."

Riley waved a hand and aimed for the west side of town.

Penny headed back to the store, counting the board members. Eight. She was one short.

The light was on in the toy store. She could see Nate putting price tags on rolls of wrapping paper, dropping them into an old wine barrel. The bell rang out when she opened the door and stepped onto his welcome mat, bits of mud and slush clinging to her boots.

"Hey, Nate."

"Hi, neighbor. I was just wondering where you went off to. Someone stopped by and said your door was locked. I said you probably ran out for lunch. They said they'd be back."

"How long ago was that?"

"Just a minute or two."

"Thanks. I'll make this quick then. Morgan came by this morning and said we need a town board to vote on the festival so he can issue a permit. Wanna be on the board? Can you come to the park tomorrow by sundown?"

"I can do that." Nate added a newly discounted roll of pink gift wrap to the barrel. "I have a question I've been meaning to ask you, too.

Thanksgiving isn't far off, and I usually spend it on my own. All these years, I've gotten used to having no place to go. I figured if you've got nowhere to run off to, you and me could cook some turkey and stuffing, maybe some mashed potatoes. We could drink some wine. What do you say?"

After years of volunteering to work so other people could spend the holidays with their families, Penny finally had someone to spend a holiday with. She didn't hesitate. "Absolutely. I'll bring the wine."

CHAPTER TWENTY-NINE

Nate walked with Penny to the park. The sky took on a faint pink hue, painting the sailor statue ahead. People passed them in small clusters, walking with their families and neighbors. Ahead, others were already gathering in his shadow, clutching cups of coffee.

This nervous silence between them was new. She felt as if she ought to fill it with some excuse for not being closer, for protecting the distance that kept them apart like magnets that repel each other. There was some need to draw close, a need greater than convenience or neighborly affection, but even stronger need to stay away compelled her to quiet.

She'd agreed to Thanksgiving, to cooking and wine, without considering the repercussions. The incremental increase in proximity.

She could accept responsibility for someone else's health, for the repair of the bones and the attachment of tendons. But she couldn't accept responsibility for anyone else's emotional well-being, not when she couldn't account for her own.

They stepped onto the soft earth and climbed the gentle hill to the park. Water squished up around the toes of her boots. If she stood still long enough, it could swallow her whole. She almost wished it would.

JENNIFER M. LANE

But she needed the town to vote. Without the festival, the fraction of money she kept from Anderson would have to last her a lot longer than six months. And she needed the boost to help her pay students loans and face a new economic reality, one in which Jake didn't have to go on a diet.

What would her mother have thought of all this? Of her quitting medical school and taking over the old hoarding store? It was hard to reconcile what her mother would have wanted for her with any desire to see her happy, because by the time Penny was old enough to seek that happiness, her mother was gone. And Penny was left to seek that approval and live out her mother's dying dreams come hell or high water.

Both hell and high water were on the way, and Penny would have to meet them at the door. Sure, she could ask Warren questions about running a small business. She could ask Carol what to do when the building fell apart. Grey could fix the plumbing. It would take a village to fill in the gaps between what she should have and might have learned and the swamp she found herself in. But who would she turn to when she was afraid of drowning?

They paused at the corner and waited for traffic that didn't come. Penny stepped over the cracked curb and into the street with Nate at her side.

"Can I ask you a random question? Did you ever meet my mom?"

"Nah. Never met her," said Nate. "I was too young, and she was long gone before I opened the toy shop. Your gran talked about you, though. She told me when you got into medical school. She was pretty proud."

She'd wondered about that, where her grandmother got her information. Some mysteries never get solved. "I wonder how she even knew. She wrote me letters over the years and never mailed them. I found them in the attic. She seemed to know things. Like, one of them sounded really disappointed that I chose medical school over Ramsbolt. Mom and I saw her once just before my mom died, and she didn't seem very proud of either of us. I guess I let both of them down, my mom for leaving medical school and my gran for coming to Ramsbolt too late."

"You probably didn't let them down. Not really. Your feelings about people change, right? There aren't any absolutes in life."

"People are just as capable of changing their minds about people as they are about their stuff, I guess. She could have read about medical school in the paper, I suppose. But my mom cut her out of our world. Do you think someone in town could have known my mom so word got around?"

Nate shrugged. His hands were still in his pockets so his jacket scrunched up around his shoulders. "Maybe. She never talked about your mom, but she'd chatter up a storm about you if you'd let her. It was generic grandmother stuff. She told me how much I'd like you. She was right. She was right about a lot of things when it comes to you."

Penny stopped at the backside of the statue, her arms folded across her middle for warmth. "What do you mean?"

"That you'd love Ramsbolt. She said it's like a pendulum swing, and kids don't turn out like their parents, that you'd get mad that your mom kept you away from here eventually, and you'd swing toward Ramsbolt and come looking for your roots."

Muddy water oozed up around her feet. She shifted her weight to find drier earth. "Maybe that's true. I didn't know it when I got here, but it's kinda true, I guess."

"She was right that I'd like you, too."

Golden rays of sunset found Nate and picked up the early grays that peppered his hair. Nate's shadow mixed with the sailors and stretched across the park. Kids squealed with delight, running around a weathered bench.

"That's nice of you. You're…" What? He was a good neighbor. A good friend. Not like Lee and the people she hung out with at Otley. None of them even cared she was gone. But Nate checked in on her every day. He invited her to walk to lunch and helped her get the chairs from the rafters over a couple of beers. He even offered to set up an old television he had in his apartment for her to watch, not that she ever watched television. After so many real-world emergencies, the fake ones on TV weren't very captivating. He was the first thing she thought of in the morning, if it was too early to pay him a visit or too late at night to knock on his door. He was more than a neighbor to her.

Nate's smile faded. The glint in his eye faded, replaced by something serious that looked and felt like want. But Penny couldn't go to that place. Not while she was trying to keep from sinking.

It felt like torture to lead him on. "You *like* me, don't you?"

Nate shuffled his feet like a scolded child. She wanted to reach out to him, to heal the hurt of revealing his heart. "I do. I'm sorry. I hope you're not offended. I would like maybe for there to be more between us someday, but saying it is really just me getting it off my chest. So I can move past it? I know you're still sorting things out and maybe you don't want things to be more complicated than they are."

"It means a lot to me that you would say that." Those weren't the words she wanted to say. They all eluded her. The gratitude, the astonishment that someone so kind and welcoming and who had their life together would be enchanted by the catastrophe that her life always seemed to be. Lee had been attracted to her mishaps, but Lee was a fixer. He saw her as a malleable doll he could pose in any image. Nate wasn't out to change her life. He just wanted to be in it.

Her heart clenched at the sting of rejecting someone. She wanted to keep him just as he was. "I'm not sure where I am, Nate. I was between things for so long. Between the city and here. Between being a doctor and not. Between being buried by all of this and digging my way out." She reached out and touched the sleeve of his coat. "I'm not really between things anymore. I'm definitely finding my way. I may be a little messy right now, but I won't be forever, and I hope I don't miss my chance when I'm ready."

"I get it. I wouldn't have said anything if you hadn't asked. I didn't want to lie to you—"

A shrill whistle cut through the air. Morgan stood on a warped bench with a clipboard in his hand.

"God, I hope that bench doesn't break." Nate stepped around the statue to join the crowd, and Penny followed.

"He looks like a chaperone taking attendance at a field trip." Penny giggled.

"Everybody, quiet down." Morgan called for calm. All around him, panicked voices called out for answers.

"Are you really stepping down?"

"I heard it was something with the sewers."

Penny whispered to Nate. "What did Riley tell these people?"

"Probably anything just to get them here."

"Guys!" Morgan stamped a foot, and the bench shook. "I am not quitting, and there's nothing wrong with the sewer. Listen. According to town code, all permits for large gatherings need to be approved by a board before I can sign off on it. So before we can have the festival in May, we need a board of officers to vote. The law also says the permit has to be requested six months before the event, so that's why we're here. We have to vote on this today. Some of you may know, Penny went around town and found nine volunteers to serve on the board. Warren, Nate, Sean from the market. Diane and Carol. Marissa. Grey. Helen and Arvil."

"Arvil?" Someone from the crowd protested.

"What good is he gonna do the festival?"

"I'm right *here*." Arvil, wrapped in his dark gray coat of wool, leaned on an umbrella in the last of the sailor's shadow. "I can hear you, you know. Ungrateful bastards."

Morgan dropped the clipboard to his feet, raised his hands, and wiggled his fingers.

"Is he doing jazz hands?" Nate shot Penny a knowing grin, and she returned it.

"Everybody!" Morgan begged for quiet. "Geez. These nine volunteers have agreed to be on the board so we can vote. Can we get a show of hands from people who vote to accept these nine volunteers to be the board? Helen came all the way out here on her bum knee. Can we vote?"

Hands shot into the air. Kids screeched and circled the statue in a game of tag.

"The ayes have it. So can the nine of you raise your hands if you're okay with the town having a festival on Memorial Day weekend?"

Eight hands shot up. Arvil, the only dissenter, folded his arms in disgust.

Morgan picked up the clipboard and handed it to Grey. "Can you nine sign this piece of paper? Eight of you, anyway. Then I'll issue the permit."

"Is that it?" A mother bounced a child on her hip, one eyebrow cocked. "That was the emergency?"

Sandy made her way through the crowd and stood by the bench. "It *is* an emergency." She gestured at the statue. "Degory Howland is highly underrepresented. Someday, the world will know who he is, and it only makes sense for Ramsbolt to host the Degory Howland Memorial Arts Festival. It could put us on the map."

"The map of what? Sailor statues?" A man in a heavy plaid coat took off his knit cap. "I never heard of no Diggory Howling."

Sandy gave an exaggerated sigh, frozen air turning to mist as she snorted like a dragon. Her lips twisted, and she gestured at the statue. "He was an artist."

"Whatever." The man pulled his hat down over his ears.

Sandy rubbed her forehead. "He was."

"I think it's perfect." The woman with the baby on her hip shot Penny a broad smile. "We need something like this. Something we can look forward to every year. Something that puts money into the town's pocket instead of all this trash and litter they throw in the park on their way through town."

"I agree." Sandy beamed. "An arts festival is perfect for Ramsbolt. Art is independent, fierce. Just like us."

"One last thing," Morgan yelled over the crowd. "We will be renting tables to artists here in the park. Word is spreading through the arts community, and people have been calling already. There will be sidewalk sales, things for the kids to do, and a concert at night. If you want to volunteer to set up, clean up, help make signs, go down to Eliza's old store and see Penny."

Morgan stepped from the bench and took the clipboard from Grey.

It was real, all the sudden. Painfully real. There would be an arts festival in their tattered park in the spring, and it was all on Penny to pull it off. A lump formed in her throat, and she tried to smile through it.

"You did it," Nate whispered in her ear. "You're bringing an arts festival to the smallest town in the country."

"I don't know what I'm doing. What if I screw this up? I've never finished anything before." Her lip trembled, and her hands shook. She held in a breath to steady her racing heart. If she failed, she wouldn't just let herself down. She would let down the whole town. "What if no one comes?"

"They will. I believe."

CHAPTER THIRTY

The sun blazed hot for early June, streaming through the windows of the antique store, limning hurricane lamps and chandelier crystals, painting the room in rainbows. Penny sat on her stool behind the counter, a new book in her hands and Jake at her side, sprawled out so his belly absorbed the sunbeams. A man in an orange cardigan browsed the store. He was the tenth tourist that day to wander through. But it was the summer months and tourists, it turned out, did stop for the bathroom, for trinkets, and sundries, just like Nate said they would.

"A friend of mine came in here when he visited the arts festival." The man turned a small glass globe in his hands. "He said you were really good at helping people find the perfect thing."

He rested the globe on the counter. His eyes wrinkled at the corners and a friendly smile spread across his face.

Penny rested her book by the register. That happened sometimes, someone hoping she could help them fill a void or soothe a need. They hoped she could cut through the clutter, though there was much less of it now than there used to be, and find the thing to transform a porch into a place to rest or a kitchen into a vibrant space that gave the outward appearance of all the love they cooked with. Other times it was an emptiness that itched at the edges, a longing for the contentment of being surrounded by things. Not just any things but curated pieces that had a feeling to them. Nostalgia, perhaps. A homesickness for places long gone.

Sometimes it was easy, but oi…the pressure. "He said I was good at that, huh? I can try. What kind of thing are you looking for?"

He scratched his neck. Razor burn. "I just moved into a new place, and I'm looking for some affordable things to decorate with. Comforting and inspiring at the same time, if that makes sense."

"Like the stuff you grew up around?"

"Yeah, maybe. Stuff I remember in my grandmom's place. Classic furniture? I need everything."

Her hair, held in a bun with a pen, bobbed when she nodded. "Starting over, huh? Tables and dressers and whatnot are scattered around. Those shelves there have dishes and utensils. You'll find the nicer ones, the ones without chips and dings, on the bottom shelves. Pots and pans are in the back. Decorative stuff is all around. Everything outside is ten percent off, and I'll give you an extra ten percent off because starting over is hard enough."

"That's generous. Thank you." The man was already pulling dishes off shelves. A set of thick blue plates. "I like these. Nice weight to them."

"They'll look nice on a breakfast table."

His smile faded, shaded by the past. Penny could almost see it etched in the lines on his forehead, the things he had lost. Things he couldn't replace with someone else's cast-offs.

"A record player just came in. A bunch of records, too."

"Yeah? God, I haven't listened to a record in…thirty years, I guess."

"Ella Fitzgerald. A few Louis Armstrong. Haven't listened to all of them, but I know the player works fine. Wanna see it? It's on that table, behind the china cabinet. Can't miss it."

The man clutched two plates and wound his way through furniture. "I used to sit on the living room floor and listen to records through an old pair of headphones. Remember those giant things with all that padding? Of course you don't. You're too young."

But she did remember. Stretching headphones over her mother's head and closing them softly. Playing James Taylor while tears streamed down her mother's cheeks. She kept the memory to herself. Why add her own seasonings to the man's bittersweet?

"I'll take this," he said. "I need some utensils, too. Some cups. Bowls."

"I'll bring the record player up front. I've got boxes and packing material behind the counter. You can leave everything else on the counter here, and I'll ring you up." Penny found a cardboard box just the right size. It was the one she'd brought shoes from her old apartment in.

"This is just the thing I need. A little bit of time travel." The man flipped through records, extracting every fifth one.

"Time travel is a potent cure." Penny loaded the record player into the box. "You need help to your car with all this?"

"No, I'm good. It's not far. I'll be back for furniture in a day or two. I have to rent a truck for that. But there's plenty of stuff I like here, and the price is right."

He paid, and she gave him his change. "If you see Jaleesa a block east of here she may have a truck she can rent to you."

"Thank you. My friend wasn't wrong. You are good at this."

"Thanks. Listen, if any of the records skip, bring 'em back. I'll return your money."

"Nice of you to offer."

The bell rang out, and the door swished to a close behind him. Penny grabbed her keys. "Jake, it's time for lunch. I've got a craving for an everything bagel. I'll bring you back a tiny schmear of lox."

There wasn't any need to lock the store, but old city habits would die hard. She shoved the keys in the front pocket of her messenger bag, hoisted it onto her shoulder, and aimed for Main Street, stopping to wave at Adelle who pruned pansies in window boxes outside the flower shop. Weighed down by her laptop and manila folders full of papers, the bag's strap cut into Penny's shoulder. She paused at the bench outside the post office to adjust.

"You got a lot of stuff there." Riley fumbled with a bag of his own. Mail for southwest side of town.

She let it fall to the bench, not wanting to hold it any longer than she had to. "Old laptop takes up a lot of room."

"You recovered from the festival yet? Town was packed full of people. Never seen so many cars try to fit on Main Street."

"Yeah. Sorry about all the disruption."

"Didn't mess up my route at all. I'm on foot. Looked like it was good for the town. Lot of people walking around, buying things. And how great was it that Helen's bar pulled off the big reopening in time for the festivities?"

Penny folded her arms. "She was so worried. Arvil put up a hell of a fight letting them rebuild it, I heard."

"The worst. Logan's a battle-ax, in all the best ways."

"You can say that again. Makes a mean drink, too."

Riley tugged his cap down over his ears. "Morgan said he wants to do it again next year."

"It was a big profit for everybody. I paid off most of my grandmother's debt after that. Life's a lot easier now." Penny nodded at her messenger bag. "That's what all this is. We did a survey of all the vendors and the stores. We got a lot of great ideas. I'm going to help him with the business end, too. There was enough profit from artists renting tables to pay for the posters and decorations for next year and plenty is left over for some landscaping for the park. Adelle might be able to plant her dream garden."

"That sounds like just the thing to get people to stop and stay for a while. And better you than me. I'm better on my feet. Paperwork's not my thing."

"It's not mine either. Just have to be motivated, I guess." She lifted her bag, and it sagged against the weight. "I gotta run. Lotta research to do."

Riley waved and stepped off the curb. Off to deliver the day's mail to houses tucked behind Main Street. Somewhere back there was a lamp, and the lady she sold it to the day of the festival. The woman had dreamed of a light and airy reading nook, and now that her kids were grown and gone, she was rearranging to her liking. It may not have warmed the empty nest, but at least the lamp made it brighter. Dozens of houses in Ramsbolt had things from her shop now. From bed frames and baskets to wicker lawn furniture. Penny watched Riley go, knowing small corners of the world were better, warmer for her work.

She hauled her bag down the street. The smell of fresh-baked blueberry pie growing stronger the closer she got. It was almost enough to make her abandon her need for an everything bagel. Almost.

Inside, all but a few tables were taken. A retired couple arguing over coffee. A woman splitting a muffin with a crying child. Penny dropped her bag at an empty table by the window and waited in line behind three teenage girls who talked over each other and giggled at a cell phone. The sound of baking tins hitting countertops, and the creak of oven doors resounded from the kitchen. Marissa appeared in the doorway with a box of cupcakes, her hair fraying from its ponytail.

The girls fumbled with purses, pooling their money. Penny caught Marissa's eye and offered a knowing smile. There was nothing worse than being stuck in a room full of chaos without a patient, friendly face.

"Penny! It has been a madhouse in here today." She brushed hair out of her eyes. "What can I get you?"

Penny leaned across the counter for a peek at the bagel bin. "I'll have two everything bagels, toasted with cream cheese, and two cups of coffee. Please. For here."

Marissa dug two bagels from the bin and ran them through a slicer. She slid two paper cups from the top of the stack and passed them across the counter. "That'll be five fifty. Oh, and if you hold on, I'll come pour you coffee. We're out over there, and I'm making more."

Penny dug exact change from her back pocket and passed it across the counter. "I don't know how you get away with charging so little. This would be twice as much in the city."

"I wouldn't mind city profits, but you can keep the city traffic." Marissa closed the register drawer. "Want me to bring the bagels out to you?"

"That would be great. Thanks. I've got a little work to do on my lunch break. I'm over by the window."

"Good luck thinking straight in all this noise." Marissa smiled and leaned across the counter. "It might be loud, but it's the sound of profit."

"Don't I know it. If I get three visitors at one time, I'm thrilled to have the company."

"It's a gorgeous day for a window seat, too." Marissa pressed a lever, and the bagels disappeared into the toaster.

Penny stepped away from the counter. The woman behind her looked familiar. From the bar, perhaps, or the market. She'd get the names down eventually.

Her laptop barely fit on the little cafe table by the window. She opened her notebook to the list she made with ideas for next year's festival. Someone had suggested a banner and bunting to stretch across Main Street, and more food vendors. She dug her pen from her bag and tucked it in the spiral of her notebook.

While she waited for her laptop to boot, she turned in her seat and took in the town. The sun was high, and cast no shadows on the sidewalk. Across the street, Warren arranged books in a new display at the newsstand, and a small corral of puppies yipped and rolled on the sidewalk outside the pet store. A little boy dashed ahead to greet the puppies, his mother not far behind, paper bags of groceries in her arms. Logan and Grey stepped out of the hardware store and crossed the street, and Logan hopped over a pothole as she climbed into his pickup truck. The two of them were so cute together. The laptop pinged, and her desktop came to life, but Penny was lost in the scene.

She had known her city. Which sidewalks were cracked on her walk from the hospital to the club. Where the streets flooded in heavy rains. The best places to get sushi. But it hadn't been her city. Not like Ramsbolt. It had never felt like Ramsbolt.

"Sorry, to interrupt your thoughts." Two bagels landed next to her laptop, and Marissa slid into the chair across the table. "Finally got a break! I'm dying to know how the festival went for the store."

Penny closed her laptop screen so she could see Marissa. "It went great. I sold about a third of what was in the shop. Most of the stuff on the sidewalk is gone, too. A couple of guys in a van bought that rusty bike and a bunch of other stuff to decorate a restaurant."

"And all that debt? Things getting better?"

"I'll have it paid off in the next few months. I never imagined it would turn out this well."

"That's fantastic. That weekend was the most fun I've had in a while. I did about two months of sales in one weekend. Remember those cute little sheep cookies I made? We ran out of them the first day."

Penny laughed. "They were adorable, and the three I had were delicious. Arvil sat on a lawn chair in the circle with a clicker. He said more than seven thousand people stopped in town. I was in the store the whole time, worried about how everything was going, but the volunteers had everything under control."

"There were some really good artists, here, too. I got some art for the bakery, but I haven't had a chance to hang it up yet." Something beeped in the kitchen. Marissa stood, her chair scraping the floor. "I'll go get you that coffee.

Marissa took Penny's coffee cup and slipped away, into the back. Across the street, the pet store door opened, and the mother tumbled onto the sidewalk, dragged by a puppy at the end of a leash. Behind her, the little boy beamed. It was a moment he would remember forever. She kept getting swept away by moments like that, little scenes that happened in the city all the same, but they were pushed to the background of noise and stress, the rush and urgency of keeping up. There was none of that noise in Ramsbolt.

The boy settled into the back seat of a sedan, and he reached out his arms to the puppy. The scene was so bucolic that Penny didn't notice Nate when he stepped through the doorway. He gave her a peck on the cheek.

"Hey gorgeous. This seat taken?"

"Hi, handsome." She tucked her notebook and pen in her bag. There'd be time to go over surveys later. "It's all yours. I got you a bagel and coffee. You have impeccable timing, too, because Marissa's behind you with fresh coffee. Look out."

Nate leaned to the side, making room for Marissa. She poured coffee into cups and left a saucer of sugar packets and cups of creamer on the table.

"So when are you two going to Montreal? I know you said you were going on vacation after the festival."

Nate held his coffee in two hands and blew on it. "Two weeks. It was hell trying to get her to step away from the store."

"I'm not surprised. Of course, if she weren't such a workaholic, we'd have lost that store months ago. You saved that place, Penny. And us, in a way. I don't think people appreciated what Ramsbolt had to offer until someone made them see it."

Penny blushed, her eyes fixed on her coffee. "It's nice of you to say so, but it would have happened eventually."

She couldn't say she had the whole town in mind. She wished she could, but the shop, the festival…it was a selfish endeavor. An act of survival in a world that was eating her alive. She'd been terrified, having already lost one dream and clinging to the hope of finding a new one. It was a gamble worth taking, looking for peace in the last place she expected to be. And as Ramsbolt woke to its own reality, that renaissance was as inevitable as slow decay, the gamble paid off for Penny, too.

Marissa slipped away, behind the counter. Back to the bagels and muffins and cookies, to the simple sweets she crafted so well. And Nate nudged her foot with his.

"Where'd you go off to? You look happy."

She reached across the table and laced Nate's fingers in her own. With her free hand, she swirled her coffee in her cup, making a tiny whirlpool. For the first time, she wasn't drowning.

ABOUT THE AUTHOR

A Maryland native and Pennsylvanian at heart, Jennifer M. Lane holds a bachelor's degree in philosophy from Barton College and a master's in liberal arts with a focus on museum studies from the University of Delaware, where she wrote her thesis on the material culture of roadside memorials. She resides with her partner Matt and a tuxedo cat named Penny.

Receive free prequel stories, news about upcoming releases and more by signing up for the author newsletter at
jennifermlanewrites.com

OTHER WORKS BY THE AUTHOR INCLUDE

Of Metal and Earth
Stick Figures from Rockport
and the
The Collected Stories of Ramsbolt Books:
Blood and Sand